WHOEVER FEARS THE SEA

Justin Fox

SAPERE BOOKS

WHOEVER FEARS THE SEA

Published by Sapere Books.

20 Windermere Drive, Leeds, England, LS17 7UZ,
United Kingdom

saperebooks.com

Copyright © Justin Fox, 2021

Justin Fox has asserted his right to be identified as the author of this work.
All rights reserved.

No part of this publication may be reproduced, stored in any retrieval system, or transmitted, in any form, or by any means, electronic, mechanical, photocopying, recording, or otherwise, without the prior written permission of the publishers.
This book is a work of fiction. Names, characters, businesses, organisations, places and events, other than those clearly in the public domain, are either the product of the author's imagination, or are used fictitiously.
Any resemblances to actual persons, living or dead, events or locales are purely coincidental.

ISBN: 978-1-80055-291-3

For my mother

ACKNOWLEDGEMENTS

I owe a great debt of gratitude to the many people who made my various journeys along the coast of East Africa possible. In particular, I'd like to thank David Beavan and Shallo Issa for the voyage on the dhow *Jannat* from Lamu. I'd also like to thank Patrick Latham and his production team on the documentary series *Winds of Change*. Friends and family read the manuscript and made invaluable suggestions. A special thanks to JM Coetzee, Imraan Coovadia, Revel Fox, Petina Gappah, Catherine Hofmeyr, Christopher Hope, Don Pinnock, Robert Plummer, François Smith and Polly Taylor. Without the teams at Sapere and Umuzi, this book would still be bobbing face down off Mombasa: thank you to my wonderful publishers Amy Durant and Fourie Botha, and my brilliant editor, Henrietta Rose-Innes. A special thanks to my indefatigable agent, Aoife Lennon-Ritchie.

My gratitude, also, for the use of dialogue based on William C Atkinson's translation of *The Lusiads* by Luis Vaz de Camões. And for the quotation from 'Utendi' by Mwana Kupona binti Msham, sourced from UCLA's Swahili Poetry Archive.

Although this is a work of fiction, many texts were consulted. The following were particularly useful: *Deadly Waters: Inside the Hidden World of Somalia's Pirates* by Jay Bahadur, *East Africa and the Orient* by Neville H Chittick and Robert I Rotberg (eds), 'The True Dates of the Chinese Maritime Expeditions in the Early Fifteenth Century' by JJL Duyvendak, *The Swahili Coast, 2nd to 19th Centuries* by GSP Freeman-Grenville, *Dhows at Mombasa* by John H Jewell, *Fort Jesus* by James S Kirkman, *The Thousand and One Nights* by Muhsin

Mahdi, *Sailing from Lamu* by AHJ Prins, *The Career and Legend of Vasco da Gama* by Sanjay Subrahmanyam, *Sons of Sinbad* by Alan Villiers and 'The Two Piracies in Somalia: Why the World Ignores the Other?' by Mohamed Abshir Waldo.

A number of songs are referred to or quoted in the text, and I gratefully acknowledge the following:

Kikki Danielsson and Dr Alban, 'Papaya Coconut (Come Along)' (lyrics by Dr Alban), SDS Records, 1998

Whitney Houston, 'My Love is Your Love' (lyrics by Wyclef Jean and Jerry Duplessis) from *My Love is Your Love* (Arista, 1998)

Bob Marley, 'Buffalo Soldier' (lyrics by Bob Marley and Noel G Williams) from *Confrontation* (Tuff Gong/ Island Records, 1983) and 'Redemption Song' from *Uprising* (Tuff Gong/Island Records, 1980)

Safari Sound Band, 'Jambo' (aka 'Jambo Bwana', lyrics by Teddy Kalanda Harrison) from *Mambo Jambo* (arc, 2001)

Mchelea bahari si msafiri
Whoever fears the sea is no traveller
— Swahili proverb

Everything can be found at sea,
According to the spirit of your quest.
— Joseph Conrad

CHAPTER 1

The sea was a dark mirror. The captain held up his hand for silence, laid his cutlass on the deck and stepped into the wheelhouse. 'It's the World Trade Center,' he said.

The *Hispaniola* swung on her anchor in the darkness and the BBC voice trailed away, then returned as the current nudged the brigantine back towards the island.

Paul Waterson looked around at the crew and guests, cramming into the wheelhouse to listen. The fancy-dress evening had been dealt a blow. Everyone had made an effort for this, the third evening of their cruise on the chartered brig, anchored now off Praslin in the Seychelles. They'd raided the dress store and were all got up with eye patches, headscarves, earrings and great-buckled belts.

Tony Blair sounded like Churchill. Was this World War Three? Paul glanced at the German tourists clad in pirate outfits, craning their necks to hear.

Blair's voice was clear again: 'There is no doubt in my mind that we stand very, very closely with America. We should regard this act as if it was an attack on any of us, and all of us.'

Paul found his hands were trembling. *Hannah.*

Hannah, his girlfriend in New York, worked for CNN. She lived uptown and her office was nowhere near the World Trade Center, but he wanted to get off the boat and find a telephone all the same.

After the broadcast, the crew tried to make the best of it, singing a bawdy version of 'Fifteen Men on a Dead Man's Chest' while two of them performed a mock sword-duel on the main deck, but people's hearts were no longer in it and the party faded early.

In his stifling cabin, Paul found it hard to sleep. His mind conjured pictures of jets ploughing into skyscrapers. He consoled himself that if there was anything he needed to be told, Hannah or her family would have found a way to contact the boat.

Paul emerged on deck early the next morning to find the skipper sharpening the end of a broomstick with his seaman's knife to form a crude spear. 'Strange things are happening in the world,' he said. 'It can't hurt to be prepared.'

He was in the Seychelles to research a travel documentary about the *Hispaniola*. Ordinarily, he would have enjoyed such an assignment, involving a pleasant week of knocking about the islands. He was a bit of a Sunday yachtsman back in Johannesburg and loved anything to do with boats. *Hispaniola* was a hundred-foot Dutch topsail schooner, restored and refitted for the luxury tourist market. The vessel had been converted to look like a pirate brig: a painstaking two-year project by the owners.

Paul had stayed a few days on Mahé doing research, then joined *Hispaniola* for a cruise. The days were spent sailing between the islands; in the evenings they'd anchor off some enchanting beach. Each location was more idyllic than the last: crescents of perfect white sand, shaggy palm trees, granite boulders and luminous water.

One afternoon, they'd rowed to Cousin Island, a deserted sanctuary. It felt like Eden. Birds nested on the ground and allowed humans to sit beside them. They displayed no fear, only curiosity. There were fairy terns, noddies and tropic birds with long white tails. His group came upon a herd of giant tortoises grazing in a glade like prehistoric cows. The reptiles ate out of their hands, long phallic necks straining from the shells. What easy meat they'd have made for hungry sailors.

Given the theme of *Hispaniola*'s refit, and the fact that the Seychelles was once a safe haven for buccaneers, Paul's research had taken a pirate angle. In fact, the trip had reawakened his childhood fantasies of nautical adventure. He'd pictured himself boarding *Hispaniola* in some secluded cove and marauding through the islands like the cutthroats of old.

His investigation had turned up plenty of useful material. During the seventeenth and eighteenth centuries, many buccaneers had their lairs in the Seychelles: the cumbersome merchant ships that sailed to and from the East were sitting ducks. It was a hideout in paradise. Even now, everyone on the islands wanted to talk about pirates. Tourist brochures spoke of buried treasure in the grounds of one or other hotel; the beach you were sipping your cocktail on was once a pirate cove; buccaneer graves dotted the shore. The pirates' ghostly presence lent a certain frisson, and they were good for business.

Now, a day away from port, Paul sat in the bows, jotting desultory notes, a skull-and-crossbones flag waving above his head. The tropical beauty around them added a bizarre counterpoint to his imaginings. He couldn't get the horror of New York out of his head.

Paul had so wanted Hannah to join him on this assignment. She was probably working long hours at the office, covering the unfolding events in her home town. He remembered the sailing trip they'd done together in Mozambique the year before. Hannah lying on the foredeck, her auburn hair coiled across the towel, her suntanned body. He saw her dark-green eyes — how they challenged him. That bold laugh that cut through his doubt. He needed to see her. He needed to hold her.

Trade winds shook the palms and takamaka trees; wavelets slapped the side of the hull. The crew listened to music on the wheelhouse stereo. 'One papaya coconut, under the sun, come along, come along,' went the insistent lyrics and tinny Caribbean backing. 'We can fly away!' But fly away to where and to what? This was the safest place on earth right now, with plenty of sea room between them and civilisation.

On the last day of the cruise, *Hispaniola* set sail on a long beam reach towards Kenya, a thousand miles to the west. The crew pressed a lot of canvas: main, course, maintop, topsail, topgallant, foresail, staysail, inner and outer jib, and a flying jib set high on the forestay. Block and tackle creaked as *Hispaniola* began to heel. Paul's spirits lifted. Free of the channel, they rode into a longer swell and, when all the sails were trimmed, it was as though sea and wind, hull and rig, were singing one harmonious note. Paul hauled out his camera and began photographing. The brig cleaved into the steady breeze, just like one of the square-riggers or dhows that had plied these waters for hundreds of years.

Paul scaled the ratlines and sat on the topsail yardarm. Far below, the crew looked like insects. Oh, to spy a cumbersome Portuguese galleon, fresh out of Goa and packed with riches! *Hispaniola* would run her down in no time and have her gold in their hold with hardly a musket shot fired.

The image of an aeroplane swooping towards a building intruded into Paul's vision and his piratical fantasies quickly lost their lustre. He climbed back down the ratlines to the deck.

The following afternoon, Paul sat in Mahé Airport awaiting his flight back to Johannesburg. A television set tuned to CNN in the departure hall ran continuous footage of jets scuttling skyscrapers — slow-motion images of aircraft ploughing into façades. A fireball, then people throwing themselves from windows, tiny specks against the perfect autumn blue. One moment, they were furiously alive. The next, they were shattered bodies on a pavement. Buildings fell in upon themselves, tall grey ships sinking into clouds of their own making. A wall of ash billowed through streets in a storm of incinerated concrete and glass. Paul felt a shortness of breath and a dull ache in his stomach.

Those sitting around him had already had three days to process the images. It was his first exposure. He watched people in white masks walking through the moonscape of lower Manhattan, the makeshift shrines of flowers and candles, the homemade posters of the missing on walls and lampposts. A firebombed mosque, Arab Americans keeping their children indoors, rumblings from the Middle East.

Paul needed to speak to Hannah. He found a payphone, but didn't have much change. At least he'd be able to hear her voice, briefly. After two rings she picked up.

'Hannah, it's me.'

She was barely awake. It was early morning in New York.

'Are you all right?' he asked. 'How's the family?'

'Yeah, we're all okay. Badly shaken, but okay. No one was downtown, thank God.'

'I've been thinking about you non-stop,' he said. 'If only you could have been here —'

'Things have been bad, Paul.'

'Do you want me to come to New York? I can book a ticket when I get back to Joburg and be with you in a couple of days.'

There was silence at the other end of the line.

'Hannah? What's wrong?'

'I… We… Paul, we can't go on like this,' she said in a flat tone.

'What? Just like that? We haven't seen each other in months, Hannah. It's distance, not us —'

'I'm really sorry, Paul. I've made my decision. We haven't been good for each other for a long time. And now this … and everything.'

'I can spend more time in New York.' There was desperation in his voice. 'You can spend more time in Joburg. We can talk about something more permanent, like me moving there.'

'No, Paul, it's not going to work.'

'Is there someone else?'

'I wish you wouldn't ask.'

'Hannah, is there someone else?'

'Yes. I'm sorry.'

There was a long pause. The line went dead. He'd run out of rupees. Paul banged the phone box with the palm of his hand, then leant his forehead against the cool metal. There were no tears, just numbness. In the background, he could hear his flight being called.

CHAPTER 2

It was a fortnight since 9/11 and Paul had spent much of the time brooding over the breakup. At least things on the work front were looking bright. The day Paul returned from the Seychelles, he'd received a call from Johan Visagie at Africa Moon Films.

'The documentary is gonna be part of a series on African civilisations,' said Johan when Paul went for a meeting in his Rosebank office. The man was only partially visible behind a bushy beard, cloud of cigarette smoke and chaotic desk. 'It's about the Swahili coast, for National Geographic. I'm gonna need you to go to Kenya.'

Paul was delighted. Although he'd worked on many wildlife documentaries, he preferred the cultural and historical assignments, with research he could sink his teeth into. He'd studied history as an undergraduate at Wits University in Johannesburg, and a film on Swahili culture was right up his street.

'We'll show how Africa had this full-on maritime culture long before Europeans rocked up. Our doccie will prove that the Indian Ocean was like this centre of civilisation. And today's Swahili people inherit that history. Am I going too fast?'

Paul was scribbling on his notepad. He shook his mop of blond hair without looking up. Johan described how the Swahili had built palaces and mosques, sailed across the ocean and traded with Asia for centuries before Vasco da Gama arrived on the coast.

'See what you can dig up. Mostly, I want us to focus on the stuff we can take pretty pictures of, like forts, boats, tropical islands. Nat Geo also wants something on Rhapta. Apparently, it's this lost city that's never been found. We want stories of cannibals and slave girls: Sinbad the Sailor comes to Africa. You get my drift?'

'Sure, Johan, just like the doccie we did on Great Zimbabwe.'

'Zackly. Same style, same mood, grander scale. You fly up in two weeks' time. For once we've got a decent budget. You'll be able to stretch it for a month, maybe six weeks if you're careful. Do the location scouting and check out hotels while you're at it. There's lots of good material across the border in Somalia, but things are too hairy there at the moment and there's the threat of pirates.'

'Pirates? Are you serious?' Paul raised his eyebrows.

'Just stick to Kenya and don't get any funny ideas. I know you.'

Paul gave him an innocent grin.

'Don't look at me like that,' said Johan.

'Like what?'

'Never mind. I want us to shoot a lot on those old boats —'

'Dhows?'

'*Ja*, dhows. Ask around about hiring one for a week or so. *Lekker* cheap. And not one that leaks. Set the whole thing up for us. We'll want to interview a dhow captain, chat about his culture and whatnot. A good-looking bloke with a beard and a dishtowel around his head, you know the type.'

'You got a title yet?' asked Paul.

'A working title, for now. *People of the Monsoon*. But let's see what the Nat Geo boys think. Washington will probably want something sexier.'

Paul had worked for Africa Moon Films many times before and knew what Johan liked. Over the next two weeks, Paul spent his mornings at Wits Library doing research. The documentary started to take shape in his head. It soon became clear that most of the shooting should take place in and around the Lamu Archipelago, where Swahili traditions seemed to be strongest and dhows remained the principal mode of transport. Crossing into southern Somalia could be just as fruitful, but the security situation prevented it and Johan had been firm on that point.

The more Paul read, the more intrigued he became by this urbane, peaceful trading culture with its beautiful architecture. He was surprised by how ancient its roots were. On a dusty shelf, he came upon a copy of the *Periplus of the Erythraean Sea*, a Greek sailors' and traders' handbook written in the second century AD. It talked about the thriving port of Rhapta:

Two days' sail beyond the island of Menouthesias lies the last mainland market-town of Azania, which is called Rhapta, a name derived from the small sewn boats. Here is much ivory and tortoiseshell. Men of the greatest stature, who are pirates, inhabit the whole coast and at each place have set up chiefs.

Sewn boats? Paul was immediately intrigued. He did some more reading and discovered that the last mtepe was probably built in the Lamu Archipelago in the 1930s. Not a single nail was used in their construction. How fragile and leaky they must have been — and yet they were able to make transoceanic voyages. Mtepes were mostly used for coastal trade, though, and could take large loads into relatively inaccessible coves. The flexible hull was said to be faster than a rigid one and, with its shallow draught, the boat was able to run ashore or over shoals without much difficulty.

The craft had a square, matted sail made from palm leaves and a palm-frond deck housing. Its swan-like prow represented the she-camel which, according to the Koran, was sent from heaven to admonish some or other Arab tribe. Apparently, the elders refused to accept it as a divine token and hamstrung the beast. The use of red paint on the hull signified the blood of the camel, tortured by the impious Arabs, while the tassels hanging from the prow represented the camel's reins and head stall.

Early chroniclers remarked on the air of flamboyance about the mtepes, which often carried bunting, streamers and flags. They sailed in convoy and drums were beaten hourly through the night so the boats could keep station. Paul tried to picture a flotilla of these oceanic camels, drums throbbing as they glided into harbour at dawn. What a sight they must have made.

Delving further, Paul came upon an article about mtepes written in the late 1970s. The author mentioned hearing stories of the remains of a wrecked mtepe near the dhow-building town of Galoh in southern Somalia. Paul felt a prickle of excitement. Could its skeleton still be there, twenty-five years later? A fabulous find in the arcane world of maritime archaeology. He imagined presenting his discovery via the movie. National Geographic would have a scoop, courtesy of Paul.

The ancestor of all dhows, Paul thought. *At the very heart of Swahili commerce, of Swahili culture. What a great image for the movie.*

An idea started to develop in Paul's mind. He loved sailing. He'd grown up racing Optimist dinghies and, as a teenager, had spent every summer holiday with his parents in Richards Bay, where he crewed on keelboats and helped out as an agile foredeck hand during weekend races. More recently, he took part in round-the-buoys racing on the Vaal Dam on Sundays.

Rather than simply flying to Lamu, why not start in Mombasa and hitch a ride to Lamu on a dhow?

Thoughts of Hannah plagued him when he wasn't working.

He's really, really nice, said her voice. *I think you'd like him.*

Perhaps all three of us should have tea sometime in the misty future, he said to the creature that now lived in his head and vaguely resembled Hannah. *Milk and arsenic with that, dear?*

She was running fast and hard into the arms of another man and another life. Not looking back. He'd made it easy for her, cutting ties and walking away. Would she miss his voice down the line from Africa, their sporadic meetings in exotic places, or feel only relief that this long, painful, transatlantic tale had come to an end?

For three years Hannah had been the epicentre of his life. Her base was New York and she'd been adamant that this was where their future home would be, close to her possessive Jewish family. Paul had lived the *soutpiel* life that English-speaking South Africans have always been accused of: one foot in Africa, one foot abroad, and his saucy bit dangling in the Atlantic. His reluctance to emigrate and embrace her world had been part of their undoing. Geography compounded the loss. He wasn't good enough: not for her, not for the USA, nor the First World. In the end, he couldn't cut it.

Paul had resisted that existence, but it had promised a life beyond Africa. He could have become a New Yorker. The possibilities had seemed dangerously enticing, but now her glamorous, jet-set life was closed to him. No more dinners in the Village and weekends in the Hamptons, no more SoHo parties with coked-up soap stars. No more weekends in Miami with Porsches and poolside petting. Now America, and by extension the world, had sunk, Atlantis-like. His global reach had contracted, and a tenuous form of belonging to a foreign land had finally been severed. He felt like a boat person, turned away from an alien shore by the coastguard and packed off back home, or simply tossed overboard. Melodramatically, he retallied the debt he could never escape: AIDS babies, Robert Mugabe, Rwandan genocide. They were all his baggage again. Paul had lost his lover and the world, and been awarded Africa as consolation, as booby prize.

He found it impossible to be alone in his apartment at night. Each evening, he drove the short distance from Killarney to Orange Grove, where he sat on his regular stool at the far end of the Radium Beer Hall's battle-scarred counter. Paul drank long and hard, but only ever got halfway drunk. He never spoke to anyone other than the barman. But it was better than staying in. It was better than thinking.

CHAPTER 3

The alarm clock bleated at four-thirty on the morning of his departure. Paul opened his eyes, not believing it was time to go. His head throbbed. He desperately didn't want to get out of bed. All through the night, he'd writhed in intermittent sleep, plagued by half-dreamed images of a blade penetrating flesh, the splash of a body over the side, a dhow sailing away into the darkness.

The departure seemed more like an ending than a beginning. He knew it was mostly Hannah, but the journey appeared opaque. Certainly, there was an element of danger: he was venturing alone into the Muslim world with nothing but a wallet full of dollars and a desire to go to sea, possibly into pirate waters. A pale Christian boy with an air of betrayal about him, calling himself an African, alone on the Muslim African wave.

Then again, perhaps this was exactly the time to take on an adventure.

The alarm clock sounded again. Paul's outstretched hand knocked it to the floor. He rolled out from under the duvet. His bags were packed and standing at the door — all the usual stuff plus anti-malaria tablets, insect repellent, his rusting seaman's knife, a big hat. Passport. Ticket. Camera. Dollars. And a box of condoms — *You never know,* thought Paul, *maybe climb back on the horse.* Anything else he could do without. *A last will and testament? No, pull yourself together, man.*

He took one last glance round the bedroom. The cupboard doors stood open. He could see Hannah's things stacked in a corner, some of them collected on their journeys together. The capulanas from Maputo, Thai flip-flops, earrings bought in Bamako, a basket from Antananarivo, the box with her face creams and perfumes, wine-dark lipstick, bottles of vitamins and Valium packets. There was the Dogon door bought in Timbuktu on their last trip, and an inlaid wooden replica of a *Tintin in the Congo* cover. The Belgian reporter looked a bit like Paul with his blond coif, piles of luggage and camera paraphernalia, heading into darkest Africa with the same troubled frown. At least Tintin had his own jalopy and Snowy, a loyal and trusty hound. Paul had nothing.

'Fuck this,' he said under his breath as he flipped the light switch. The airport shuttle was waiting in the street below.

Nairobi Airport. Paul threaded his trolley from the international to the domestic terminal through a scrum of touts and taxi drivers. The air was muggy and clouded with insects; his clothes stuck to his body. Once inside the departure hall, he bought a beer and found a plastic seat where he could wait for his connecting flight to Mombasa. He noticed a pair of amorous Italians sitting opposite him. The woman had a hairclip in the shape of a fake tropical flower; the man wore cream loafers without socks. The two nibbled each other's ears and cooed like overheated pigeons. Irritated beyond reason, Paul felt like pulling out his seaman's knife and ambling over to lop off their earlobes, so they'd have something more substantial to munch on. Then he remembered the knife was buried in his check-in luggage. Bloody 9/11 security measures.

Paul was exhausted and angry. Angry at the flight's delay. Angry at the Italians and their edible ears. Angry at Hannah. Angry because he was thirty-one years old and hadn't sorted anything out yet. Angry that he wasn't leaping gratefully at this opportunity, or at least sucking an Italian lobe.

He was fuming, too, about love and the mess it left behind when it sailed over the horizon. The second beer wasn't helping his mood. Love. The swept-off-your-feet species of love, the walking-through-walls kind. Would he ever experience that again? Paul figured he'd blown the one or two shots that were his due and was staring down the barrel of a lonely dotage.

Which didn't necessarily mean he'd given up on the hunt. Case in point: a pretty Indian woman across the hall whose eye he may have caught. She was flying to Mombasa too. Maybe he should try to chat to her in the queue, if and when it formed. Single again and the old reflex was still working, but with none of the pleasure. He got up and went to buy another beer.

It was already dark when they boarded the plane for the short flight to Mombasa. Paul had requested a window seat, but after the lights of Nairobi receded, everything beyond the wing was black. He stared at the darkness. He was good at torturing himself. A bruised heart was not something to take into Africa, he concluded, asking the air hostess for another drink. Yes, famously, there was catharsis in travel: turning a page, finding yourself and your destiny 'out there'. As if the act of wandering were the greatest university on earth. It was hogwash: the traveller packs all his woes in his knapsack and carries them along on his back. He should be nursing himself at home, going on a few tentative dates with old, still-single friends. He needed to be building himself up, instead of being drop-kicked into a dark corner of Kenya.

After landing, he emerged with a headache into the Mombasa terminal parking lot. A taxi driver called Ray separated him from the tourist herd and promised the cheapest rates in town. Paul gave the name of a beach hotel and was ushered into the back seat of an ancient Toyota. Ray eased along in the fast lane, allowing his hooting competitors to speed by on the inside.

'So, how's the big man?' he said, flashing a set of enormous teeth at Paul in the rear-view mirror.

'The big man?' Paul was reluctant to chat.

'Yes, man, your big man, our big man.'

'Mandela?' Paul hazarded.

'Of course!'

'Oh, he's fine, he's great. Busy as always. This and that. Here, there, everywhere. Never stops.'

'He needs to take a rest, you know. Slow down. Spend time with the sexy new Mozambican wife,' he said, as though entrusting Paul with the task of speaking sternly to Mandela upon his return.

'Tourism is very down nowadays,' confided Ray. 'This Osama business. Oowah, not good for business.'

'What do you think will happen next?' asked Paul.

'America must be very careful. It must go for the terrorists, but not start a war. There's too much talk of revenge. We had the same thing here after they bombed the American embassy in Nairobi. Revenge, revenge, revenge.'

Ray was weaving his way slowly down a shopping street thronged with pedestrians.

'Are you from Mombasa?' asked Paul.

'No, I'm not from the coast. From inland, Lake Victoria. My father came here to work in the docks. How many big harbours you got in South Africa?'

'Five,' said Paul, doing some mental arithmetic and discounting, on consideration, Coega.

'Yow, that's a lot. We only got this one,' he said, pointing at the orange dockland lights. 'They want to build another one up near Lamu, but we will need lots of money for that.' Ray made it sound as though he were passing round a hat, and would Paul consider chipping in for the deep-water terminal?

They turned left at an open-air church crammed with worshippers, despite the late hour. A jam of taxis and tuk-tuks filled the surrounding streets, ready to spirit the faithful home after the service. Ray crossed back to the mainland on the northern causeway. Here the suburbs were smarter, the walls higher.

The Reef Hotel offered standard beach-holiday package fare. There were low-rise white blocks set among palm trees, swimming pools, lawns and loungers. Frangipani trees poured their scent into the air. It was nice enough, in a bland, resorty sort of way. Paul dumped his bags in the room and found a stool at the poolside bar. He could smell the grassy aroma of the sea, sloshing away behind a line of nodding coconut palms. The BLT sandwich, when it came, was dreary, but the beer was cold. *Tusker: makes us equal, has no equal,* read a sign above the bar. Damn right.

A bosomy Dutchwoman sat at the far end of the counter with a muscular local. Paul watched how she ran her eyes over the man's body. Nothing stealthy about her; she was a B-52 with bomb doors wide open. The pub began to fill up and it became apparent they were about to be treated to some sort of performance. A pair of Geordies from a village outside Newcastle took the stools beside him. They were forty-something women on their first trip to Africa. One was unmarried, the other divorced and 'on me first holiday in ever so long', having left the kids with the grandparents. Sharon, the prettier of the two, had been to London only once in her life.

'A lovely trip. Four whole days, for me work. It was a course. I'm in customer services for a mobile-phone company. Buck House, Tower o' London, 'Arrods — weren't nearly so expensive as I thought. We've done Spain, a coopla times. Tory Molenos, Costadelsol. But Africa, gosh, it's way different. We booked before 9/11, otherwise we'd never have come.'

They chatted aimlessly for a while — the usual exchange of tourist pleasantries. Paul was vaguely formulating the idea of pitching for a snog and tried to ignore the content of the conversation. 'Sue's feet blew up awful on the plane coming over,' said Sharon, making it sound like a terrorist attack. 'Had to soak 'em in cold water. I've always loved wild animals. Sue too. We love watching the BBC programmes; just love the hairies and furries. I thought I had to come see for meself, once in me lifetime.'

The next moment, five lithe young men twirled out of the darkness, somersaulting and flick-flacking into their midst. The acrobats swallow-dived through rings, then through fiery hoops, wearing fixed grins and emitting self-congratulatory yelps. Muted applause echoed into the night after each death-defying tumble. Paul looked at Sharon and she caught his eye. There was, he thought, half the suggestion of a smile. But he knew he'd have to work for it, buy a few more rounds of drinks, spend the next day at the crocodile farm with both of them. A candlelit dinner for three with lots of nattering.

What the fuck am I doing? he thought. He downed the warm dregs of his beer, bade his goodnights and took a turn round the lawn before bed. From a low bluff he could see the beach stretching away into the darkness. The water was ruffled, the sea breathing softly. Shards of moonlight jiggled in the shore-break.

With his air-conditioner set to high, he stood naked in the bedroom spraying his body with Tabard, then a squirt of Doom around the room and under the bed. There was no mosquito net. He climbed into bed and lay there with a hard-on and nothing to pin it in. Sharon? The Italian lobe-nibbler? Anyone but Hannah. Should he get some moisturising cream from the complimentary goodies basket in the bathroom? It was too much effort. Trapped in paralysing indecision, he nodded off.

CHAPTER 4

The morning provided a groggy start, and it took a force of will for Paul to lever himself out of bed. He swallowed two Panadols. Today, he had to kick-start his research. Down in the dining hall, he struggled through a bowl of fruit and yoghurt, then made heavy weather of an omelette, conjured before his eyes by an egg magician in a silly hat.

A rabbit sat staring at him from the lawn as he ate. By the time he'd finished eating, the rabbit still had not moved a whisker. Was it a statue? Maybe it was dead? Behind the bunny, clouds began to boil above the palms like empty thought bubbles. His mind was in slow motion. The punkah-punkah fan went round and round above his head. He was having enough trouble focusing on his dishwater coffee, let alone the job at hand. *Get up from the table, go into town, find a thread, write some notes, take some photographs, get your arse into gear.* The rabbit had gone. *'Alive!' she cried,* he wrote in his notebook, the first entry for *People of the Monsoon*.

An hour later, the taxi dropped Paul in Nyeri Street. The gate to the old harbour was guarded by hordes of police. Paul had to pay to enter and was directed to the ramshackle Kenya Ports Authority building. At the top of a flight of wooden stairs, he asked for the dhow registrar and was directed to an office. He paused in the doorway of a spacious room with tall ceilings and a row of windows overlooking the jetty.

Mombasa's dhow registrar was on the phone. He was a well-built man in his fifties and spoke with a deep, authoritative voice. He was elegant and well-groomed in a formal, old-world way. A faded photograph of President Moi gazed down from the wall above the desk, next to it the picture of a kitten staring at itself in the mirror. The reflection it saw was that of a full-maned lion. The caption read, *What matters most is how you see yourself.*

The registrar waved to Paul but gave no indication of being disturbed by his presence as he got on with his business. Employees came and went from the office, some bearing cash, which was deposited in a Victorian safe standing in a corner of the room. Through the windows, Paul could smell the stench of dried shark issuing from a Somali freighter's hold. Men had formed a chain, carrying the sheets of grey flesh ashore on their backs. As the cargo piled up on the quayside, planks were offloaded from a lorry and manhandled aboard, replacing the sharks in the hold.

A model ship sat atop a filing cabinet. It resembled a rowing boat with a vertical prow, short bowsprit and flat transom. Paul took a closer look. It had intricate woodcarving, a colourful paint job and delicate rope work.

'You like my Lamu dhow?' said the registrar, replacing the receiver. 'It's a jahazi, the largest of our local dhows. Magnificent vessels.' The man held out a hand. 'Rasul Hussain. You must be Mr Paul, from South Africa. I received your letter. *Karibu*, you are most welcome.'

'It's a pleasure to meet you, Mr Hussain.'

'So, you still have this ambitious plan of sailing to Lamu? Why don't you just take the bus? It's seven hours on bumpy roads, but at least you will get there.'

'In our film, you see, we want to retrace the old trade routes. The dhow idea sort of brings it all together.'

Mr Hussain cleared his throat with the sound of a scraping spatula. He stood up, walked to the window and launched a projectile of phlegm between the bars towards an empty anchorage where ghost ships rode the tide. 'Look at the harbour,' he said. 'In a good year, more than four hundred dhows used to visit, boats of all kinds — mostly booms, but also lots of sambuks and jahazis. Kotias, zarooks and ghanjahs too. Their cargoes were unloaded all along the waterfront: dates, salt, Mangalore tiles, carpets, everything.' He returned to his chair. 'There was lots of smuggling too. Fast badans used to creep into the inlets at night to meet the ivory and gold dealers. In the olden days, it would have been slaves —' Mr Hussain lowered his voice — 'and also in the not-so-olden days. Look here.' He gestured at a large leather-bound register lying on the desk.

Paul saw that it held names — *Harambee*, *Zubeida*, *Shiraz*, *Inaiya*, *Jada al Karim* — the countless, long-since-vanished dhows that once frequented Mombasa. *Just like a cemetery register,* he thought.

'But now?' A sweep of Mr Hussain's hand encompassed the entire anchorage. 'This morning there are only two motor dhows and a freighter from Somalia.'

'What happened?'

'Oil. Black gold. The Gulf states no longer need to trade with Africa in old wooden boats. Just one tanker or container ship dwarfs the whole East African dhow trade. In the 1980s it dried up. Trade that lasted a thousand years disappeared in one decade.'

'Do any booms still come?' Paul asked.

'No, they are all gone.'

'Jahazis?'

'Yes, we still get a few jahazis, but they are mostly up north.'

Paul sighed. 'So you don't think I'll find a dhow to Lamu.'

'It's not likely but let me see what I can do. Ghalib!'

An elderly man with a kofia skullcap and walking stick appeared in the doorway and, after a brief discussion, was despatched to ask around the harbour and find out if anyone, perhaps a northbound fisherman, would be prepared to take him to Lamu.

While they waited, Paul studied the model, taking in the details of mast, rigging and a yardarm that was longer than the vessel itself. He craved to see one. Whether by bus or dhow, he needed to get to Lamu.

'So, tell me, Mr Paul, how's your economy back in South Africa? A weak rand, no?'

'Yes,' said Paul. 'But that makes it cheap for tourists. Have you ever been?'

'No,' Mr Hussain said, stroking his chin. 'But I would like to. When I retire I want to visit Johannesburg, the city of gold. Tell me, what are the hotel prices like and how much does a steak and chips cost?'

Paul offered a few numbers and out came Mr Hussain's calculator, converting the prices from rands to shillings. He looked pleased.

Eventually Ghalib returned with news. Mr Hussain looked angry and answered brusquely in Swahili. He turned to Paul: 'The verdict is not good. There are no sailing craft available, only motor dhows, and no one wants to go as far as Lamu, or even Malindi. Ghalib *did* find a fisherman who is prepared to get you as far as Kilifi, where you could try to find another boat.'

But Kilifi is only fifty kilometres away. And I'll have the same problem there. Paul thought for a moment. 'How much is he asking?'

'Five hundred dollars.'

'But that's insane!' Paul spluttered. 'I could fly to London and back for that.'

'I know, it's crazy. The bus to Malindi will cost you one dollar.' Mr Hussain shook his head. 'Maybe you must forget about a dhow.'

Paul stood up and shook Mr Hussain's hand. There was nothing more to be done. Still, he hesitated at the door: 'I was also thinking about trying to get to Somalia —'

'You certainly won't find a captain willing to take you up there.'

Paul wandered up Mzizima Road, fuming. Mr Hussain had not even permitted him to look around the port and take photos: 'I'm afraid not. We've had to tighten security. If you'd come with an official letter, perhaps, but my hands are tied.' Paul imagined a suicide bomber singling out Mombasa dhow harbour for attack. He could eliminate the Somali freighter and send exploded bits of shark meat raining down on the town — a potent, if enigmatic, symbol. Koranic manna, perhaps? Next thing they'd have anti-aircraft guns protecting the bloody anchorage.

Paul walked past Vasco da Gama kiosk and Schmuck Laden Curio Shop. A red banner strung across the street read LIVERPOOL FC. A group of teenagers at Leven Steps offered him marijuana, but Paul didn't hear them. He was too busy cursing his lack of preparation. Had he really thought he could simply swan into Kenya and hop on a northbound dhow? He'd read too many books by venerable travellers who took every mishap in their stride. They always had a Plan B.

His notions of African sail had come up against an empty anchorage. This was not Mozambique, where dhows were still plentiful. Better economies quickly lose their commercial sail power. What fisherman or small-time merchantman wouldn't swap his patchwork sail for an outboard engine?

Paul reached the old dhow anchorage down a flight of steps. Piles of smouldering plastic leaked an acrid smoke. Cats and crows picked through the filth on the beach. Just then, a load of rubbish was tipped from the bluff and avalanched past him.

He walked along the water's edge. A man in holey underpants stepped from a dinghy and threw a few undersized fish on to the sand, where they flapped like wind-up toys. A vagrant shuffled across the beach towards him. 'Hi, Mister, I'm also a producer,' he said, flashing a rotten smile and pointing at Paul's Nikon. 'I've been in the movies.'

'Yeah, right, send me your show reel, buddy,' Paul said through clenched teeth, and quickened his pace.

At the end of the beach he came to an upturned rowing boat and sat on the hull. Paul closed his eyes and felt the sun on his face. He listened to the wind ruffling the palm fronds, the wash of water on the sand. It was low tide, and he imagined a row of dhows from different centuries and from across southern Asia propped upright on the beach for caulking and repairs. Behind them lay a fleet at anchor in the shallows. He pictured Kuwaiti booms offloading dates from Basra, sambuks from Sur with deck-loads of cows and boriti poles, ornate baghlas with carved stern-castles and any number of jahazis from ports along the African main. Here was a ghanjah making ready to slip anchor with a deck full of fierce-looking Bedouin passengers with scarred cheeks. There, a straight-bowed Mahra badan creeping into the anchorage; and beyond it, the longboat from an ababuz, rowed by a span of muscular black men and steered by a dainty Arab in a pink turban.

Was that a sea shanty he could hear from a departing Omani boom? He squinted at the glittering water. Her silhouette swarmed with activity. There was the beating of drums and tam-tams, the rhythmical stamp of dancing feet, the snapping sound of handclaps echoing around the anchorage. On the poop stood the nakhoda, a proud figure in gown and gold-embroidered cloak, watching the raising of the yardarm. With the anchor aweigh, the sail was released and fell like a stage curtain, immediately billowing to a breath of hot wind.

That blue offing, studded with departing sails … gone forever, blown away by the monsoon of time. He felt the loss as if it were his own. All that maritime industry had shrunk to a few leaky ngalawa canoes and a dozen horis with sails made from plastic bags and sackcloth. He needed a beer.

Paul wandered the narrow lanes looking for a bar. In his dejected mood, the picturesque buildings with their Zanzibar-style doors made no impression on him. Eventually he found a dingy hole in the wall with a sign that read: *New, New, New! Nairobi-Style Lap Dancing!*

He paid the entrance fee. The hallway was dark, and a large room at the back not much brighter. Pop music pulsed within. A couple of middle-aged foreigners sat at tables and five women in garish outfits perched at the bar nursing long drinks. Paul found a sofa in the corner and ordered a Tusker from a waif in a bikini. There was no sign of any lap dancing, but Paul didn't mind. He had nothing better to do, and a few cold ones would see him through an otherwise barren afternoon. The whole dhow-voyage adventure looked like a dead end.

He was already on to his fourth beer when things started to liven up, if the arrival of two more greying patrons and one buxom dancer could be considered enlivenment. The woman had all the moves and a pleasant face. She wore a white sequinned bra and miniskirt, which nicely contrasted with her dark skin. The dancer latched on to a German sitting near the bar and began to work her magic, so to speak. The music had been turned up loud. She approached him with swaying hips, sliding across the room, hands rubbing her thighs. Then she swung around and leaned over until her head almost touched the floor. The dancer seemed to have no joints in her body. She jiggled her buttock cheeks in the man's face. He wore a stupid, slightly embarrassed grin.

Her eyes now locked on to Paul and she slunk across the floor with the exaggerated gait of a ramp model. The dancer knelt in front of him, caressing her body with stiffened fingers. Paul was not particularly turned on by this. However, he did, despite himself, feel the first awakenings of an erection.

Next, she stepped up on to the sofa in her stilettos, legs on either side of him, and wobbled her hips. She unzipped her skirt and pulled it over her head to reveal a pink G-string. Her hips continued to sway back and forth as she grabbed a handful of his hair in her red talons and drove his head towards her crotch. Then, with the swift movement of a predator, she swivelled to vibrate her buttocks in his face. She crouched down and coaxed his hands on to her breasts as she rubbed her crotch against his groin.

Somehow the woman's bra came adrift and she turned to bounce her breasts in his face. They were large and elongated. Paul pictured a pair of Zeppelins fighting a gale. Each enthusiastic nipple seemed to have a slightly different interpretation of the music. Paul's head was spinning. From somewhere, the dancer produced an ice block and slid it across her chest. She circled her nipples until they were hard, then slipped the remains of the cube into Paul's mouth.

The music changed. It was, inappropriately, the happy tourist song, 'Jambo Bwana'. Paul groaned. He'd already heard it half a dozen times since arriving in Kenya. The ditty seemed designed to teach basic Swahili to pink northerners in three comprehensive minutes. The dancer mistook his groan for pleasure and reached down to give his bulging jeans a playful tweak. She winked. He winked back. He found himself mouthing the inane lyrics:

Jambo
Jambo bwana
Habari gani?
Mzuri sana

Hi
Hi sir
How are you?
Very fine

The dancer stood over him and, with hips still gyrating, dragged off her G-string.

Wageni mwakaribishwa
Kenya yetu
Hakuna matata

Visitors are welcome
Our Kenya
No worries

She leant over him and said, 'Maybe a little something for the little lady?'

He fumbled in his wallet and drew out a ten-dollar bill. Rolling it tightly into the shape of a cigarette, she slipped it between her legs. She gave him a peck on the cheek, picked up her garments and sauntered off, the refrain '*Hakuna matata!*' following her across the floor.

Back at the hotel, Paul lay on his bed and looked at the ceiling. His head throbbed. His throat was parched. He tried to empty his thoughts of Hannah and the arguments that chased themselves around in his brain like rabid dogs. The pain of her leaving was no longer constant. It came in bouts, like malaria, which he'd once contracted during a shoot in western Zambia. At such times he felt her on his skin, felt her eyes scalding him, felt her in his stomach. In fact, he registered her as a form of nausea.

Into his thoughts floated a dhow. She was a graceful Kuwaiti boom, her tall lateen sail bulging in the breeze — the first of the Gulf vessels to arrive in Mombasa with the summer monsoon. Paul pictured himself as her nakhoda, standing on the poop, calling commands to the crew and guiding her into port. He was a descendant of Sinbad the Sailor, the last in a long line of mariners stretching back into the dim origins of Indian Ocean navigation. He made an impressive sight with his dishdasha flapping in the wind and ghutra of white cloth fringed with tassels wound around his head. It was a vision that calmed him, and he drifted to sleep.

CHAPTER 5

Feeling nauseous, Paul rested a cheek against the taxi's windowpane on the way into town the next morning. Today, the plan was to forget about dhows and focus on historical research. The best place to start was Fort Jesus: a centre of Portuguese power, the perfect symbol for Europe's expansion into Africa and the clash between Islam and Christianity on the continent.

Paul made his way towards the portal of Fort Jesus Museum, feeling the muggy heat weighing at his legs. He climbed the ramp, passed through an iron gate into a courtyard flanked by barracks and a chapel. Large-calibre cannons lined both sides of the *praça*. He found a table beneath a tamarind tree in the courtyard café. From his daypack, Paul pulled out a pile of readings about the great siege which he'd photocopied at Wits, but not had time to read. As he worked, he jotted an occasional note, testing sound bites on a separate sheet of paper:

VOICE-OVER: *The Portuguese arrive in the Indian Ocean in their caravels and carracks, armed with cast-iron cannons that fire shot weighing ten pounds at a speed of six hundred feet per second. Swahili and Arab traders have no defence against this. The Europeans smash a peaceful maritime network that has existed for centuries and stretches from China to the gold fields of Zimbabwe.*

Then comes 11 March 1696: Omani Arabs arrive off Mombasa with a force of three thousand men in seven ships, backed up by armed Swahili dhows from Lamu and Pate Islands. Portuguese civilians and loyal

Swahili flee to Fort Jesus and the protection of a tiny garrison of fifty men. The great siege has begun.

Months drag by. Smallpox decimates the Omanis and the Portuguese commander succumbs to malaria. Finally, in December, a relieving fleet arrives from Goa. Attempts are made to bring reinforcements ashore in longboats, but the sailors are cut down by Omani musket fire. The few that get through find only twenty surviving Portuguese men, many weakened by venereal disease contracted from local women who'd taken refuge in the dry moat. After a few weeks the fleet, led by a cowardly commander, pulls up anchor and sails away. The defenders watch in dismay as the ships disappear over the horizon.

By the middle of 1697, only six Portuguese remain in the fort, with a few dozen Swahili men and about fifty women, who are taught how to use muskets. When the last of the Europeans dies, a young local sheik takes command and remains loyal to the defence with his band of female soldiers.

It takes the Portuguese a year to prepare another fleet. When it arrives off Mombasa on 13 December 1698, a terrible sight awaits them: the red flag of Oman flutters over the bastions of Fort Jesus. The fleet turns about and sails away.

VISUAL: *Renaissance paintings of caravels. Pikes and swords, battle-axes and halberds. Shots of Prince Henry the Navigator's fortress-cum-navigation school in Sagres, Atlantic waves exploding below the battlements. The camera glides down the length of a cannon. We see the ball being loaded into the muzzle, the touchhole ignites, smoke belches.*

SOUND EFFECTS: *Gregorian chant and wailing fado music, the sound of marching feet and an echoing martial song in Portuguese.*

Paul remained in the café all morning, immersed in the history and only dimly aware of his surroundings. Since childhood, he'd developed a knack of transporting himself into another time or place, able to conjure all the details, and he found his imagination slipping in and out of the seventeenth century and the great siege of Fort Jesus.

Every so often, an elderly waiter, in black trousers and neatly ironed white shirt, strolled over and Paul would order something to keep from flagging: 'Another Coke please, Anwar.'

'I'm sorry, bwana, we've run out of Coke and the besiegers won't let us collect more from the harbour. The last party were all killed. We only have water from the cistern. One pint ration per day.'

'That will do fine, thank you, Anwar.'

Later, the waiter brought news from the battlements. José had been shot in the eye with a poisoned arrow and would not make it. A group of attackers using siege ladders had been driven off. The captain was suffering from hay fever. Paul chronicled each snippet of news in his notebook.

VOICE-OVER: *More than 6,500 people fell in a defence that lasted thirty-three months. Portugal's power in East Africa was broken. After two bloody centuries, the Europeans were chased from the western Indian Ocean, and all that remained of the empire initiated by Vasco da Gama were a few backwater ports in Mozambique. Between 1631 and 1875, Fort Jesus was won and lost nine times. Innumerable accounts of heroism, treachery and resistance cling to its ramparts. And so on, and so on...*

The cloud of Paul's hangover had lifted somewhat and he needed to stretch his legs. He left his papers in the care of Anwar and went exploring. At the far end of the courtyard, he came to a room adorned with charcoal drawings by Portuguese soldiers and sailors. There were doodles of crucifixes and churches, tents and sea creatures, the like of which any schoolboy might sketch. The drawing of a frigate had meticulously worked rigging and ratlines, no doubt a clue to the lower-deck identity of the artist.

Paul found a heart with an arrow through it: a sailor longing for a sweetheart back home. Many years would pass before he saw her again. Would he make it safely down the Indian Ocean, around the dreaded Cape of Storms, and all the way back up the Atlantic to his love? Would she still be waiting for him and was it worth the wait? He'd have no choice in the matter, stuck on that infernal, reeking ship with only male company. How else to occupy his mind, other than with the thought of their reunion, perhaps years hence, on the banks of the Tagus? *She's going to dump you, poor bastard.*

Paul entered the guardroom. Its ceiling was fashioned from planks laid side by side; the edges had holes drilled in them and were stitched together with rope. Of course! He'd read somewhere that Fort Jesus housed the only surviving remains of a mtepe. He stared up at the dark beams, the intricate stitching that held them together, and marvelled at the ancient maritime engineering.

He left the guardroom and climbed the battlements. The walls were tall, ochre-coloured redoubts punctuated with musket slits and bristling with cannons. He stopped to peer through an embrasure above a secluded corner of the moat. Closing his eyes, he pictured the unfolding scene from three centuries ago. A young African woman was talking to a Portuguese soldier. His musket lay to one side and he'd undone his sword. She leant against the wall and hitched up her skirts to reveal large brown buttocks. The man let his breeches fall and pressed himself against her. With his knees he forced her legs wider and both bodies began to gyrate. They looked like some strange insect with two torsos and four legs.

The white bottom bounced back and forth. Black arms were spread against the coral wall. The soldier yanked roughly at her blouse and two breasts fell out. After a few moments, there was a faint moan and the man pulled up his trousers, looked around furtively and handed her a small leather pouch.

Paul opened his eyes, shook his head and walked on. He found a stone seat where the walls were at their lowest and where the Omanis had finally breached the defences. Paul had watched enough war documentaries on the History Channel to have a fairly good idea of how it went: ragged musket fire, the occasional harrumph of a cannon, the shouting, smoke and chaos. He felt the fear: an enemy swarming over the walls like cockroaches and racing towards him, brandishing muskets and swords (pikes? scimitars? he'd better check); the bloodcurdling screams. There on the bastion, Paul could feel the axis of power shifting to the east.

Blood, blood and more blood was all he could think about.

A graffito on the wall opposite the fort read WESTOXICATION. He walked down to the water's edge. The fort's seaward defences overlooked a line of blossoming frangipani trees; beyond them, boys swam in clear blue water. Large 'ship-breaker' cannons and stubby carronades sat close to the water, protecting the narrow channel to the anchorage.

Outside Schmuck Laden Curio Shop, an American woman — leathery skin, khaki shorts, sneakers and backpack — asked him where he was from. She ignored his answer and got straight to the point, as though they'd already been conversing for some time.

The woman was from Santa Cruz, California. *An older version of Hannah,* thought Paul. The same searching eyes, the same hunger to be understood. Her name was Pamela and she was perfectly nice. The questions came thick and fast. What did Paul think of 9/11? What should America's response be? What would Muslim Africa do if they bombed Afghanistan? Pamela had been 'talking with the locals', questioning, fact-finding, seeking approval for her president's next move. It was as though she were on a PR mission from the White House.

'America has a historic opportunity to improve its image in the world, to *join* the world!' she said, touching Paul's arm. 'It's a chance for us to really understand other nations, what with all the sympathy directed our way in the month since 9/11. We must seize this opportunity, don't you think?'

Her attitude was something new to Paul. There was a vulnerability, a need to be understood, accepted, even in the back streets of Mombasa. It was as though the destruction of two towers had pricked a bubble in the same way Pearl Harbour had done. Paul liked what he was hearing.

They talked for a while on the pavement, Paul giving his cautious two cents' worth, Pamela almost listening. Then, all of a sudden, she turned on her heel and trotted up the street, pumping her sneakers and looking for more sympathy for America.

Half a block further on, he overheard an argument taking place on a veranda. He'd stopped to take a picture of a carved wooden door and lingered for a moment of eavesdropping. The tiff was in Swahili, but the words 'Osama' and 'Bush' were unmistakeable. After a minute, the pair of arguers in flowing white kanzus stormed off in different directions: no common ground had been found. Paul felt war was close. He pictured a box of dynamite and a sizzling spark gliding along its fuse like a mamba through long grass.

He wandered deeper into the backstreets, where little appeared to have changed in centuries. There were diminutive mosques and darkened shops selling chests, fabrics, soapstone sculptures and carpets. Here was a living link to the slaves and ivory, hides and horns that passed through these streets long before the first Europeans set foot ashore.

Insistent salesmen talked the age-old talk of trade — extra-low price, only today, especially for you, your last chance, how much you think it's worth, name a price, go on sir, name your price. So too, the insistent refrain of *'Jambo!'* from passing men, offering to be his guide, to show him the secrets of the town. Less forthcoming were the women, often in head-to-toe buibuis. The sparkle of kohl-lined eyes from slits in their black robes; the glimpse of a gold bracelet, henna tattoo or dainty, sandal-strapped ankle. *So sexy and so damned aloof,* he thought.

Paul took a taxi back to the hotel. He decided he deserved some pampering by feminine hands, even if he had to pay for it. Joyce was his masseuse, a buxom Kikuyu matron who'd hoped to knock off early — but along came a down-in-the-mouth, bag-of-bones mzungu just before closing time. It was not the feel-good, New Age experience he knew from his regular in Joburg. There was no incense, no candles, no tinkling music; just a brightly lit room and a metal bed. It looked more like a surgery. They stood facing each other under the neon glow.

'Take off clothes,' she commanded, more gruffly than he thought necessary. An assistant joined her, and both stood watching him with their arms folded. Paul pulled off his T-shirt as nonchalantly as possible, but struggled to slip out of his jeans. He climbed on to the bed in his jocks. The women made no move to get to work on him.

'Is this okay?' he asked.

'Yes, you lie still,' said the matron.

The assistant left and slammed the door. Paul cleared his throat authoritatively.

Joyce was rough, pummelling him as though his flesh were recalcitrant clay. He cringed and winced, but her fingers read none of his resistance. When he directed her to his sensitive bits, like the middle of his back, she saw this as an opportunity to try to split his skin with her thumbs, then with her elbow. 'Is it better?' she asked.

'Yes, much!' he gasped. 'That bit's really fine now.'

She had poured a tub of oil over him, which attracted the dusk mosquitoes. They attended to every part of his body not being flayed by Joyce. When would it end? There was a knock at the door and Paul had a moment of respite, which he used to kill a mosquito slaking itself on his calf. There was a hissed exchange: it was after five, why was she still here? A muscle-bound man peered round the curtain and eyed Paul suspiciously. Joyce returned to renew her onslaught, more urgently, more painfully.

Paul crawled out of the spa forty-five minutes later, wondering how long it would take for his muscles to recover. So much for the milk of feminine kindness he'd been craving. Passing through reception, he bumped into Joshua, the hotel's entertainment manager. On the off chance that the man might be able to help, Paul imparted his dhow woes.

'*Hakuna matata*, my friend, we'll find you a boat,' said Joshua, picking up the phone to call one of his contacts. Paul asked him to try Kilifi harbour first, then Malindi.

Half an hour later, Joshua came to find him at the bar. Kilifi wasn't an option. It had only yachts and live-aboard dive boats, not the experience Paul was looking for. However, Joshua had secured a possibility of sorts: big thumbs-up and a wide grin. A certain Mr Yusuf in Malindi would be able to organise something.

'It'll be expensive, because any dhow that takes you up to Lamu will have to tack back down the coast into the wind after it's dropped you,' he warned. 'Day after tomorrow good for you?' Paul had no other plans and nothing to lose; in forty-eight hours he'd make sure he was in Malindi.

Dinner was another big, bland buffet. He sat alone at a table on the terrace with a romantic candle for one and palms swaying their skirts alluringly. *Lady-boy palms with hairy coconut testicles,* he wrote in his notebook. Everywhere he looked were honeymooners, each one transfixed by the candles in their partner's eyes. Elton John gnawed away at the edge of his hearing like the bloated mosquito that he was. If only he, too, could be swatted. The omelette man now carved fat slices of desiccated lamb. The éclairs were as floppy, and as tasty, as his lopsided chef's hat.

Paul remembered Bangkok with Hannah — an evening like this, of sticky air and swaying palms. It was early in their relationship, a virtual honeymoon after months apart. There was an expensive dinner at the water's edge, following by nightclubbing and then love-making. Good times. Before the indeterminate times. Long before the bad times.

Paul helped himself to another éclair. Then he walked through the palms down to the beach, only to find the moon almost full and casting an ethereal path across the sea. It looked too romantic for a stroll, so he headed for the safety of the bar.

A television set flickered above the counter. KBC showed footage of Ground Zero, where teams picked through the rubble. The newsreader was saying all eyes were on Afghanistan and the retribution to come. A studio guest talked about preventing a clash between East and West, Islam and Christianity, and how Kenya was home to both communities, able to see both sides of the story.

Relief arrived in the shape of the girls from an Abidjan dance group who began contorting their bodies, dislocating shoulders, tumbling about and snaking across the floor between the guests. At least they were a distraction, and kind of sexy. And the beer was nice.

A couple from London, who'd been having a spat about wallpaper colours over dinner, were making up over G&Ts at the end of the bar. There was a light sucking of lower lips, a darting of chameleon tongues, a fogging of eyes. Their electricity coursed down the bar to where Paul sat. *Enough*, he decided, taking himself and his heavy head off to bed.

CHAPTER 6

The matatu minibus taxi pulled away in a cloud of black fumes and triumphant hooting. It zigzagged through a maze of parked tuk-tuks and stalls selling fruit, sofas and bed frames, paused at a ramshackle Shell garage to put more air in the tyres, then pulled over at a bus stop on the edge of town. By Paul's reckoning, the taxi was full. It would be a three-hour drive to Malindi and, with twelve passengers and all their luggage, the vehicle was chock-a-block. The gap-toothed driver with wraparound sunglasses stood on the pavement chanting 'Malindi, Malindi, Malindi,' as though auctioning the town, and manhandled ever more passengers through the door.

By the time they left, there were nineteen people on board. Paul wondered whether the $500 boat ride wouldn't, in fact, have been a bargain. There were survival-of-the fittest seating arrangements. Paul had a portly man half-sitting on his lap and a mound of luggage at his feet. He hoped the driver's supplication to Allah, inscribed on the windscreen, would see them safely to their destination.

Just beyond Mtwapa Creek, they came to a roadblock where a traffic cop directed them into a lay-by. Surely their driver would be fined for smooth tyres, overloading, a lack of seat belts? But money seamlessly changed hands and the policeman smiled, waving them on. *Fine us, damn it, we're a tin coffin!* he wanted to shout.

The Kikuyu man beside Paul ran his arm along the backrest and let his hand brush the shoulder of a buibui-clad woman. She shot him a lethal glance and he quickly withdrew his arm.

The windows were kept shut and the air grew close. Passengers were squeezed together, sweating and jostling for buttock-cheek advantage on the seats. When Paul leant forward, his travelling companion's flesh spread out behind him. When he sat back, the man hunched forward, ballooning across his vision.

The landscape flashed by. Paul glimpsed baobab and mango trees, sisal plantations and patches of forest, but paid little heed and derived no enjoyment from the scenery. The driving conditions were too uncomfortable. A woman in black sat on the seat in front of Paul and her cute baby daughter stared at him over her shoulder, transfixed. Paul didn't particularly like babies — or dogs, and he was allergic to cats. Amazingly, all three species knew this and homed in on him, especially at social gatherings. Babies wanted him to play with them, cats made a home in his lap and dogs wasted little time with crotch-sniffing foreplay before getting down to trouser copulation.

However, he had to admit this baby with cherubic cheeks and pigtails was a charmer. He winked and she blinked; he stuck out his tongue and she stuck out hers; he grinned stupidly and she almost reciprocated. This was splendid entertainment. He found himself imagining, in an abstract sort of way, having a child, one day ... until he pulled a face that was clearly not to the baby's liking. Her face crumpled in dismay, then the crying started, then the screaming, followed by vomiting and attendant smell. Paul had seldom craved a destination so wholeheartedly.

Finally Malindi hove into view and the occupants disembarked at a taxi rank. Paul asked the driver to drop him at the waterfront, but the man wanted another hundred shillings, thereby doubling the fare from Mombasa. The two got into an argument, which Paul lost. He was carrying three bags and didn't know how long the walk might be. 'I'm not an American with dollars,' he grumbled. 'Fleecing visitors is no way to encourage tourism.'

The driver shrugged. Paul relented and paid the money. It was only five hundred metres to the waterfront. He got out in a huff, slamming the door.

Malindi was a scruffy place, a far cry from the prosperous Portuguese town of the sixteenth century he'd read about. Loaded like a pack mule, he stomped along the waterfront in a foul temper.

He'd been given the name of a café beside the main jetty and told to ask for Yusuf Abdulrazak. Paul went from door to door until he found the place. Yusuf was sitting in a plastic chair on the café's veranda. He was a big man with a white kikoi and blue kofia skullcap and the prematurely lined face of a smoker. '*Salaam alaikum*,' he said gruffly and held out a hand.

'*Alaikum salaam*,' Paul returned the greeting.

'They tell me on telephone you want to go to Lamu. They say you want to go in dhow.'

'Yes, Mr Yusuf, I'd like to get there the traditional way. Maybe even sail further, to Somalia, if possible.'

'You are too late. The man you need is gone to Mombasa. He left by taxi in morning. You come again at five.'

Yusuf directed Paul to a nearby backpackers' hostel. Walking through town, he was approached by earnest young men wishing to be his guide. '*Jambo, habari*, where you from?' The refrain echoed up the street. He returned the greetings but kept walking. Many establishments along the main drag had signs in Italian and German, but there was little evidence of tourist activity. In the month since 9/11, Muslim destinations had slipped off the map and most Westerners had changed their vacation plans.

Ozi's was a spartan establishment set around a courtyard opposite the town's main mosque. Paul's room was on the top floor. The bed was a bare mattress, but sheets and a pillow could be rustled up for the guest who arrived with no sleeping bag. Paul threw open the windows to allow in a sea breeze. From the terrace he surveyed the mosque and beach beyond, as pigeons fluttered between the minarets, cooing lustily.

Once he'd unpacked, Paul decided to go for a swim. Bathing towel over his shoulder, he followed an overgrown lane which narrowed to a path and led on to a headland where Vasco da Gama's pillar dominated the anchorage. Paul clambered over a coral outcrop and down on to a sweeping stretch of beach. There was only one other sunbather. He laid his towel on the sand nearby and went for a swim, then stretched out on the towel taking notes, whiling away the afternoon waiting for his appointment at Mr Yusuf's café.

'Do you have the time?' Her voice was soft and melodic. She stood over him, silhouetted against the sun.

'I'm sorry?' he said, flustered by her sudden appearance.

'The time? Do you have it?'

'Oh, yes, sure.' He fumbled in the daypack for his watch. 'Four-fifteen. I'm Paul, by the way.'

'Dalila.' She smiled.

'Are you from around here?'

'I'm a hairdresser in town. It's my day off.'

Dalila Kariuki had an oval face with full lips, dark eyes and short dreadlocks. They chatted for a few minutes, then she returned to her towel. Paul watched her go, watched her bum and the loosely tied strings of her bikini top. *Damn*, he thought.

He went for another dip and walked back to his towel via Dalila.

'May I sit?' he asked, dripping from his swim.

'Of course.' Her grin was playful. She rolled on to her side and put down the romantic novel she was reading. He struggled through a series of pleasantries, registering the breathlessness between them. She adjusted her bikini top, dragging a triangle of material over a nipple that was in danger of exposing itself. Paul found the gesture almost unbearably alluring.

They talked awkwardly about Johannesburg and Kenya, this and that. She was a Kikuyu from Nairobi and had moved to the coast to start a career.

On an impulse he leant towards her. She hesitated, widened her eyes in mock astonishment, then leant closer. Her lips were duvet soft, feather soft, something-or-other soft. How would her romantic novel put it? So much for the Swahili adage of *pole-pole* — 'slowly, slowly'. Which suited him just fine, as there was no time for the prescribed three dates. After all, by the next morning he could be sailing for Lamu.

Mid-kiss, Paul suddenly noticed how low the sun had sunk. It was almost time for his meeting. He apologised, arranged to meet her the next day at the jetty, then jogged back to town feeling happier than he had in weeks.

'*Jambo*, Mr Paul, you are late,' said Yusuf, standing with hands on hips outside his café. 'I introduce you to Mr Husni Issa. He is my friend. He will take you to Lamu for $120.'

Paul shook the man's hand, which reeked of fish. Husni was in his late forties, wore cut-off jeans and an ancient Liverpool FC shirt. He was a stocky man with a powerful build and very dark skin; his face had refined, handsome features and a pencil moustache. Husni carried a foot-long dagger in his belt and did not look him in the eye. Paul didn't have a good feeling about any of this.

'All right, Husni, it's a deal,' he found himself saying. 'What time should we meet?'

'Day after tomorrow at sunrise. Next to the jetty. I will need some of the money now. To buy food for the trip. For the crew.'

Paul handed over some cash and a few dollars to Mr Yusuf as reward for his facilitation.

'Is there something special you want to eat?' asked Husni.

Paul couldn't think of anything. Besides, what on earth was on a dhow's menu? He'd just go with whatever the crew ate.

'No, nothing special,' he said.

They shook hands again. Paul watched Husni walk up the street and into the shadows. The man didn't glance back.

CHAPTER 7

Paul had a day to spare and wanted to visit the Gedi ruins, a likely location for one or two scenes in the documentary. Gedi was a legendary Swahili city, founded in the thirteenth century and mysteriously abandoned in the seventeenth. So many questions still lingered among its eerie, forest-bound ruins. Not surprisingly, local people considered it a place of ghosts and evil spirits.

Paul joined a tour group from one of the beach hotels. The bus dropped them at the gates, where a jocular guide called Harith introduced himself. 'Gedi means "precious" in the Galla language,' said the diminutive man. 'Today, my good people, I will show you its treasures. This way, please.'

Brightly coloured Sykes' monkeys trailed behind the group, badgering them for snacks. Harith bent down and handed a banana to a pretty young female. 'My favourite,' he said with a smile, patting her on the head.

The ruins began to materialise from thick foliage and the group stopped at an overgrown mosque, where Harith gave a short introduction to the site. Dappled light shafted down from a canopy of trees. Paul found it utterly captivating. He let the others walk on and sat on a piece of toppled masonry to write in his notebook.

VISUAL: *Subjective Steadicam. The camera moves through trees, brushing aside leaves ... and comes upon Gedi. It follows a ruined street towards the remains of a mosque. Cutaways of birds and monkeys peering from foliage overhead.*

Paul trailed after the group, marvelling at the city as it slowly revealed itself. Gedi lay in the heart of the forest, baobabs and tamarind trees towering above the ruins, the tentacle roots of strangler figs climbing over walls. The bark of the trees was the same grey colour and texture as the stonework, lending an organic aspect to the city, as though the buildings had grown from seeds. Streets were narrow, the walls pressing in to create cool shadows and draughts in the humid climate. Every now and then an alley would open on to a small square with a well. Harith pointed out evidence of sophisticated plumbing: lavatories that made use of the tide, and even underfloor, water-cooled air conditioning. Some houses were grand affairs with sunken courts, panelled walls and carved stonework. In one ruined home, Harith showed them a graffito of a dhow which had been dated to the fifteenth century. Paul took a closer look. The vessel had a square sail, not a triangular lateen. It was obviously a mtepe.

He broke away from the group, wanting to let his imagination people the spaces without interference. His mind rebuilt the houses and palaces. Shade extended across the narrow lanes once again as homes rapidly grew around him, stone upon stone. He ghosted through an open doorway. There was the master of the house, clad in a striped caftan and silk turban, reclining on cushions in the courtyard. Paul roved through the apartments where the wives had their bedrooms and private lavatories. One woman sat at a table, applying kohl with a bronze eye-pencil. Gold bangles covered her arms to the elbow, crystal and carnelian beads adorned her neck, and gold chains were wrapped around her ankles. She stood up, sprayed herself with Damascus rose water and, after carefully appraising herself in the mirror, strode through to the kitchen. Paul followed discreetly and heard her talking to the cook, something about using the good blue-and-white porcelain as guests were expected for dinner.

He climbed to a viewing platform in the branches of a tree from where he could survey the ground plan of the houses, the sultan's palace with its sunken courtrooms and the remains of a double ring of city walls. These ramparts were designed to protect Gedi from attack — but at some point they had failed. The archaeological evidence, Harith had told them, suggested the inhabitants had left in a hurry.

Although the citizens were long dead and the ruins silent, Paul felt that, in a strange way, almost nothing had been lost. Of course, there were still mysteries surrounding Gedi, and its demise remained a riddle; but this form of Swahili urbanity persisted. In Mombasa Old Town and Zanzibar, and on islands to the north, the essence of the culture lived on in the architecture, dhows, Islamic traditions and language. Gedi's spirit had simply reincarnated itself elsewhere along the coast.

A site-museum housed artefacts that showed the extent of trade. Paul picked his way among displays of glazed earthenware from Persia, furniture and beads from all corners of the Indian Ocean, and intricate silver jewellery. Ming porcelain from China reminded him how far the dhows and junks had travelled. A poster on the wall described the great Chinese voyages of exploration, especially those of Grand Admiral Zheng, a court eunuch with the auspicious title of 'Three-Jewelled Eunuch of Pious Ejaculation'. Zheng's seven expeditions in the early fifteenth century put Vasco da Gama's exploits into perspective.

The fourth of Zheng's voyages had reached Africa. Here he sought rare commodities such as rhino horn, ivory and 'dragon's spittle' — ambergris. Malindi, and perhaps Gedi, became the source of goods that would astound the imperial court. Not only did his ships return home with a miraculous striped horse and the sabre antelope of Eastern myth, they also brought a beast so strange it had the residents of Peking in raptures. Could the tall creature really be the magical qilin, the unicorn-like creature of Chinese legend? Its appearance was thought to be a good omen for both emperor and country. Crowds thronged the streets of Peking to watch the gentle animal with the elongated neck pass by like a visiting royal.

Paul took notes:

VOICE-OVER (Chinese quote):
'Now in the twelfth year of which the cyclical position is chia-wu,
In a corner of the western seas, in the stagnant waters of a great morass,
Truly was produced the qilin *whose shape was fifteen feet high,*
With the body of a deer and the tail of an ox, and a fleshy boneless horn,
With luminous spots like a red cloud or a purple mist.
Gentle is this animal that in all antiquity has been seen but once,
The manifestation of its divine spirit rises up to Heaven's abode.'

The bits of broken porcelain in Gedi museum were no less a link to Ming-dynasty Peking than the Malindi giraffe which caused such a stir. Their journey across the oceans was just as miraculous.

Back at Ozi's, Paul took a cold shower, dug out the cleanest shirt and jeans from the bottom of his backpack, and applied less insect repellent and more deodorant than was malarially prudent. He hated the aftertaste of Tabard on the end of a kiss. He found he was both excited and a little nervous.

Paul waited at a bus stop above the jetty. Dalila came walking up the coast road with a lazy swaying of the hips, her short dreads bouncing against her cheeks. White shirt and black miniskirt, sparkling eyes and gloss on her lips.

They walked along the beach for a while, carrying their sandals and holding hands. The sun had dipped behind the palms, casting long, shaggy shadows and a choppy shore break slapped the sand. The sky turned salmon, then purple. They stopped and he kissed her lightly on the forehead, then the lips.

'Do you want to come back to my room?' Paul asked impulsively. 'Or should we go to dinner?'

'What are you doing tomorrow?'

'I'm leaving at sunrise, by dhow. To Lamu.'

She looked confused. 'You mean, this is the last time we'll see each other? You mean this is hello and, really, goodbye?'

'I might come back to Malindi, after ... one day... But yes, this is maybe the last time. I'm sorry.'

'I'm sorry too,' Dalila said. She glanced down at her feet, then took his hand and seared him with a look that was deadly serious. 'Let's go to your place,' she whispered.

They walked back to Ozi's in silence. There was an awkward moment at reception. A notice above the desk said no visitors were allowed in the rooms, so they pretended to be collecting something Paul had forgotten. The befezzed concierge gave them a filthy look as they scuttled up the stairs.

Dalila thought his room was 'wonderful' and threw open the shutters with glee, which made his heart ache. If this unfurnished shell appeared glamorous to her, what kind of living conditions did she have to endure? He felt suddenly empty, as though all energy had drained out of him through his shoes. Dalila stood in the terrace doorway and unbuttoned her shirt to reveal a cream-coloured bra.

She came over to undo the top buttons of his shirt and began kissing his neck. He ran his fingers down the notches of her spine. Should he go through with this? Was she having the same thoughts? Paul undid the last buttons of the blouse and slipped it from her shoulders. He looked at her small, perfect breasts, cupped by the cream material, then unclipped her bra with a squeeze of thumb and forefinger. She caught her breath as it fell to the floor ... melodramatically killing the lights.

Or so it seemed, for the bedroom was suddenly plunged into darkness. They looked out of the window and saw that a power cut had blackened much of the town. If there had been hesitation before, the darkness was taken by both of them as a sign. He hastily undid her belt. His thumbs manoeuvred miniskirt and underwear over her hips.

Dalila gently pushed him backwards on to the bed. He lay still as she straddled him. Leaning back, her hair clip got caught in the knotted mosquito net. She laughed, extricating her dreads. Their eyes became accustomed to the gloom and the last of the dusk cast a soft glow across her body.

Paul rolled Dalila on to her back and slid down her body.

There was a knock at the door. They froze.

'Mister?' came an obsequious voice.

Paul put a finger to her lips. Of course the concierge knew they were there, must have heard the squeal of the bed, but Paul wasn't going to respond.

'Mister, are you here?'

What if he had a key? There was a long pause. Perhaps the man had his ear pressed to the keyhole. 'A lamp for you,' he whined. 'I'll leave it at the door.' His feet scraped down the steps, pausing every now and again as he descended to the lobby.

They waited a full minute, their bodies locked together. He bit her earlobe when the pleasure became too much, feeling the clink of an earring against his teeth. Once Paul felt sure the man had gone, he hooked his elbows behind her knees, lifting her. Dalila's head was pressed against the wall. He arched his back, drawing his head away from her. Then he collapsed on top of her, gasping for air.

'I'm sorry. It's been a long time,' he mumbled, then got up to go to the toilet.

When he returned, she was standing beside the bed, holding her clothes.

'Can I use your shower?' she said softly.

'Of course, of course, I'm sorry, I'll get you a towel,' he said. 'The hot water's not working.'

'It doesn't matter.'

She closed the door and he got dressed, feeling wretched. When she emerged, fully clothed and with wet hair, Paul took her in his arms. He didn't know what to say, so he said nothing and kissed her. Dalila's body pressed against his. He felt the affection streaming back, took her hand and led her down the stairwell. Each landing was lit by a single paraffin lamp. Laughing, they ran through reception and ignored the accusing glare of the concierge.

They had supper at the I Love Pizza Restaurant, just down the road from Ozi's. Their conversation had become awkward again and strangely formal. After a while, they fell to holding hands for long stretches. With the second glass of wine, conversation returned. They told each other about their homes.

'My father works in a factory in Nairobi,' she said. 'My mother is a nurse, a very good nurse.'

'What language do you speak at home?' asked Paul.

'Kikuyu. Swahili is my second language.'

'So English is your third?'

'Yes. But in Nairobi it's mostly English. I don't like Nairobi. The crime. My father is also very possessive. He is always angry when I go out at night, so I moved to Malindi. My eldest brother lives here. He's married, one child. It is more free for me here. The hairdressing job is just the beginning. I've only been here a few months and haven't made many friends yet. But I love the beach and I go almost every day.'

'Has there been a man in your life here?' asked Paul.

'No, not really, but I am looking. Perhaps, one day, someone like you, you know —' she said shyly.

Did she mean rich, white, older, foreign? How much distinction did she make between him and the middle-aged Italians, bristling with medallions and machismo, walking the Malindi streets arm in arm with teenage beauties? Was there any difference at all? He thought of his receding hairline, his wallet of dollars, his growing beer gut.

Their waiter was an older man who watched Dalila suspiciously from the corner and was rude to her when they placed their orders. She spoke English to him, not Swahili, and did not look him in the eye. Paul guessed he was making assumptions about her intentions, perhaps even about her profession. He felt a wave of anger, mostly directed at the waiter, but also at himself.

Paul turned the conversation to politics. Was there tension in Malindi between Muslims and Christians, Swahili and Kikuyu? No, as far as she was concerned, there was no discrimination and hardly any tension. In turn, she wanted to know about racism in South Africa. He made similarly vague statements about a rainbow nation. He told her about the world he'd grown up in. She had only the sketchiest idea of what apartheid was. When he explained the details of discriminatory legislation, her eyes registered an implausible fiction of mixed-marriage acts and segregation. At times, it seemed she only half believed the mzungu storyteller with his tall tales of a faraway tribe of white Africans.

They left the restaurant and walked to the bus stop, where they sat on a stone bench and said nothing for a while. Paul felt trepidation about the next morning, and a strange guilt at leaving Dalila. They lingered, arms around each other, until a taxi pulled up and the door squawked open. They stood up and kissed goodbye. Dalila's hand was out of the window, his at half mast, waving until the taxi turned the corner. He sat back down on the bench and stared at his feet for a long time.

CHAPTER 8

Paul took a walk along the beach and out on to the headland where the padrão stood out, white like a tooth in the moonlight. He climbed on to the plinth and looked out to sea, imaging the first arrival of the Portuguese in this bay half a millennium ago and letting his mind slip back through the centuries to an evening in 1498…

A dark figure was sitting on the seaward side of the pillar. The man was dressed in a big-buttoned tunic with billowing sleeves, long stockings and a codpiece. Olive-skinned and bearded, he wore pointy leather shoes and a circular cap.

'Hi there, I'm Paul,' he said. 'What's up?'

The young man stared back blankly. Then recognition dawned on his face: '*Bom dia,* I no spick *inglês.*'

'*Ola, muito prazer, Senhor.*' Paul's Portuguese was rusty, but passable. He'd spent enough holidays in Mozambique to get by and had studied the language for a year at university. 'That's a very smart outfit,' he said.

'This is my shore garb,' said the young man in Portuguese. 'But your vestments are far stranger.'

'Are you from Portugal?'

'*Sim*, from Lisboa, but it's been long since I was home. It has taken us many months to get here.'

'You came by sea?'

'*Sim, Senhor,* our ships are anchored in the bay. Some of the crew are in the town. Our commander and his captains have remained on board. They won't come ashore. We had some trouble in the south. These Mahometan infidels ... you must know how they are.'

'Um, kind of.'

'They are treacherous. Never trust them. All along the coast they have tried to betray us: at Musa Al Big's Island, at Kilwa, and again when we anchored off Mombasa. My captain had to pour boiling oil on those we captured to extract their villainous intentions. They are all dogs. We had hoped to find evidence of Prester John, or at least some Christian people along the coast. But all is infidel.'

'You have been fighting your way up the coast?'

'Yes. When we were betrayed, we opened fire with cannons and razed their buildings to the ground. At Musa Al Big's Island, we set the town alight. At Mombasa, the infidels laid a trap, but the Lord showed us their treachery and we were spared.

'Trust me, good sir, all the towns that have plotted against us will be forced to accept the yoke of Portugal. The island kingdoms of Africa will be overrun and subjugated. The Mahometan, in his hate, will find himself transfixed by his own arrows. Mark my words. When we set sail from Mombasa, my commander prayed to our Lord to show us some safe haven and that is how we came to fair Malindi. It is by the grace of God alone.'

'The people have been good to you here?' said Paul.

'Yes, they seem a trusty, warm-hearted race. The sultan has welcomed my commander. He has showered acts of friendship upon us and gifts of fat-tailed sheep, poultry and such fruits as are in season. But we never let our guard down.

'It was a great honour bestowed upon me by my beloved commander, that I be the first envoy to meet the sultan. Yesterday I came ashore with gifts of scarlet cloth and wrought coral. I told the sultan, through an interpreter, that we were not pirates but proud mariners from the continent of Europe. I must confess that I made an exceptionally good impression on the sultan. He agreed to come and visit aboard our flagship, the *São Gabriel*. Last night there was great rejoicing on the ships. You may have heard us?'

'No, I didn't.'

'Oh, we had fireworks and exploding firebombs! Those on the beach made reply in kind, letting off rockets and Catherine wheels. This morning at dawn I returned to the shore, feeling a little the worse for wear after such revelry, and escorted the sultan to my commander's ship.'

'I wish I'd seen it.'

'It was magnificent. His barge was decked with multi-coloured silk awnings and the sultan himself was resplendent in robes of damask, dyed a lovely Tyrian purple. I have an eye for such things. At his belt hung a beautiful dagger, its haft glittering with diamonds. His velvet slippers were studded with gold and pearls. In the prow of his barge, men drew from bow-shaped trumpets a strange, festive music that was discordant and even fearsome to the ear. Well, to my ear at least. Some of our mariners appeared to enjoy it, but they had been imbibing.

'My captain, no less resplendent, put out from the *São Gabriel* to meet us on the water. His dress was after the Iberian style, though on top he had a French cloak of crimson Venetian satin. My captain wore his gold sword and in his cap a feather was set at a jaunty angle. Such a handsome man. I wore my favourite purple shore-going garb with green breeches. Being properly attired can be so important, critical even, don't you think?'

'Yes indeed,' said Paul, painfully aware of his own casual attire.

'There were grand speeches on both sides. My commander thanked the sultan for his hospitality and told him about Portugal, how it had risen as a nation by defeating the followers of Islam on the Iberian peninsula. He concluded: "Mahometan might shall never again raise its head among the descendants of Lusus!" Though the sultan was of that faith, he could not fail to be impressed and he wished only goodness upon my captain. "How came you by our shores?" asked the ruler of Malindi.

'My commander replied that the king of Portugal had sent ships to compel the African to recognise by ordeal of battle how superior was the Christian faith to that of Mahomet. Once the rulers of North Africa had been bent to his will, our king sought a passage around the continent to bring Christianity to the East. Upon hearing our story, the sultan agreed to help us with all that we required and promised to replenish our vessels.'

'What is your position on the ship, if I may ask?'

'I am scribe and chronicler. I keep the log too. I have an education. My commander trusts me and I have his ear.'

'Where are you going next?' asked Paul.

'Our king has charged us with finding a sea passage to the East, to bring back spices, gold, riches.' Then, in a whisper, 'You're not working for the English king, are you?'

'No, no, I'm just a simple traveller.'

'Nor the Dutch dogs neither?'

'No, I assure you, I work for no one.' (*Except Africa Moon Films,* Paul thought, but he didn't consider it relevant.)

'Ah,' said the young man, eyeing Paul warily. 'My captain is looking for a pilot to guide us to India. Towards the cradle of the sun. We have heard of a great trading city. Its name is, I think, Qualecut. That is where our destiny lies.'

'Calicut, yes. It's a city in India, many days' sail away.'

'Praise be! I have no doubt Captain da Gama will bring us to that enchanted shore. And you, good sir, where are you bound?'

'North, up the coast. To the islands of Lamu, perhaps beyond.'

'Do you not think it foolhardy? To the north is all pirates. Mahometan pirates. Which is why our ships turn east from here. A Christian like you, all alone on the coast ... this is surely not a wise thing.'

Paul looked out to sea, uneasy. When he glanced back, the man had disappeared. Below him the black waves pummelled the coral. *To the north is all pirates...*

What was he letting himself in for?

Paul woke to a crackling sound. He opened his eyes and saw the grey shades of dawn through the slats of his shutters. What on earth was that noise? The Tannoy crackled again, squeaked; then the call to Mecca broke into his slumber like a wave. He cursed the wailing voice and pulled a pillow over his head in frustration, trying to force himself back to sleep.

The words, without meaning, washed over him. After a while, Paul found himself listening for the incantation of '*Allahu Akbar*', God is Most Great, even mouthing the words as a pantheistic prayer for himself. Indian Ocean matins. '*Hayya 'ala 'l-falah, Allahu Akbar!*'

He reached the beach just before the sun. Already the air was warm and a gentle breeze ruffled the sea. After a few minutes he was joined by Husni and four shipmates, who were perfunctorily introduced to Paul.

'This is Omar, Kijoka, Swaleh and Shekh, all of them Malindi fishermen, all good sailors,' said Husni.

They were a motley bunch in torn shorts and faded T-shirts. The bearded Omar was second mate. The rest were muscular deck hands who barely acknowledged Paul.

'You ready to go?' asked Husni.

'Yes, I guess so.'

'Okay, we go.' Husni picked up Paul's backpack with one hand and strode down the beach. The men followed. As the sun's first rays stole across the water, inflaming a line of palm trees, the crew dragged a flat-bottomed mwuo dinghy into the surf. Paul scrambled aboard and his luggage was piled in the bows. Shekh started paddling fiercely as a small wave loomed ahead of them. It sucked hollow. The mwuo had minimal freeboard and did not rise up to meet the wave, but rather cleaved through the middle, wrapping a wall of green water around them. They emerged on the other side as wet as if they'd swum. Only the sunglasses perched on top of Paul's head were dry. Shekh wore a wide grin. Paul's bags were soaked. Thank goodness his camera was wrapped in plastic.

They drew alongside *Fayswal* and climbed aboard. She was a well-maintained mashua dhow, a little under thirty feet in length – certainly not the jahazi Paul had hoped for, but attractive nonetheless. The paintwork sported recently touched-up detailing in checks and triangles, and the sail was new-white. His bags were dumped in the fish drums amidships, where they were to acquire a nasty aroma.

The lanky Swaleh attached a rudder to the stern while the crew prepared the rigging. Paul found a seat beside Husni at the tiller. Shekh pulled up the anchor, coiling the rope in the bows. At the cry of '*Chukua!*' the yard was hoisted and the lateen sail unfurled to a loud whoop from first-mate Omar. Husni bore away and a light offshore breeze filled the sail as *Fayswal* threaded between anchored dhows that danced on their mooring lines in the short swell. A puff of wind caught them, and the acceleration took Paul by surprise. Mangrove and mahogany creaked, the sail billowed. *Fayswal* bowed to the gust, picking up speed.

Paul looked astern and caught sight of the padrão on the headland. With a shiver he remembered his conversation with the gentleman from the night before. It was in Malindi, he knew from his reading, that Da Gama had found his pilot. When the Arab navigator, Ibn Mãjid, showed the Portuguese a route across the sea to Calicut, he inadvertently initiated half a millennium of European domination of the Indian Ocean.

Paul cast an eye over the crew. Who were these African sailors and what did they make of him? For now, they seemed to be ignoring their passenger. Swaleh and Shekh were coiling rope, Rafiki sat in the bows sharpening two long knives against each other. Paul tried to catch Husni's eye to pass a remark about the wind, make some sort of contact, but the man was staring fixedly at the horizon.

Da Gama had found his navigator in Malindi; for better or for worse, so had Paul.

CHAPTER 9

Fayswal wallowed uncomfortably as they changed course. Gybing is a precarious manoeuvre on a dhow, calling for the yard to be swung around the front of the mast. Shekh stood on the bucking foredeck, feet apart on each rail, trying to keep his balance. The yardarm was raised, its foot pulled back by hand until it was almost vertical, then flipped on to the other side of the mast. At the same time, the main sheet was carried in a coil around the front of the yard. It was a tricky business, neatly handled by the crew. Gybing completed, the dhow headed for open sea.

They were sailing *tingi*, off the wind, in a considerable swell which saw *Fayswal* pitching and rolling exaggeratedly. Once clear of the reefs and sandbanks, they turned north, and took the swells on the starboard quarter, occasionally riding them — to the delight of everyone on board. Despite feeling awkward with the crew, Paul was beginning to enjoy himself. Now and then, a bigger crest would lift the vessel and lob it into a trough, creaming a tall bow wave that had the men cheering. At such moments, they took water over both weather and leeward rails. Kijoka, the youngest on board and general dogsbody-cum-galley slave, was set to work bailing between the ribs with a plastic container. If they ran out of food or got stranded on a desert isle, Kijoka would be the first to be eaten. Or was it non-believing kafirs first, and thus Paul?

An anchored dhow being tossed about in the swell appeared on the horizon. As *Fayswal* drew closer, they could see a group of men fishing with hand lines. Omar was at the helm and bore off to pass within hailing distance. Greetings were called and fish held aloft. Then the dhow was lost behind a rolling wall of blue; when it emerged again, it was out of shouting range.

The rocky headland of Ras Ngomeni stood out grey to the north. Beyond it lay a line of coral outcrops and Omar steered for deeper water. Past Ngomeni, *Fayswal* crossed the wide mouth of Ungwana Bay. They were far offshore now, cruising on a longer, undulating swell.

Biscuits were passed around and Paul managed to get chatting to some of the men. 'How stable are these dhows, I mean, in rough seas?' he asked Omar, who sat peering at the shore from beneath a ragged peak cap, the uneven tufts of his beard blowing in the wind.

'Not too bad. Mmm, sometimes not so good.' He spoke sparingly, as though his words were knots tied in a rope.

'Do they ever capsize?'

'Mmm, sometimes. In the winter Kusi, when the wind is strong, they go over. Some sink. Some float. The men hang on to drums. Maybe cut free the mast, try to swim to shore. If they're not too far. Some make it across the reef to the beach. Alive. Look, that's Zeboma Reef over there,' he said, pointing across the port bow. 'Very dangerous.'

Paul's eye traced a line of breakers. It was difficult to see where the white horses ended and the more serious combers, raking across shallow coral, began. He imagined an unsuspecting dhow heading into that maw at night, how quickly the keel would be ripped out by the knife-edged reef. Suddenly there would be men in the water, and shouting, and black waves detonating on coral.

'The elders always warn about Zeboma,' said Omar.

For most of the year, Omar explained, the current was from the south. Sometimes it swept fishermen out to sea. Ngalawas from as far as Zanzibar would be found drifting, with only the desiccated remains of their crew aboard. However, there was an offshore current from the north at this time of year, so northbound vessels tried to hug the coast, bringing them perilously close to Zeboma's razors.

The swells shortened and sharpened as *Fayswal* shaved past. Everyone had eyes only for the reef until they were well clear.

The morning drifted by. *Fayswal* clipped along in a shallow sea, a line of surf crumbling over coral to port, a firm blue horizon to starboard. Husni and Kijoka rigged a makeshift awning to provide shade. Flying fish leapt from the waves, looking surprised at being briefly transmogrified into birds. Paul sat leaning against the mast, scribbling notes. He loved the way he could feel the mast moving in its seat. There was play in everything on boats like *Fayswal*, where rope, canvas and wood all had give. This pliability gave the vessel life, allowing it to flex and respond to the water.

Watching the crew work, Paul mused about the pioneering Portuguese and the Swahili sailors they encountered. There would have been so many similarities between crews and boats. Life on board would have followed identical rhythms, with the same jokes and stories about women, food and the incompetent chef, about reaching port safely and seeing loved ones again; the same endless diagnosis of wind and water, or how to squeeze another half knot from their lateen rigs. That abandoned laughter, echoing across the water … was it Henrique and José or Omar and Shekh? Those hands working the splice with a marlinspike were tough, intuitive sailors' hands, whether from Malindi or Lisbon.

'This is a very fast mashua,' said Husni as they surfed down another swell. 'She does well in the Malindi races.'

'The Swahili are mad about racing, aren't they?' said Paul.

'Yes, it's in our blood,' said the skipper. 'In the old days, the first boat from Arabia at the beginning of the season got the best prices, so racing was like, how can I say, business. We must know how to use the wind, make our dhows go fast.'

Paul had read lots about the monsoon winds — the summer Kaskazi that brought the dhows from Asia and the winter Kusi that blew them home — but the unsteady easterly they were experiencing didn't seem to fit.

'This isn't still the Kusi, is it?'

'No,' said Husni, 'we would be using a smaller sail if it was Kusi.'

'And it's not the Kaskazi either?'

'No, not yet, next month. This we call Matlai, the in-between wind of springtime, mostly from the southeast. It blows in October and early November. The Matlai is lighter, not so reliable.'

As the day wore on, the crew became chattier. Paul asked them to teach him Swahili sailing terms and jotted them down. Shekh came to look over his shoulder and corrected him as he wrote. '*Changa* — sail, *mangoti* — mast, *foromani* — yardarm, *kana* — tiller, *omo* — bows.' To Paul's ear, sitting on an open deck with a fair following wind and a lateen tugging above his head, the names were pleasingly lyrical, the sound of the word identical to its task, as though object and name had been born of the same monsoonal breath. Swahili was a language that caught the romance of the tropics in its every utterance. Paul tried the words on his tongue, relishing the way they rode his lips. Shekh giggled and shook his head at the terrible pronunciation.

Swaleh took over the helm from Omar. The young apprentice helmsman sat on the stern apron, steering with his foot and hardly ever looking ahead. Husni pulled out two fishing rods from under the thwarts and cast his Rapala lures. Anticipating the catch, baby-faced Kijoka returned to sharpening his pair of knives: scrape, scrape, scrape. Paul recalled his earlier throat-slitting fears and chuckled guiltily at himself.

'We fish for sharks, tuna, kingfish,' said Husni. 'The best places are off Somalia. Lots of trouble there. Boats from Kenya still go, but you must be careful. No one sails as far as Mogadishu any more. Just the southern part.'

'I was hoping to go up there,' said Paul. 'There are some important Swahili settlements and ruins.'

'That is not a good plan,' said Husni as he reeled in one of the Rapalas, then cast again.

Paul decided to let it drop, but the idea of sailing to Somalia still lurked at the back of his mind.

Husni chatted to Paul about fishing and the strange methods employed by his forefathers. For instance, some of them would use sucking fish, like remoras, on a line with a ring around their tails. The fish were trained to hunt green turtles. When they found one, they attached themselves to its throat and all you needed to do was pull in the line.

When a human-looking dugong was caught, an elder in the village would cleanse the fishermen. Crews had to swear on the Koran that no one had indulged in sex with the creature. Only after the ceremony could it be eaten.

One of Husni's lines began to sing and, after a short skirmish, a barracuda was brought alongside. Swaleh grabbed a gaff, impaled the flailing fish and dragged it aboard where it thudded about among the ribs, splattering blood. Kijoka came aft and bludgeoned it to death with a belaying pin. Then the carcass was slid under the stern apron along with the boathook and gaff. Soon after, Husni hooked a second barracuda. Lunch was sorted.

Swaleh set about preparing a makeshift stove just abaft the mast. A wheel rim was lodged between the ribs, lined with sacking and filled with sand. Swaleh used his knife to split firewood into kindling, then doused the pyramid of sticks with paraffin and set a match to it. A pot of water was placed precariously on the flames, forcing the helmsman to sail more conservatively so as not to upend the meal. Meanwhile Kijoka descaled, gutted and chopped the barracudas into manageable chunks. The spines snapped with the same sound as the kindling. Pieces of fish were tossed into the pot, which slopped boiling water every time they crested a big swell. There were no condiments, accompanying vegetables or utensils.

When lunch was ready, the men picked pieces of meat straight from the pot. They'd already been at sea eight hours and Paul was hungry. But he felt queasy and couldn't face the soft, insipid flesh, so Kijoka butchered a papaya for him, deftly cleaving and gutting it with a long blade. Paul dunked the fruit over the side to rinse off the fish blood and ate. The sailors chewed with open mouths, sucking loudly on the meat and smacking their lips. Kijoka clearly enjoyed watching how well his meal went down.

'When we are not fishing, I'm a windsurfing instructor in Malindi,' said the lad.

'I'd love to learn,' said Paul.

'When you come again, I teach you. It's easy-easy.'

Kijoka was a lively teenager who bounded about the deck, keen to help and eager to gain experience. Paul had been just like him when he was learning to sail as a kid on the Vaal Dam, first in Optimist dinghies, then Sprogs and finally L26 keelboats.

The fire was doused with a bucket of water and they could sheet in again. '*Chia damani* … pull in the sail!' cried Husni. Kijoka and Shekh sprang to the sheet and hauled it in, taking a turn on a belaying pin slotted into the gunnel. *Fayswal* healed over and the bow wave began to boil. Paul helped them shift the ballast, in the form of sacks of sand, to the starboard side. The short luff at the foot of the sail quivered as the dhow crested each swell. They were tearing along.

The colour of the sea turned from aquamarine to murky green and Husni said it was from the silt of the Tana River, disgorging into the ocean. For mariners sailing far offshore, such signs helped them fix their positions. Omar spotted three dhows on the horizon, sailing evenly spaced, line astern. The vessels were hull down, flying towards the mushroom-shaped rocks of Ziwayu islet. As *Fayswal* approached the outcrop, Paul noticed a number of craft anchored in its lee. Husni explained that fishermen often sought overnight shelter at this oceanic rendezvous spot.

'You want to stop at Ziwayu and sleep on the dhow?' he asked. 'Or you want go for Lamu?'

'How long will it take?'

'We won't make it before dark. Maybe nine o' clock tonight.'

The wind was freshening and the sea getting rougher. Paul knew they had no navigational instruments, lights or safety equipment, but he didn't fancy a night sleeping on the narrow thwart of a tossing dhow. He reckoned his shipmates were experienced enough night sailors.

'Ziwayu won't be nice in these conditions,' he said. 'Let's push for Lamu.'

The ocean grew moody as evening approached. Ramparts of grey cloud lined the horizon. Ahead of them, the coral outcrop of Tenewi ya Yuu was bathed in orange sunlight. The rocks, carved by wind and water into the shape of two lateen sails, glided past them to starboard. They looked like dhows frozen in the act of running aground.

'You can just see Lamu, there, in the clouds,' said Husni, pointing over the port bow.

Fabled Lamu. Kiwa Ndeo, the Proud Island, as it is known to sailors and poets. Here, at last, was the archipelago Paul had yearned for, the Seven Isles of Eryaya. Unspoilt, uncorrupted, far from the beaten track, an archipelago of ancient towns and overgrown forts, mangrove creeks and pearly beaches. More than anywhere along the African coast, this cluster of islands was the home of seafarers, a living piece of maritime history. Here at last was the *sawahil*, the heartland of the Swahili. Paul felt a surge of elation. Lamu. Lamu at last.

The sun dissolved into the mainland like melting butter, followed by an eerie twilight. The wind turned chilly. Then, quite suddenly, the light was gone. The swells grew more threatening in the dark. Their sail billowed like a black wing, blotting out a triangle of stars. *Fayswal* was racing headlong into troughs whose depth Paul could no longer discern. He began to shiver. Hannah had returned with the darkness. If only he could shift the ballast, change tack. Why did the touch of a woman mean so much more when at sea, he wondered? Was it an inheritance borne by all sailors?

Fayswal was beam-on to the set of the ocean, riding the crests awkwardly, dropping heavily into troughs, blind to what they may hold, for the night was now black as charcoal. Having foregone the barracuda, Paul's stomach growled. Spray coming over the bows set his teeth chattering. The sailors' occasional laughter at some witticism in Swahili only served to isolate him further.

A tangerine moon interrupted his thoughts. Briefly unhinging itself from the cloud bank, it bathed *Fayswal* in pale light. The sea fizzed with lunar sparkles. Lamu appeared close, a dark, upturned dish on the water ahead. Paul noticed they were bearing away, keeping clear of the reefs and mjabalis lining the entrance to the channel that separated Lamu from Manda Island.

The spring tide was ebbing fast to reveal shoals to port and sandbanks to starboard. To make matters worse, the swell had increased. *Fayswal* bore off on to a dead run with the wind directly behind her, aiming at the middle of the channel. Lamu's feeble lighthouse beam provided no help in ascertaining their position, and errant fishermen, Husni told him, had stolen the solar panels from the leading lights which once marked the entrance.

With the ebbing tide, there was now less than a fathom's clearance over the banks and waves broke all around them. 'Those are the Mtanga wa Papa shallows in front of us,' said Husni. 'In some places it's only three feet deep. We must be very careful. When the swell is big, it sucks dry.'

Paul's sailing companions, so animated and chatty only minutes earlier, had fallen silent. The lateen flogged as Omar spilled wind, slowing their progress and trying to get his bearings. Husni was up in the bows, peering ahead. The black outline of the island drew closer.

Something made Paul look astern. What he saw made his hands clench the rail in fear. The dark shadow of an enormous wave slid towards them. It jacked up and exploded into white with a loud crack. Husni screamed something. Omar started to push the tiller for a gybe to bring them into deeper water, then realised it was too late. The wind had all but died and they were bobbing helplessly. The line of white water bore down on them, spitting spray and foam. Everyone braced themselves, hanging on to thwart or rail. The roaring filled their ears. Paul closed his eyes.

It felt as though they'd been boxed by a giant fist. Water smashed over the stern and into the bilges. The dhow was given an almighty shove and they shot ahead of the wave like a cork, ploughing along and kicking up improbable bow-wave sheets. Omar and Swaleh held on to the tiller, trying to keep her straight. If the dhow slewed round, they would broach and capsize. But *Fayswal* rode the slope like a surfboard. The crew held on tight, wide-eyed. As the wave lost its power, they broached hard and cleaved through the froth, taking a torrent over the leeward rail.

By now they were perilously close to Lamu's shoals. Paul grabbed a pot and joined Kijoka, who was already bailing furiously. The rest scrambled into position for a gybe. After a slick turn, hastened by fear, the dhow angled across towards Ras Kitau on the Manda shore, away from the shallows. The ebb was against them, but the breeze was picking up and they were able to claw free of the surf.

But which was the right course? Omar was finding it difficult to keep the vessel on a dead run in such a lumpy sea. Husni couldn't afford securing the lateen at three points in case they needed another quick gybe. Mast and yard bounced uncomfortably as *Fayswal* plunged into the troughs. Waves broke along the Manda shore, just off their starboard beam. The sailors kept glancing nervously over their shoulders. Another wave now could sink them.

They didn't have long to wait. A comber loomed astern, unbroken, brimming. Paul looked at Husni. There was probably enough time to harden up and take it head on, but the skipper gave no such command. Perhaps he'd decided Omar's surfing skills were sufficiently honed. *Fayswal* had just enough speed to catch the big, hollowing wave. The dhow skated down the face, threatening to bury her prow. Paul and the crew instinctively scrambled to the stern to bring the nose up. Now everyone was shouting in a mixture of excitement and terror. Paul emitted an inarticulate howl that came from somewhere deep inside his chest.

When *Fayswal* slid off the back of the wave, they found themselves beneath the lighthouse, gliding into calmer water. The light's comforting beam raked the channel in a sweeping arc above their heads. The moon poked through the clouds again like a cheerleader and the crew responded, breaking into a Swahili shanty that lifted the hair on the back of Paul's neck. Shela village lay to port, along with a few dhows tugging at their anchors. Guests at the colonial Peponi Hotel sat on the terrace sipping cocktails and watching them pass. The men on *Fayswal* sang even louder and Paul joined in with any refrain that was repeated, imitating the seductive sounds.

'Fishing louts,' he imagined the drinkers muttering into their drinks. Fishing louts indeed, and thank Allah he was one of them! Tears of emotion brimmed in his eyes.

Omar and Paul leant against the *dasturi*, looking at the moon. 'They say people have landed there,' he said.

Paul nodded.

'Americans,' Omar said, a hint of disapproval in his voice.

'Yes,' said Paul, laughing. 'Damn Americans, up to no good again.'

He looked at the American moon: full, confident and engorged. The slimmer Islamic version was lean and lethal, with a sharpened edge.

But the loneliness was gone; Hannah had receded. Their dhow was running crisply, propelled by a tropical zephyr into an ancient anchorage. Wherever he looked, boats of every shape and size were anchored in the channel. *Fayswal* slid past a big jahazi with a tree-trunk mast and Omar gave a low whistle of appreciation. At last, a jahazi in the flesh. Paul marvelled at her graceful lines. At that moment, there was nowhere on earth he'd rather be.

The dancing lights of Lamu stone-town drew closer. Faint Arab music reached them across the water, followed by the smell of spicy food. Paul could make out a line of cannons along the waterfront. Most of the dhows they passed were attractive mashuas like *Fayswal*, with straight prows and transom sterns, but there were plenty of other types too. They might just as well be approaching any nineteenth-century harbour, where the age of sail had not yet been eclipsed by steam and iron. The crew were buoyed, chatting loudly and calling to fishermen in the anchorage. Paul felt included, one of the out-of-towners creeping into an exotic port.

Shekh and Kijoka lowered the yardarm in a flurry of canvas. The sail bellied out to leeward and engulfed the crew. It was quickly brought under control and furled with strops to the yard. *Fayswal* described a graceful turn towards the shore, slowing until the prow bit gently into the sand at the southern end of the waterfront. A row of two-storey buildings lined a promenade to their right. His bags were carried ashore on the shoulders of the sailors. Husni said the crew would sleep at a local dosshouse, but first he'd help Paul find a room. Paul felt torn. Earlier, he'd chosen to sail on and not stop at the fishermen's anchorage of Ziwayu. Now, leaving the crew seemed premature.

Paul bade the men farewell, shaking hands with each one, before a barefoot Husni led him north along the waterfront. Soft lamplight issued from doorways, voices murmured below the seawall. Dhows by the dozen bobbed in the shallows or were tethered to bollards. After the disappointment of Mombasa, Paul was thrilled by what he saw.

Husni ushered him into the lobby of Sunsail Inn, a cheap and clean establishment with an upstairs terrace. Paul had planned to make Lamu his base for research, and decided there and then that this would be his home for the coming weeks. The proprietor showed him to a second storey room. There was a four-poster bed, an overhead fan billowing the mosquito net, and shutters that opened to reveal the waterfront.

Back at reception, Paul handed Husni the rest of the payment. They shook hands and Paul gave him a hug. Husni looked sheepish, but smiled broadly.

'Thank you for everything. It's been a pleasure sailing with you. Have a safe voyage back to Malindi.'

'Maybe we will hang around and do some fishing, catch some more barracuda for you,' said Husni.

Paul offered an embarrassed grin.

'Actually,' Husni continued, 'I'm thinking of staying on in Lamu for a while and letting the crew sail *Fayswal* back.'

'Maybe we'll see each other around town then?'

'Yes, maybe. Goodbye. And forget about Somalia.' They both laughed.

Paul had a quick shower before stepping out to find a restaurant. The New Minaa Top-Roof Café was the only place still serving food. There were plastic tables and chairs, neon lighting and a Kenyan soap opera blaring from the television. The place was packed with locals, all gathered around the set. The chicken tikka and chips filled the gap nicely. Paul jotted notes as he ate, trying to capture details of the voyage. He was watched by a curious waiter who intermittently asked him what he was doing, perhaps in the hope that his answer would eventually change to something more interesting. The soap opera meandered to an incongruous ending and Paul trooped out with the rest of the patrons.

CHAPTER 10

Early the following morning, Paul was woken by a commotion outside his room. It sounded like an invasion by the Pate islanders. Half asleep, Paul stumbled to the window. Pushing open the shutters, he stared down on a jovial horde embarking and disembarking from a pair of overloaded motor dhows. Sunsail Inn evidently overlooked the water-taxi rank. *Just my luck,* he cursed, inserting earplugs and ducking back under the net to try and find a few more hours' sleep.

He emerged mid-morning and set off along the promenade, photographing the dhows and trying to get a feel for the town. Much of the documentary would be filmed here, so he wanted to find plenty of potential locations. It wasn't going to be difficult: everywhere he looked were beautiful images. Paul used his notebook, camera and annotated map to keep a record.

Initially, dhows were his main interest. They stretched the length of the waterfront, often moored two or three deep. Vessels were being built, repaired, caulked, talked about and compared. Paul decided that the Swahili, left to their own devices, could not design an ugly boat. No one built from plans. Everything was done by hand using eye and instinct. Large jahazis, workmanlike mashuas, flat-bottomed daus or tiny hori dinghies: all of them graceful.

The government buildings and double-storey homes along the waterfront received the full face of the morning sun. He paused to jot down the details: colonnades, crenellated walls and studded Zanzibar-style doors. All these elements would make for a good town-montage sequence. Architecturally, little had changed in centuries.

However, the signs of the new millennium and its troubles were there. *Down with the power of money*, read one graffito. *USA is dead 2001!* shouted another. Beside them were crudely drawn American and Israeli flags with red lines through them.

At the northern end of town, Paul looked over a wall and saw a dozen mules lounging in the shade. A sign read: *Our sanctuary treats ill and injured donkeys, and works to improve harnesses, reduce overloading, and generally promote good husbandry and care among Lamu's donkey owners.*

He was busy trying to coax one donkey into a more accommodating pose for a photograph when a woman tapped him on the shoulder. She lowered her scarlet veil briefly to reveal a lined face and vacant eyes. 'You go with me, back in your hotel, good price,' she said in a whisper. He shook his head and returned to photographing the donkey.

Paul was one of the few foreigners on the waterfront that morning. World events had crippled Lamu's tourism. In the absence of clients, every available tout, guide, dhow captain and facilitator set to work on Paul, sometimes singly, often in pairs. A simple 'no', or even a complicated one, did not deter them. They offered a range of services, the most useful of which appeared to be keeping other touts at bay. He continued to fend them off all morning as he strolled up and down the promenade. Even on his sixth pass, the same questions would be asked, and the same conversations struck up using the same refrains. Paul grew irritable. His idea of an old-world, embalmed Lamu slipped a notch with each pass.

Then he chose another tack and began to play the game. 'Do you have a dhow going to London?' he asked.

'Mister, you are being unreasonable. All our boats are going to Paris today.'

'How about a cruise to visit the pirate dens of Somalia, then?'

'But sir, October is their time of rest, before the season begins. We do not like to disturb them.'

When it came to prices, Paul also played hard to get. 'I never pay more than a dollar for anything!' he'd say. Or conversely, 'I'll give you ten times your asking price and not a shilling less.'

It became a game of wit and banter that would be picked up where it left off each day for the rest of his stay in Lamu. Their refrains grew increasingly tongue-in-cheek and his stock responses more jocular. He asked for camel trips to the Yemen and flights to Afghanistan, and the touts responded with equally absurd offers. They reached an impasse of sorts, like an old, nagging couple. The agents weren't going to get any business out of him and he wasn't going to persuade them to shut up.

When the incoming tide was high enough, dhows began to make sail all along the front, cleaving away from the shore and beating down the channel towards Shela. Paul came upon *Fayswal* at the end of the waterfront. Instead of sailing straight home, the crew were making ready to head north on a fishing expedition around Pate. Husni was going to visit his parents, who lived in a village on the north shore of the island. Paul climbed down a flight of stone steps for a chat. The crew were awkward with him, perhaps feeling, as Paul did, that he'd somehow broken ranks. There were a few pleasantries, before he climbed the steps and walked on.

Paul left the promenade to explore the back streets. A warren of narrow alleys and closely packed buildings offered a window on the workings of a traditional Swahili town: tiny cafés, hole-in-the-wall fabric stores, courtyard markets and carpentry workshops. Peeping into darkened doorways, he saw hookahs and coffeepots for sale, Persian carpets and Indian brassware. Some buildings had annexes that bridged the lanes on mangrove-pole beams. This was the heart of stone-town, a private quarter whose grand coral houses were owned by the waungwana, the patricians. These fortress-like suburbs with their inward-looking homes kept the outside world, and modernity, at bay.

Paul was soon lost in a maze of labyrinthine alleyways. He didn't mind. It was charming and intimate: whitewashed steps, glimpses of courtyards and small gardens with pomegranate and tamarind trees. A strangler fig climbed out the window of a derelict house, spilling its muscular roots into the lane. Unaccompanied donkeys brushed by, knowing the way home. He squeezed past cart pushers selling goods from door to door and hawkers of coffee and khat. A man ambled by, walking his goat on a lead. Chickens clucked behind high walls, tabby cats snoozed in doorways, men played dominoes in open daka porches. Occasionally the call to prayer would echo down the lanes. Paul felt he was being borne along in some romantic scene from the *Arabian Nights*.

The day was growing uncomfortably hot, so he found an open-air restaurant on the waterfront where he could sit and read. He had a handful of books and a folder of photocopies marked *Lamu* in his daypack. A dhow had lowered its sail and was gliding in to anchor directly in front of him. He picked up his pen and began to write.

VOICE-OVER: *The Lamu Archipelago is home to a long line of nakhodas, dhow captains who have plied their trade along this coast for centuries. It is from here that we will set sail and rediscover the great city-states of the Swahili. Lamu, Manda and Pate were central to the northern* *trade. They had little sweet water, but one great advantage: they were islands. At one remove from the continent, they escaped the raids of inland tribes. Coral reefs protected them from the force of the ocean, and strong currents made for excellent fishing. Mangrove trees, in demand in the East, grew in abundance. Slaves and ivory were also easily attainable from the mainland.*

The tide had turned and was ebbing fast, draining the shallows. One dhow crew, not wishing to be grounded, poled their jahazi into deeper water. A dau coasted in and dropped anchor. Given this craft's flat bottom, the crew was happy to let her settle on the sand as the tide fell. The young men aboard a nearby mashua were sound asleep, not caring whether their vessel was afloat or aground. All the while, the offloading of cut stone and lime continued from the enormous belly of a motorised jahazi.

VISUAL: *Slo-mo shot of a dhow. Sepia sequence of turbaned nakhoda, eyes screwed at the sun, watching the horizon. Old sea chart of the western Indian Ocean, a line is traced from the Persian Gulf to Kenya.*

SOUND EFFECTS: *Call of the muezzin's dawn adhan fades into mournful Arab music, bleeds into African drums, insistent. Behind it the moan of the wind, softly. Fades to the sound of water sloshing on a beach.*

CHAPTER 11

Paul fell into a comfortable daily rhythm, starting with an early-morning walk along the promenade, stopping to ask the touts and captains if there were any dhows heading for Somalia. An image of the ancient sewn boat kept surfacing in his daydreams and wouldn't go away. He'd started to contemplate searching for the last abandoned mtepe. Despite everything he'd heard about Somalia, he wanted to push the idea of going, if not the act, as far as possible. If the journey happened to present itself, then he could weigh up the safety concerns and make a decision.

'No, Mister, still no one is going that way,' was the invariable reply.

Back at the inn, he had his usual breakfast of mango, papaya and toast, followed by a few hours of writing and reading on the terrace. Paul had started the first, tentative scripting of scenes. He was frequently interrupted by a man from reception, who'd call him to the television for CNN newsflashes from Washington and Pakistan, or live crossings to the clearing-up operation at Ground Zero. Fiery politicians insisted that Osama, the Taliban and Afghanistan would soon be brought to heel. To Paul, it seemed the scenario was being presented in cowboy terms: *We've got you surrounded, come out with your hands up.* As the days wore on, the crowd in front of the television grew. At times, there were up to thirty men gathered around the set, commenting loudly on developments.

When CNN or Al Jazeera became too repetitive, he'd wander the town. The main square seemed to him the epitome of 'Swahiliness', with its daily market, Omani fort, waterfront of dhows glimpsed through the town gate, and hubbub of conversation interspersed with the muezzin's call to prayer. Here, men whiled away the day beneath big-leafed trees, playing endless games of bao or simply watching the world go by, fingering their amber prayer beads.

In the produce market, women in bright sarongs presided over equally bright tropical fruit. The stalls were a patchwork of colour: striped awnings, scarlet tomatoes, bowls of chillies, outsize avocados and piles of de-husked coconuts. Everything was ripe and in joyous abundance. The market was alive with chatter and wafted by the scents of dried fish, grilling meat, aromatic spices, rotting bananas and livestock dung. Shopping trolleys in the shape of long-suffering donkeys stood amidst the throng, baskets strapped to their flanks, waiting while their owners haggled for the best prices.

Next to the market, Lamu's fort was a picturesque building with pointy towers, sawtooth crenellations and gun slits. Paul climbed to the highest ramparts, which offered vertical views of the market below. There were vignettes into Lamu's back alleys and courtyards as well as panoramas of the harbour and Manda Island beyond. He gazed over the rooftop terraces and palm-frond makuti roofs, some scruffy and half collapsed, others a collage of rusty corrugated iron. Through the shimmering heat haze, distant palms bent to a breeze which propelled a handful of sails towards the offing.

Later in the day, he might return to his spot on the terrace and watch the passing fray, paying special attention to the water traffic. A mashua might tie up to offload crates of Coca-Cola or receive a consignment of coral blocks. He thought how little such scenes had changed over the centuries. With the slightest recalibration of the eye, the mashua could be replaced with a Persian boom, the labourers with Bajun porters, the cold drinks with mangrove poles.

Paul loved it that so few of the dhows were motorised. The tourist trade was helping to sustain the lateen rig — mzungus preferred the romance of sail. There were dhow ferries and dhow airport shuttles, dhows acting as motorised taxis and as pleasure craft.

Paul spent hours simply watching the vessels manoeuvring in the Lamu roadstead. He never grew tired of it, especially when the wind was strong and skippers' skills were tested in the confined waters. Back and forth the dhows would fly, tacking and gybing, their sails crisscrossing his field of vision like mutant question marks. Spider-like, the crew would hang far out over the water, often without a rope for safety. During a gybe, there'd be a flurry of activity as ballast was shifted, the yard swung and the outrigger plank passed from one side to the other. Sometimes, particularly if the wind was light and the distance to be sailed on the opposing tack not too far, a skipper might elect not to swing the yard and continue with the sail backed against the mast, a dangerous manoeuvre as a strong gust could bring the whole rig down on top of him.

On one occasion, a crew member makes a hash of things, snagging the sail round the top of a mast. The sail begins to flog, rifle cracks echo across the channel. Heads look up all along the promenade, advice is shouted, a joke about shoddy seamanship is bellowed from a rowing boat. Eventually, a foredeck hand shins up the mast to free the sail. The dhow keels over with too much weight so high above the centre of gravity. Water pours over the gunnel and the skipper barks a command. The masthead monkey drops to the deck like a stone and the dhow rights itself. Capsize is narrowly averted. Derisive comments are shouted from the shore, no doubt having something to do with where the crew learnt to sail. A few minutes later the dhow slinks into the anchorage, the men bailing sheepishly, the sail still flogging. There'll be plenty of jokes at someone's expense in the mosque this evening, you can be sure.

Afternoons were a quiet time in Lamu when locals withdrew from the streets and took their siestas. In the early evening, when the air began to cool, people reappeared. Friends and family visited each other, thronging the promenade, playing games and chewing betel or khat. Women filled the shops and the sound of animated gossip poured into the lanes. Paul loved Lamu at this time of day and usually took a stroll before supper. All along the waterfront, groups of men in long white kanzus and embroidered kofia skullcaps stood chatting. Again and again, Paul caught the words 'Bin Laden', 'Bush', 'Taliban'. The imminent attack was on everyone's lips.

He'd often find a bench on the promenade and watch the Lamu world stream by. On one afternoon, a squadron of little boys took to the water below him. Some played with toy dhows made of wood with plastic sails. A pair of twins wearing water wings helped push an overloaded motor dhow away from the jetty. Other children hung on to its fenders and were dragged some way into the roadstead before letting go. One lad even clasped the bows between his thighs and, clinging on tight, was propelled backwards through the water like a living figurehead. Water babies all, he marvelled.

When the tide came in, there was an ad hoc diving competition off the end of the pier. At times it looked as though it were raining children as little bodies dropped from the sky like gannets in a feeding frenzy. A screaming infant, barely out of nappies, was hurled over the edge by a laughing boy. Paul leapt to his feet, ready to perform a rescue, only to see the spluttering child bob to the surface, shouting with delight. The tiny tot scrambled back up the steps and picked on someone even smaller to toss into the drink. International strife seemed a million miles from such happy scenes. How long, he wondered, could such innocence last?

Paul set aside a full day for visiting the Lamu Museum, housed in a rambling three-storey villa on the waterfront. Exhibits presented the history of Swahili city-states. Paul wandered through the rooms, dutifully taking notes. He soon grew bored by the tiresome descriptions of building styles and furniture and his mind turned easily to Hannah. He caught himself writing her name over and over in the margin of his notebook. Trying to snap out of it, he found an information board about building materials. *Soft, reef coral is used for lintels and carved elements*, he noted. *Hard, terrestrial coral goes into foundations and walls. Hannah, why are you so hard, hard like terrestrial coral? Ceilings are carved with plaster friezes, floors are covered with carpets whose decorations often depict Arab society. Below the floor you'll often find an earthenware pot in which the fingo lives. This beneficent jinni guards the home against those with evil intent. Like an unwanted suitor, come to steal her away? A suitor who is, quite frankly, so many of the things you're not.*

Hannah, Hannah, why did you have to go? They could have been here in Lamu together. She would have loved this place. Paul trailed through the rooms, absent-mindedly photographing the items on display.

He climbed the stairs to find the top floor dedicated to Swahili seafaring, its rooms crammed with model boats. This was more like it. Some of the captions were long out of date, still referring to 'the current export of mangrove poles to the Gulf states and Persia by dhow'. There were miniature booms, sambuks and baghlas, and one large replica of a magnificent, double-masted jahazi which traded with India until 1944.

Perking up considerably, Paul noted the specs and drew sketches. He knew his notes were getting too detailed for the movie, but he was now so fascinated by his subject that he couldn't help himself.

VOICE-OVER: *Every summer for a thousand years, the inhabitants of East African coastal towns looked northeast. The arrival of dhows with their merchandise marked the start of the trading season. Graceful, round-hulled vessels would glide into the anchorages under a cloud of sail. The nakhodas and crew, dressed in their finest robes, would break into song as horns echoed across the roadstead and townsfolk lined the waterfront. The mood on both sides was electric.*

A new season had begun. The engine of change was the monsoon cycle: the summer Kaskazi that brought the dhows from Asia and the winter Kusi that propelled them home. An intricate network of political and social ties between Indian Ocean ports grew up around this commerce. Families intermarried, Islam was imported, a culture was disseminated along routes determined by wind and tide, and a distinctive society of coastal people was born: the Swahili.

Walking back to the inn, feeling buoyed and on top of his research, Paul passed a telephone box set into a coral wall. He had a pocket full of coins and, on impulse, picked up the phone and dialled a number in New York. He heard the receiver being lifted. 'Hannah, I —'

'Hi, this is Hannah. I can't come to the phone right now, but if you'd like to —'

He slammed the handset back into its cradle, his heart pounding.

CHAPTER 12

Paul began frequenting Hapa Hapa, an open-sided, beach-style restaurant on the promenade, from where he could watch the comings and goings in the channel. Backpackers played chess and cards while sipping iced punch, crushed from piles of tropical fruit that stood knee deep behind the bar counter. Donkeys would poke their heads into the restaurant to see what the tourists were up to and maybe receive a nibble or a scratch on the snout. Bob Marley throbbed in the background without interruption, day and night. Among the Lamu dhow crews and beach boys who hung out with the tourists, the most popular frame of reference was Jamaica and reggae music. Many grew dreadlocks, wore Rasta colours, spoke in affected accents and used catch phrases plundered from their favourite tunes. One song got the most airplay and its words had become ingrained in Paul's brain:

There was a buffalo soldier in the heart of America,
Stolen from Africa, brought to America,
Fighting on arrival, fighting for survival.

A group of American exchange students used Hapa Hapa as their hangout. They were a loud bunch and colonised the tables around Paul. He quickly grew irritated by them and tried to steer clear, picking a table at the opposite end of the restaurant. He resented the way the Americans tried to ingratiate themselves with the locals, making any number of instant friends and singing along enthusiastically to the reggae songs.

The women students' garb was almost a uniform: baggy T-shirts, blonde dreadlocks, kikois, bandanas, leather sandals, moon bags round their waists, henna tattoos and bellybutton rings. A young woman from upstate New York hardly let go of her Swahili lover, whispering never-ending sweet nothings in his ear. *Jah Will Provide* read the lover's T-shirt. Failing Jah, this week's mzungu fuck buddy would do just fine.

The Americans had acquired an entourage of local brothers who were showing them the haunts, getting them the requisite herbs. Which was all kind of okay with Paul, but the effusive greetings, coded handshakes and pat Swahili phrases sounded glib, as though everyone was acting a part. Or was he being too cynical as he eyed them from his corner table? Why didn't he, too, find himself a brother who'd slap him on the back, provide the ganga and show him the ropes? Was he too aloof, a stuck-up white South African looking down his nose at the Americans going native? He was probably seeing too much of Hannah in them, her naïve immersion in other cultures, her passion for the 'real' Africa, whatever that might be.

Paul tried to counter his own prejudice: weren't they actually getting a better take on the people and culture, getting under the Swahili skin in a way that his own inhibitions prevented? He'd had a brief engagement with the sailors on *Fayswal*, but hadn't he recoiled? Was his pursuit of dhows and dusty African history less rewarding, and safer, than the Americans' active involvement, their forging of bonds with real live Swahili people, not with old books and pieces of carved wood? Maybe he could learn from them.

Despite his reservations, Paul edged a bit closer each day. After all, he'd been feeling kind of lonely. Eventually, he was able to pass the odd comment to one of the African-Americanos. However, he was not, once they found out he was a *South* African, fully embraced as one of the brothers. They seemed to view him with circumspection, suspicion even. A lone, white, note-taking man from the racist south who claimed to be African — better be careful of that one.

After a few more encounters, Paul was able to join the conversation. On the fifth day, he learnt the details. They were on a semester abroad from various American universities and were doing a course on Swahili culture and history. The group had been studying in Mombasa, but was currently on a field trip.

'Brought to America, fighting on arrival, fighting for survival,' sang Bob in the background. Then the whole of Team USA hit the refrain, along with their tame waiter: 'Woy yoy yoy, woy yoy-yoy yoy, woy yoy yoy, yoy yoy-yoy yoy yoy!'

Suddenly, a tropical shower burst overhead and drove the pedestrians from the waterfront. The ground turned to steam and bedraggled donkeys stood about looking more long-suffering than ever. Perhaps because of the rain, the barman moved from the soul-searching of Marley to more fun-in-the-sun reggae: Eddy Grant, Shaggy and other beach-party hits. Led by the students, everyone in the restaurant was singing along to the easy lyrics — even Paul.

That was the problem. These damn Americans did have a way of building camaraderie and team spirit. It was one of their greatest strengths, from the clean-up at Ground Zero to Hapa Hapa Restaurant. He found himself secretly envying their gregariousness, their way of drawing people in. In the long run, they got further and achieved more than a cynic like himself.

As Bob said, 'all their wicked intentions are destroying the human race' — but when they're singing it, it's somehow okay.

Right? And the Kenyan lads, chanting down wicked Babylon every lunchtime, would do almost anything to emigrate to one of those Babylons, be it New York, London or even Joburg.

Paul found evenings harder than the days. Hannah still visited his thoughts when he wasn't working. Beer took the edge off. Paul sensed that each day he was doing better, getting stronger. Then she would find him again, often late at night, or in his dreams. She'd come strolling in, all playful and coquettish, and wreck his equilibrium. Each visitation would set him back.

One muggy, windless night, he lay on his bed, unable to sleep because of the heat. Images of Hannah, and Dalila, spooled through his head. The bedclothes were wet with his sweat; even the overhead fan offered little relief. Finding sleep impossible, he got up and took a walk along the promenade. It was after midnight, but there were still a few islanders about. Candles flickered from windows overlooking the water. The sea gave off a musty scent and sounded like a leviathan taking tiny sips.

His imagination spiriting him back through the centuries once more, Paul noticed a woman in black seated on a bench at the end of the pier. She was staring towards the mouth of Lamu Channel and the open ocean beyond. As if in a vision, he was drawn along the jetty towards her.

She was quietly singing a traditional love song to herself:

Yana nalikikungoja
Kamaria
Hata goma likapigwa
Khasindia
Saa ya sita mbeja
Ikangia.

Yesterday too I waited for you
O shining moon
When they beat the drum
I went to sleep
It was midnight
O lady.

Having got so close to her, Paul couldn't very well turn around and steal away; she might notice and assume he'd been eavesdropping. He called a greeting and she turned. Her face appeared ghostly, her expression absent, as though she didn't recognise the place and time they inhabited. It was a disturbing look. Was there disappointment in her eyes: perhaps she'd been expecting someone else?

The woman had pale brown skin, S-shaped eyebrows and full lips. A lock of black hair curled from beneath her headscarf.

He sat down beside her.

'Hello, I'm Paul.'

She looked down. 'Maryam,' she said softly.

'What a lovely name.'

'Back home they called me Mariamu.'

'Home?'

'A long way from here, the mountains. Tigray, in Abyssinia.'

'That's very far.'

'Yes. I was, ah … brought here. I am Christian. The Muslim raiders came. I was given to my master. I was lucky. He is not a bad man. His sons, well, they are not as good. I have been given a Muslim name and I am part of the household. There is a daughter of the house. She is fifteen and I am her personal servant. You will not tell my master I was here, will you?' Her voice was suddenly anxious.

'Of course not. But why are you out so late?'

She hesitated.

'I … you see … it's him.' She started to cry and shielded her face in her hands.

An embarrassed Paul glanced round to see whether there was anyone near enough to notice the mzungu and a local woman in what must look like a love tangle. Finding no one, he reached out to touch her shoulder.

'What's wrong?' he asked lamely. When her crying subsided, she spoke hesitantly.

'He is a Muslim and I am a Christian, you see. He is a prince from far Arabia and I am merely a slave girl, hardly fit for his bed, let alone anything more. He is from a great merchant family in Oman and has been schooled in the Koran. He has his own ship. And me? What am I? What can I give him?' she asked, sniffing and starting to cry again.

Paul didn't know what to say, so he asked her to tell him more about the man she loved. She appeared eager to talk. It was clear that her secret love was weighing on her and during the nakhoda's absence, there was no one to speak to. As a *faranji*, Paul would soon be gone and was thus a safe confidant. The story that unfurled was a familiar one: rich boy meets girl from the wrong side of the tracks. Only the temporal frame was wrong.

His name was Ahmed and, according to Maryam, he was the bravest and most handsome of the merchant captains who sailed from Oman to Africa each year. His family had close links to her master and, during the weeks or even months that his dhow lay at anchor in Lamu, he lodged with them. Two years earlier they had fallen in love. But she was only a house slave and they kept their affair secret.

Maryam had been entranced by Ahmed's description of his home. He came from the port city of Sur and lived in a mansion built by his father's father. It was a grand house with many slaves. In the evenings, the ground before it was swept and watered, the air grew temperate and town notables gathered to talk and listen to singers and lute players. Sometimes there would be feasts in the garden where tables were garnished with sweet-scented herbs and flowers and laden with meats and fruit. Beautiful slave girls danced for the guests deep into the night.

'Ahmed told me that one day he will take me home with him across the sea,' she said. 'To make me his bride, but I am not so sure any more.'

Ahmed's father wanted him to remain in Sur, take over the business and run their small fleet from home, but the son had always been captivated by the sea. Since childhood, he'd loved dhows and had wandered the shore, talking to fishermen and merchants about their voyages and about the vast ocean that washed their doorstep. His eyes would follow the departing fleet at the start of each season, heading south to trade with wondrous foreign lands, returning again after many months, their bellies swollen with riches. He was sure his destiny lay beyond the horizon.

'Ahmed has seen many an adventure on the high seas. He has told me of the things that have befallen him, and I fear for his safety. The ocean is dark and dangerous. There are pirates. He has had narrow escapes. He might not always be so lucky. The people here and in his homeland know and love the sea, but I am from the highlands. For me the mountains hold no terror, but the sea is a bad place. I am scared of it, and what it can do. Look, he gave me this.' She held up a tortoiseshell comb.

'It's lovely.'

'He will return soon. The Kaskazi will start to blow any day now. It will bring him to me.'

'And this time, will you return to Sur with him?'

'I … he … I do not know.' Just then, a donkey let out a loud braying. He saw a flash of fear cross her face. 'I must go. If they find that I am gone, they will beat me. Thank you for listening, Mr Paul. Goodbye.'

She stood up and walked briskly away, dissolving into the darkness. He had asked the wrong question.

CHAPTER 13

Paul was sitting at his usual table on the first-floor terrace when a dhow taxi tied up below. Three young backpackers disembarked and made their way across the wharf towards Sunsail. He watched their progress and, a few minutes later, heard them being led up the stairs to their rooms. They emerged on the terrace and greeted him.

Katja was an attractive blonde with an open, engaging face. She was a Dutch lawyer who'd spent the last few months in northern Kenya helping an NGO involved in aid work. Her friends, Lorike and Pieter, both worked for a law firm in Amsterdam and had joined her for a three-week tour of Kenya. Pieter was a lanky fellow with round, wire-framed spectacles. Lorike was a petite and pretty brunette.

'How long will you be staying on Lamu?' asked Paul.

'About ten days,' said Katja. 'It's the last leg of our trip before we head home for the winter, so we want as much sun as possible.'

The Dutch chatted to Paul for a while about the usual backpacker concerns: where to find alcohol in a Muslim town, cool things to do and the cheapest prices for everything. Katja was the more gregarious of the three and did most of the talking; Pieter made a few comments about dhows. Lorike remained aloof and didn't say a word. Paul had to force himself not to stare. He decided Lorike was not, after all, pretty; she was beautiful. Katja announced that they were going to find a dhow to take them to the beach and they trooped off downstairs. Paul thought about asking if he could tag along, but decided against it.

That night he dined at The Mangrove, another open-sided, makuti-roofed establishment on the promenade. The Dutch arrived and sat at a table in the far corner. Paul kept glancing at them over his plate of chicken and avocado milkshake. Lorike had her back to him. *A lovely back,* he thought, *with shoulder blades like angel's wings.* After their meal, Pieter came over and invited him to a game of pool.

There was a sloping table in a mosquito-filled back room of the restaurant. It was boys versus girls and Paul kept catching Lorike's eye across the table. It was Hannah all over again; dark hair falling in loose curls round a wide face, a well-defined jaw, high cheekbones, big green eyes and the same wretched Cindy Crawford mole above the lips. Her voice even had some of Hannah's huskiness. The girls beat the boys, Pieter went off to bed and a beach bum called Roy latched on to them, offering a great disco just outside town. He wore a Manchester United FC jersey and kept brushing back his dreadlocks and drawling, 'Yeah man, is cool.' Roy was so stoned he needed the walls on both sides of the darkened lane to stay on course.

Beyond the town, a sandy path led through palm trees to a white house. A couple of dozen locals sat on plastic chairs under an awning. The lights were bright neon and Celine Dion rent the balmy air. Most of the men were far gone on khat, which they chewed endlessly like ruminating cows. There was no sign of a disco and many patrons seemed to be in the process of leaving. Paul bought a round of beers.

'Do you like living in Johannesburg?' said Lorike when they were seated at a table. 'I hear it's a dangerous city.' Clichéd, but at least they were speaking.

'Yes, I do, actually. It's crime-ridden, crazy and dangerous, but it has real energy. The people are amazing, not at all like the snooty Capetonians and dopey Durbanites. What about Amsterdam?'

'Yes, I like it, I suppose. But it's so urban; there's no nature. I want change. Something completely different, like Africa. Kenya has opened my mind. I really envy Katja working for the NGO. I would give my right leg —'

'Right arm,' he corrected her, grinning.

'Right arm, yes, to spend a year in Africa.' Lorike half-smiled. She had perfect teeth. They were the most perfect teeth in the world.

Paul and Lorike sat on one side of the table, Roy and Katja on the other. The loud music created a barrier between the two couples, for which he was grateful. After Celine came a Whitney Houston love ballad. Paul tried to talk over the song, but was shushed by Lorike, who said she liked it. He thought about how popular love songs were so effective at fixing time and place, a certain emotion from a particular moment. Their transience, being pop, was their embalming mechanism. 'Your love is my love, And my love is your love. It would take an eternity to break us,' crooned Whitney, and Paul sat squirming with a fake grin and the inside of Hannah's apartment etched in his mind.

Lorike spoke of a Greek lover who'd broken up with her when she left to study law at NYU. So she, too, had a problem with New York. They had something in common: heartache and New York. Every now and then, Lorike's pale green eyes caught his like a lighthouse beam. 'I have not been able to be friends with him,' she said. 'I know it's bad, but I just can't.'

The undeserving Greek bastard, he thought, but said, 'It's hard to remain friends with the big loves, much easier with the small ones.'

She nodded.

'You have beautiful eyes,' he said, regretting it immediately. Too soon, too lame.

'Thank you,' she said under her breath. Then she realised that Katja was looking at her quizzically across the table and they rejoined the conversation with Roy.

The music — country and western now — was turned down and chairs were being stacked on tables. They drained their beers, left Roy with a friend and strolled back to the inn, where they sat on the terrace. After a while, Katja said she was tired and went off to bed. Lorike lingered, then yawned and said she too should get some sleep.

'Would you like to take a walk before bed?' asked Paul, his heart beating so loudly he thought she might hear.

Lorike looked at him doubtingly. 'I don't think it would be right.'

Paul backtracked and apologised. He'd misread the signals.

'But yes, okay, let's go for a short walk,' she said.

They quietly descended the stairs, stepped out on to the promenade and turned left. Even at this late hour, a few men sat on benches enjoying the warm night air. As they strolled along the front, away from the streetlamps, it grew darker. Paul put an arm around her. 'We really shouldn't,' she said.

He retracted his arm. She took his hand, kissed it and placed it back on her shoulder. His breathing grew shallow. Tethered dhows rode easily beside them, brushing each other's fenders, then parting, before being drawn together again by their mooring lines. They walked to the end of the waterfront without saying another word. Once past the donkey sanctuary, there were no lights and he suggested they head back. In the process of turning, their bodies came together and they kissed. Her breath was warm and her lips felt like satin against his. 'This shouldn't be happening,' she moaned, then kissed him again.

'Why?' asked Paul. 'Do you have a boyfriend or something?'

'Of course,' she whispered.

Paul had no idea why it was 'of course'. He thought of Hannah, his own 'of course not', but she seemed a long way off, packed in cotton wool and utterly harmless.

'I feel so guilty,' she said, holding his face with both her hands. 'We must not let on to Katja and Pieter. They know my boyfriend. He's a lovely man.'

She kissed him hungrily, her tongue urgent. His arms drew them together tighter, her breasts pressed hard against his chest. He could feel her nipples stiffening through the vest.

'Sorry about the bristles,' he said.

'It doesn't matter. I like the feeling.'

He suddenly felt self-conscious about his grooming. His toenails were filthy. Tomorrow he'd make more of an effort. She ran her fingers along his chin and up into his salty blond locks.

'I need a haircut too,' he said.

'My beach boy. My white, African beach boy,' she said with a delicious smile that sent a shiver through him.

'I can be whatever you want me to be,' he said, and meant it.

'The others must not know about this. And we cannot make love, you understand.'

'But we can do this,' he said, pulling her closer and kissing her neck.

'Yes, sometimes we can do this.' She closed her eyes and let him kiss her on the mouth again.

'You're sure you don't want me to come back to your room?' he said when she began kissing his neck. 'I could unwrap your kikoi, I would love to see all of it. The colours look amazing. All those blues. I love pale blue.'

'It is a nice kikoi and I'm sure you'd like to see all of it. But no. Besides, the three of us are sharing a room.'

'You could come back to mine for a while.'

'I know I could, and a part of me wants to. But it must be this way.'

'Okay.' And he really was strangely okay with it. Paul did not need a grand, replacement love affair right now, just someone like Lorike.

Back in his room, he lay on the bed. He felt Lorike's beauty as a force that was not exactly sexual, not yet anyway, but deeply compelling. Basking in the glow of being wanted, half desired even, was enough.

Paul thought about how each journey, each documentary he made, was a thing external to himself, a drama in which he participated. On each trip, he chose the role he wanted to play: interesting filmmaker, mysterious Don Juan, resourceful backpacker, whatever. On this journey, the role had been written for him. But now he could rework the script. *That's what travel is all about,* he thought. *A constant rewriting. In each new place and with each new encounter you can remake yourself.* It was an old idea, but it was true.

CHAPTER 14

The next box to tick on Paul's research agenda was dhow construction. One morning at spring low tide, he climbed down the foreshore stairs to stroll among the vessels that lay stranded like beached whales. Crews took the opportunity to paint, oil, caulk and tend to rigging on the sand. The tropics are not kind to wooden boats and their undersides need regular treatment for teredo worm, while their upper works also require a coating of shark oil and paint.

The end of the beach, where the sand was hard and the high tide did not gather for long, served as a repair yard. Paul spent hours photographing details, noting characteristics and speaking to sailors. He loved the dhow names carved in the bows and transoms: *Asakher*, *Muscat*, *Al-Iman*, *Nashikuru*.

He got talking to a first mate called Zahir who was overseeing the work on a dhow tied up in front of the customs house. 'If you treat it well, a mashua lasts twenty-five years, maybe more,' he said, pushing back a straw hat and wiping his brow. 'But we sail them hard and the sun, the humidity, the sea animals, they all eat away its life.'

'What's this decoration?' asked Paul, pointing to a wooden strip on the prow painted green and carved with arabesques.

'That is the boat's moustache. We have many patterns — flowers, birds, lions.'

'And the round one?' said Paul, pointing to a circular carving painted with a crescent moon and star.

'That is the *jicho*, the eye,' said Zahir. 'A ship must not be blind, you understand. How can I say? The eyes are like a protection that helps the dhow to see danger.'

Paul wanted to arrange for the film crew to shoot a vessel under construction. He'd heard there were yards at Matondoni on the west coast of Lamu and at Kizingitini on Pate. Of course, the prize would be to visit the dhow-building village of Galoh in southern Somalia, where the mtepe had supposedly been found, but that seemed an impossibly long shot. Matondoni, at least, was close by.

On the appointed morning, a certain Captain Jabari collected Paul from Sunsail and led him to the dhow taxi *Angalia*, tethered to a rusty cannon. The inscription *Keep smile, one love, I can't forget you* was painted in the bows along with a yin-yang sign. *Angalia* was a rougher, more workmanlike mashua than *Fayswal*, but she had decent lines and looked fast.

The moment Paul stepped aboard, the crew cast off with much jovial shouting and a flogging sail was swiftly sheeted in. Captain Jabari called for an immediate gybe, only narrowly missing an anchored dhow. One teenager jumped on to the foredeck apron, others grabbed the preventer and mainsheet as they swung the yard, sheeting in on the port tack without losing much way. They were a handy crew and told Paul, on several occasions within the first fifteen minutes, that *Angalia* was one of the fastest dhows in Lamu.

'I've rigged a big, eight-and-a-half-panel sail,' said Jabari, his arm resting on the tiller and a big hat pulled low over his eyes. Most sails, the skipper explained, were made of seven cotton panels. During races, or when the winds were particularly light, captains added sections of wood to lengthen their yards and bent larger sails. 'In light winds, we can beat any mashua.'

'What's your secret?' asked Paul.

'Magic!'

No self-respecting nakhoda, Captain Jabari told him, would enter a regatta without 'medicine' and 'counter-medicine' for his vessel. Nakhodas and owners sought the help of magicians, either evil wachawi or waganga medicine men; before a race, sentries were posted to guard dhows from the application of evil charms.

'Medicine can win you a regatta,' said Captain Jabari, bearing off slightly to avoid a floating log. 'We all saw it once, right here in Lamu Channel. The nakhoda of one dhow took some uchawi and threw it at the other jahazi. As soon as it touched the deck, the mast broke and the sail crashed down. Everyone in town was watching.

'Of course, there is also good magic. We have a famous story of a race between the jahazis, *Ikbal* and *Roshani*, of two different merchant houses. The owner of *Ikbal* — his name was Said Ahmed — laid down a challenge. He walked to the office of his rival. As he entered the building, Said saw an axe next to the door and cried out, "I challenge you to a race from Lamu to Mombasa! If you win, you can take this axe and chop my dhow into pieces."'

The captain explained that Said then went to one of the sharifs, who prepared a spell to protect *Ikbal*. Two days later, a racing fleet set off from Lamu. *Ikbal* and *Roshani* soon took the lead, sailing side by side down the channel towards Shela. There was almost a collision and something was thrown from *Roshani* which landed in *Ikbal*'s hold. Nothing happened. The mast didn't break. The wind didn't betray them. The Lamu crew were joyful. *Roshani*'s black magic had not worked.

But the uchawi was apparently a new, delayed-action variety. It took effect later, when the dhows were nearing Ziwayu Rocks. There was a loud crack and some of the rigging came adrift and fell into the sea. *Roshani* sailed on and the rest of the dhows overtook *Ikbal*. Her nakhoda broke down and wept while his crew tried to repair the damage. It took them eight hours.

'Now his only hope was the charm,' said Captain Jabari. 'It was in two parts. A liquid, which he splashed on the foredeck. And a kind of powder, which he burnt in the bows. The crew hoisted the sail again and prepared it for a downwind run. *Ikbal* was like a ski boat, racing along in a cloud of spray. The crew of *Roshani* watched her coming over the horizon. Old sailors who saw *Ikbal* said she was doing more than twenty-five knots. She overtook *Roshani* in Mombasa channel to win by only so much.' He held his thumb and forefinger close together, his whole face creased into one enormous grin.

'Gosh,' said Paul, 'I'd love to race a dhow one day.'

'If you want to take part in a regatta, you must come on the first day of January, or the fifteenth of August, or during our Maulidi festival. These are the three big races. The one in August, that's a good one for foreigners to join in. Next year, you come?'

'Maybe. It would be fantastic.' What would Paul give to leave a sign *Gone dhow racing* hanging on his front door?

After clearing the roadstead, Jabari asked whether he'd mind if they smoked a joint. Paul had no problem with it. A huge bhangy was rolled, lit and passed among the crew. He took a drag and handed it on. Soon, *Angalia* was zigzagging all over the channel, with the sail being left to flog for long periods. Paul asked Jabari if he could take the helm. Before long, his shipmates were reduced to giggling wrecks, seemingly incapable of even the most basic sail adjustments. For Paul, who'd abstained from further drags, it was a glorious two hours of sailing. The mashua was small enough and the wind light enough for it to be handled like a dinghy. He had the mainsheet in one hand and the tiller in the other as he weaved her between the sandbanks.

One deckhand used a petrol canister as a drum and sang the same rollicking song over and over, the crew joining in for the chorus. In the old days, he had read, there'd be a whole orchestra of drums, cymbals, trumpets and antelope-horn flutes on a jahazi. When entering port or setting sail, dhows would fill the roadsteads of East Africa with the sound of music. A large fleet leaving on an evening ebb would have been unimaginably evocative, thought Paul as the stoned crew tried to chase an ebbing tune that forever eluded them.

The channel narrowed. Gusts stole over the treetops, leaving no tell-tale cat's paws on the water, and were upon them before Paul had a chance to make adjustments. Fortunately they were light. By now the sailors had dozed off on the thwarts and ballast bags. *Angalia* squeezed past an overloaded motor dhow, weighed down to the gunnels, chugging back from the mainland with produce. Paul waved and dozens of hands waved back. Then he crept up behind a hori making for Matondoni and sailed past under its lee. The other skipper smiled a toothless grin and held up a fish. 'No thanks!' shouted Paul. The man dropped the fish and freed off, pumping his sail, trying to catch up. No Swahili sailor appreciates another slipping through his lee.

Paul roused the crew as *Angalia* neared the village. Docking was a shambles, with lines landing in the water, stifled laughter and a loud bump as they collided with an anchored dhow. A stout young man with a moth-eaten beard appeared above them on the jetty. '*Jambo*, Mister, my name is Jeremy!' he called. 'Let me welcome you to the humble town of Matondoni.'

Paul shook hands with him at the top of the steps.

'For a very small fee, Mister, I —'

'*Sawa,* okay, Jeremy. I know the story,' said Paul. 'You're hired. I'd like to see the boat-building yard.'

'Certainly, come this way, I will show you everything,' said Jeremy, drawing ahead with a waddling gait.

They tramped through a pretty village and down to an inlet that flooded at high tide. Palm trees lined the water's edge, their fronds decorated with weaver nests that dangled like faux coconuts. In one enclosure, they found two men busy repairing a hori, caulking the seams and replacing rusty nails.

'We have been a boat-making village for more than six hundred years,' said Jeremy proudly. 'The most famous jahazi ever built came from our yard. It was the year 1967.' The smooth-talking Jeremy had his tour-guide sound bites down pat. Paul made a note to interview him on camera. 'The dhow was called *Hodi* and it was supposed to sail all the way to Canada for the World Fair in Montreal. But the Suez Canal war came and *Hodi* never even got to the Atlantic. She was sold to a sheik in the Persian Gulf.'

Jeremy suggested they pay a visit to the misumari fundi. The pair came to a hut and stood in a doorway watching the elderly man bent to his work. He wore only a kikoi and kofia and was banging ships' nails into shape over a fire. 'This is a very important job, let us not disturb him,' said Jeremy in a hushed voice. 'The misumari fundi is a highly respected man. Without nails, you have no dhow. If the nails fail, you sink.'

'What about mtepes?' asked Paul as they walked on.

'They did not need nails, but I have never seen one. Those dhows disappeared long before I was born.'

They reached a boatyard where Jeremy's uncle was shipwright. Badru was busy with the construction of a mashua under a makuti-roofed ship loft. The fundi shook hands with

Paul, then went back to work. He chatted to them, hardly glancing at the chisel as it sliced into wood, the unwatched hammer rising and falling with unfailing accuracy.

Paul knew that ship fundis were important figures in any Swahili community. Their mastery was thought to be coupled with piety, which lent the men even greater stature. Although each fundi employed many workers and apprentices, the selection of wood and most of the calculating and measuring was his preserve. Getting the correctly shaped branches and tree trunks needed a practised eye. The fundi had a few simple tools to help with the measuring and fitting: a ball of string, a pointed stick and a pot of blue paint. Saw and adze were all that was needed to fashion the wood into a basic shape.

For Paul's benefit, Badru kept up a running commentary about what he was doing and the materials being used. The ribs of the vessel as well as its mast were of mangrove wood, he explained, while the hull planking was mahogany. The stem, sternpost and ribs were scarfed securely to the keel — the *utako* — which comprised one long, heavy tree trunk. Badru showed Paul how to use the *kekee* bow drill for making holes, the *tindo* chisel for shaping and the *randa* plane to smooth the wood. He demonstrated how the coconut-fibre *kamba* rope was woven and prepared for the rigging. Paul took notes and photographed. This place would make an ideal location for the movie.

Jeremy told him of the festivities that accompanied the launching of a new dhow. 'The whole village comes together and a goat is sacrificed for a feast,' he said. 'In ancient times, human sacrifice may have taken place. There's a famous story from Mafia Island about the ruler of Kisimani who captured an Arab boy from a neighbouring kingdom. He was tied up and put on the rollers of the slipway. When the dhow was launched, it crushed the child to death.'

Jeremy and Paul continued walking and ended up on the far side of the village where an unfinished mashua appeared to have been abandoned midway through construction. The keel was laid and the ribs were in place, but grass was growing up around it and the makuti shelter had collapsed. 'The owner ran out of money,' said Jeremy. 'When he gets some more, building will start again.'

'How much does a dhow like this cost?' Paul asked. He had a vague vision of sailing one from Lamu to Durban and having it trucked up from the coast to Lake Deneys Yacht Club. What a curious sight it would make, plying the brown waters of the Vaal Dam on summer Sundays.

'Between two and four thousand dollars, depending on size. I can get you a good price. My cousin —'

'No thanks, Jeremy, I mustn't even start thinking about it.'

Back at the jetty, Paul boarded *Angalia* and the men cast off, setting sail for home. The dhow hugged the mangroves on the left of the channel to avoid the meat of the tide, her flanks sometimes scraping branches. Passing a narrow creek he hadn't noticed earlier, Paul spotted a half-submerged motor dhow grounded in the shallows. The hull was blackened from fire and the line of scars along her starboard side looked suspiciously like bullet holes.

That evening, the Dutch stayed on in Shela after a day on the beach and Paul dined alone at The Mangrove. After the meal, he was standing at the counter watching a game of pool when a thick-set young man came and sat on a stool next to him.

The traveller was from Durban. They chatted for a while, but Paul didn't warm to his fellow countryman. After half a year on the road, Doug reckoned he knew all about Africa and was prepared to share his opinions with everyone within earshot. Zim was stuffed, the Malawians were nice but lazy, Tanzanians were rip-off artists. He'd travelled with Richard for a bit, but Richard had got pissed off with him back in Malawi. Richard was a fuck-up. 'Dicky didn't dig dope, dude,' he chuckled. It appeared Doug had got himself waylaid by marijuana on the Lake of Stars and Richard had hitchhiked back to South Africa.

Doug was short and stocky with a goatee and shaved head, which he adorned with a bandana in the colours of the South African flag. He wore veldskoens and sometimes replaced the bandana with a sweat-stained Sharks rugby cap. His backpack carried only the bare essentials, 'plus a mozzie net, box of condoms and Imodium for the shits — that's all you need in Africa, bru,' confided Doug.

Paul got trapped in an unwanted conversation and couldn't find a way to extricate himself. His drinking companion was dogged and slow to come to the point. Paul could almost hear the machinery of his brain, see the idea sluggishly forming, like a wobbly thought bubble. Truisms were spoken with a first-timer's conviction. 'If only we could teach them proper agriculture, give them seed. East Africa would be a bloody bread basket. Teach a man to fish ... know what I mean?'

'But why can't they sort out the time thing, hey? What's with these okes? Always late with everything.' Although patronising, at least Doug 'got his rocks off on Africa' and his covert racism was couched in a semblance of passion, pronounced 'peshin'. *A good old-fashioned mugging might change all that,* Paul reckoned.

Doug switched to pontificating about Islam. Lamu was too Muslim for his taste. You had to struggle to get a beer, everyone wore their dressing gowns in the street, the women were cold fish. Doug was talking too loudly; Paul grew uncomfortable.

'And what about Somalia, hey, just a hundred kays thataway?' said Doug, pointing vaguely out the front door. 'A failed Islamic state, breeding ground for terrs.'

'Yes, no one wants to touch Somalia,' said Paul softly, hoping Doug would get the hint and lower his voice.

'The Americans tried, back in the 90s. They got fucked up one time. Did you see the movie *Black Hawk Down*? Brilliant.'

'*Ja*, one of my favourites,' Paul had to concede.

'Fucking A!' Doug's eyes lit up. They were on familiar territory.

'Apache helicopters is what we want.' Doug was putting on a fake American accent. 'Got all the firepower a man needs. Zap 'em from the air. We don't even have to put boots on the ground.'

'The US has got enough on its hands right now,' said Paul.

'But that's the whole point. This does affect them. There are towel-heads everywhere wanting to take over the world!' Doug banged the counter. Patrons turned to look at them. Paul squirmed. 'Somalia especially,' he continued. 'Muslims are convinced their culture is superior, and obsessed with the inferiority of their power.' It sounded like Doug was quoting something he'd read. 'The only way to deal with this kind of Arab and his ideas about gee-had is to wipe him out.'

Paul answered under his breath: 'Surely that's not the way —'

'Nah, bru, don't pussyfoot around!' Doug was almost shouting. 'Nuke the camel-fuckers, that's what I say.'

'I need some shut-eye. I'll see you around,' said Paul. He downed the dregs of his milkshake and made a hasty exit, feeling the eyes of the patrons following him out the door.

CHAPTER 15

The following afternoon, Paul was taking a stroll along the promenade, daydreaming in another era once again, when he spotted a strange craft moored stern to. He stepped closer to have a look at the ornately carved stern-castle with its galleried decorations, and felt himself sliding back into the seventeenth century...

The vessel was more Portuguese galleon than dhow, a romantic creature of intricately carved teak, her hull oiled and gleaming. A tall man in his late twenties stood on the shore directing the offloading of dates. He wore a spotless white dishdasha and a pompom-fringed ghatra was wound about his head. Round his waist was a thick silver-filigree belt sporting a curved dagger with an ivory handle. He was a handsome fellow with a hawk nose, beard trimmed to a point, bushy eyebrows and a booming voice.

'*Salaam alaikum,* Captain, where is your ship from?' he enquired.

'*Alaikum salaam,* Mister. We arrived from Sur this morning.'

'I've never seen such a boat,' said Paul, marvelling at the carvings on her stern.

'It is a ghanjah, the most beautiful of all dhows. My name is Ahmed Suleiman, nakhoda.'

They fell to talking about the vessel. Paul wanted to know more about Ahmed and his crew, their passage and how they came to be trading on the coast so close to the beginning of the season.

'The Kaskazi was early this year. I left immediately and stood close inshore, using the land airs and taking advantage of the counter current. Every successful voyage across the Abyssinian Sea is a gift from Allah, praise be to Him.'

Ahmed invited Paul on board. As they strode the spacious deck, Paul learnt that the ghanjah was ninety feet long and displaced 120 tons. She had two masts, thick as tree trunks, and carried a vast spread of canvas. Her tall prow was in the shape of a bird's head with a long beak. It reminded him of a mtepe. Most of the upper parts were carved with fleur-de-lis and vine patterns, while the stern quarters were adorned with decorative plaques painted blue and white.

The crewmen — Paul couldn't help thinking they were slaves — had laid out cushions and a Persian carpet behind the brass binnacle on the poop. Ahmed invited his guest to tea, which was poured from a samovar into tiny glasses by a black man in a red kikoi. A tray of sherbet and sweetmeats was placed beside Paul. The servant wafted some incense in their direction from a burner, then retired from the poop.

The two men reclined on the cushions, chatting and watching the activity of the sailors and the unloading of goods from their hold. Ahmed told Paul that he was selling some of his cargo of dates, dried fish and salt in Lamu, before continuing south for further trading. He'd be taking on mangrove poles at whichever port offered the best price; he might even cut them himself in the Rufiji Delta. However, he was open to just about any items, as long as the price was right and the resale prospects good. There was, for instance, an order for a pair of elephant tusks from a friend in Muscat, and rhino horn always fetched a tidy sum back in Sur.

'A few slaves, too, if I can get a good deal,' he said, between puffs from an earthenware hookah pipe. 'I also have some chests and carpets for trading in Lamu, but this I will do through the family with whom I lodge. They have a room for me, very private, with a latrine of my own. It is comfortable. I do most of my trading in Lamu through the master of the house, which is our custom. They put me up each season. Our respective families have had close ties for generations. I might even make his daughter my bride, but not this year. She is only fifteen.'

'And take her back to Sur?'

'Yes, of course.'

'Will she make a good wife?'

'I think so. Hers is an eminent family, but I have not seen much of her, as is our custom. We do not have much opportunity to be with women of high breeding. Thank goodness for the slave girls.'

They discussed the sailing qualities of the ghanjah and the art of blue-water navigation. 'My father taught me the ways of piloting,' said Ahmed. 'From him I learnt the value of signs, of a change in the weather. You can tell which region of the ocean you are in by the types of fish or by the colour of the water. At night we sail by the stars. As it says in the Koran: "Allah it is who appointed for you the stars, that ye guide yourselves thereby in the darkness of land and sea."'

'Do you use a compass?' asked Paul.

'A magnetic needle? Not I. Some nakhodas do. I prefer a *kamal.*'

'A camel?'

'No, no, my friend, the *ka-maal*. Here, let me show you.' Ahmed reached into a sea chest behind the binnacle and brought out a wooden tablet with a string attached to the middle. 'You hold it out in front of you like this. The lower edge must touch the horizon and the upper edge rests on the star you are observing. The end of the string, pulled taut, is in your mouth. Like so. Knots tied along the string indicate degrees of latitude,' he mumbled, the string between his teeth. 'It is all very simple.'

Paul nodded, although he didn't really understand.

Ahmed spat the string out. 'Most importantly, a nakhoda must know the mawsim, the season for sailing. We have to know the dates of the monsoon in every different region of the ocean. Getting this wrong could trap you in a foreign port for many months.

'We must also keep our vessels safe from attack. Only last year we had a narrow escape on the Salalah coast. I anchored close in. A watchman was posted to make sure the local Bedouins didn't cut the cables and drive us on to the rocks. The guard fell asleep and I woke to find bearded men armed with swords standing over me. The crew were rounded up on the main deck by another band of ruffians. A scruffy sambuk was tethered alongside. The Bedouins demanded my cargo of dates.

'I told them they were welcome to the dates and all the ghanjah's money. They merely had to allow me to open my chest. I was desperate, thinking they would burn the ship and sell us into slavery. They crowded around greedily as I took the key from my pocket and opened the lid. In the darkness, they could not see that I was reaching inside for my small musket. I grabbed it, swung round and thrust it into the ugly face of the leader, yelling at the top of my lungs. My crew joined in the shouting and fell upon them. The Bedouins dropped their swords and fled, jumping into the sea and swimming for the shore. We were lucky.'

By now the sun was low on the horizon and the crew had stopped work for the day. They began to emerge on deck in shore-going finery, some of them carrying personal items to trade with Lamu merchants. Paul took this as his cue, bade Ahmed farewell and followed a group up the gangplank.

'*Ja, ja*, it sounds like you're having a ball and all, but stick to the topic,' said Johan down the crackly line from Johannesburg. 'It's all very well doing tons of research, but you're not writing a fucking PhD.'

'No sure, I hear you,' said Paul. 'It's just that things are pretty fascinating and I've uncovered so much good material. Like those sewn boats you mentioned —'

'Don't go chasing stuff that isn't going to make it into the movie. Listen, I think it's time you moved to that guesthouse, like we discussed. The place we gonna put the crew up: Ki-something-or-other.'

'Kijani.'

'*Ja*, that's the one. How's your budget?'

'Still okay, although the dhow to Lamu cost a bit.'

'Remember, no wine, women and how's your father. Keep the receipts.'

After speaking to Johan, Paul phoned Kijani and booked a room. The guesthouse lay three kilometres southeast of town on the beach in Shela. Johan wanted him to check out the accommodation, negotiate a good deal for the crew, arrange for meals at irregular hours, make sure there was a quiet room to review footage and the like. Paul had a last meal with the Dutch, although he'd be seeing them again: most days they visited Shela beach. Then he packed his bags and ordered a dhow taxi for the following morning.

That night Paul dreamt he was a nakhoda, sailing towards the African coast. An island has been sighted. They approach cautiously and drop anchor beside a calm lee shore. The crew sets off exploring; some busy themselves with washing and mending on the beach while others light cooking fires. He reclines on the sand: it is good to be on firm ground again.

The island begins to move beneath him. How is this possible? Terror grips him. It becomes instantly clear: the behemoth whale has been asleep for an age. So long, in fact, that sand has accumulated on its back and trees have sprouted. But the lighting of cooking fires has wakened it.

With a venting of air like an enormous geyser, a column of foul-smelling water jets into the sky. The island begins to sink and waves crash in from all sides, swamping them. He is engulfed, sucked under.

CHAPTER 16

An elderly skipper, who introduced himself as Sharif, stood waist deep in the water, holding the bows of the dhow taxi into the wind. As soon as Paul pulled himself and his luggage over the rail, the man shoved off and scrambled aboard. His pubescent grandson was the only crew. The small mashua glided down the channel past Lamu's waterfront buildings. Sharif was deep into his seventies, had a large moustache and weather-worn face with scrunched-up eyes that had spent a lifetime staring at sunlight on water. He played the breeze expertly, finding the groove of the wind and staying there, no matter its vagaries. Paul surmised that Sharif would have lived through the last years of the golden age of sail in Kenya.

'Do you remember the booms from Arabia?' asked Paul.

'When I was young they used to come, bringing dates, taking back boriti. I went down to Mombasa once, on a boom. It was hard, with my bad Arabic. Big boats. Much power.'

Sharif offered Paul a chance to steer and he immediately commented on the lee helm — the vessel instinctively wanting to bear off the wind. It was something he'd never encountered before.

'Oh, that's because of the propeller,' explained Sharif. 'When we race, I take it off and remove the engine. I also put up a bigger mast, bigger *foromani*, bigger sail.'

Paul smiled to himself. A Lamu sailor needed no excuse to bring racing into a conversation. The passion was there in their eyes, these men of the sea.

Arriving off Shela, they anchored in green shallows and waded ashore. Kijani House lay a few metres from the water's edge. It was a Swahili-style inn with courtyards and terraces set in a tropical garden. Paul found a doorway in a whitewashed wall overflowing with pink bougainvillaea. He passed a couple of guests with American accents relaxing under palm trees beside a pool.

'Hi, I'm Pierre Oberson, welcome to Kijani,' said the lanky fellow at reception, handing Paul a coconut with a straw poking out the top.

After Paul had signed in, Pierre led him down the steps and across a lawn. 'You sound German,' said Paul.

'Swiss, actually.'

'How did you end up in Shela?'

'I was an engineer back home. Fell in love with the archipelago — and with a local girl. Packed up my life and moved to Lamu fifteen years ago. Nothing would lure me back to Europe.'

Kijani comprised a cluster of Swahili houses. It was obvious that Pierre's precise skills had been brought to bear: the detailing and finishes were all Swiss standard. The proud owner led him up a flight of stairs and through a set of rooms, pointing out architectural idiosyncrasies. Some of the walls were over a metre thick. 'In the olden days, many of Shela's inhabitants came from places where they had been forced out, or had to have defences,' said Pierre. 'So the early structures were built very strong. When we dug the foundations, we found all sorts of things: chinaware, an amphora, even a cannonball.'

In the renovation, he'd insisted on using local materials — mangrove and coral. The walls were waxed once a year to create the traditional shiny effect.

'Sometimes we had to strike a compromise between authentic Swahili and making it comfortable for guests,' explained Pierre.

'Swiss Swahili,' said Paul.

Pierre said that they'd mostly opted for traditional over mod cons. Paul noticed that all the rooms were long and narrow. The length of a mangrove roof-pole is only about two-and-a-half metres, so this has always determined the size of Swahili rooms.

The spaces were decorated with bright fabrics, antiques from Arabia and studded doors. 'There's an old chap in town who used to be a dhow merchant when the booms still came from the Gulf,' said Pierre. 'I was looking everywhere for antiques and I knew this guy still had lots of stuff. He's got two ceramic bowls from the sultan's palace in Zanzibar hanging on the wall of his office. Apparently the Aga Khan offered him a fortune for them — enough to buy half the town — but he refused. He wouldn't tell me what else he had.

'Anyway, so, I kept going to him. I'd buy the odd brass lock for a door, get chatting, pass the time of day. I always dropped in a question about whether he had more stock hidden away somewhere, and he would chuckle and say no. Then, out of the blue one day, as I was leaving, he says, "Mistah Pierre, you still looking for an old bed?"

'"Of course," I say.

'"I think I might just have one somewhere," he says.

'He led me up an alley to a warehouse, pulled out one of those big, old-fashioned keys, and opened the door. There were about a hundred antique beds inside and much, much more. I couldn't believe my eyes.'

Pierre ran his hand over a finely engraved dressing table. 'This mahogany piece is from him, made a hundred years ago in the archipelago. Most of the teak and rosewood pieces in our guestrooms came on the boats from India.'

He led Paul out on to a balcony, where they watched two dhows fetching towards the horizon. 'You know, this is where the Battle of Shela took place,' said Pierre. 'Pate's soldiers were slaughtered right here on our beach.'

Paul had read about this bloody battle. Pate Island and their Mombasa allies had tried to overrun Lamu. The Nabhani of Pate, however, had fatally miscalculated the tides and the dhows were stranded, leaving the men to be butchered with no means of escape. Shela's beach had run with blood and, for years after, was littered with the bones of the dead.

'You can learn a lot about Lamu history by studying the buildings of Kijani,' said Pierre. 'Maybe you could put us in your movie?'

Each morning in Shela, Paul followed the same routine he had in Lamu, walking the streets and waterfront with notebook and camera. He'd grown more gregarious during his time on the island, less wrapped up in his own concerns, and chatted to whoever felt like passing the time of day with him. He befriended a skipper who'd recently bought a bright yellow dau. Paul would sit in the shade watching the sailor, crouched and shirtless under a tattered straw hat, hammering cotton dipped in sesame-seed oil into the seams of his new boat. Paul noticed that, rather than being hung on gudgeons and pintles, the dau's rudder was lashed to the stern — just like a mtepe. He loved finding these archaic throwbacks.

On the third morning, Paul tagged along when the man visited a group of sail makers in a square just behind the beach, to monitor the progress of a new cotton lateen. The shape of the sail was outlined with rope pegged to the ground. Every lateen is slightly different and tailored to the specifications of the owner, who chooses the kind of cloth, width of sail panel, type of rope and the cut of head, foot and leech best suited to his dhow and the conditions he expects to sail her in. Paul took photographs of each step in the process.

That afternoon, he joined the Dutch for a swim on Shela beach. They found a secluded spot near a replica Omani fort, complete with turrets and crenellations. It had been built by a reclusive Italian and it was a folly indeed, as the sands of the peninsula were constantly shifting, and who knew what a storm might bring. Like the fantastical mirage it resembled, it seemed the fort might vanish overnight.

Lorike and Paul positioned their towels next to each other, allowing fingertips to touch, brushing an arm or a leg as they got up to go for a swim. Paul found it tantalising and frustrating, like being back in a teenage romance. They both thought it strange the others hadn't noticed the currents of electricity zinging between them; or maybe they had.

Paul lay staring at Lorike, wishing he could hold her. Beautiful, aloof Lorike; she made cheap clothing look like designer wear; she made silence sound profound. She treated everyone, including the beach boys and insistent touts, with respect and charm. If only he could reach out a hand and undo her bra strap.

The woman who'd propositioned him in Lamu approached their group, her trademark scarlet headscarf clashing with her black robes. For a moment, he thought she was going to ask him again, but there was no recognition on her face. She offered henna painting and showed the Dutch a book of patterns. For a small fee she would decorate their hands or ankles, but they declined and she wandered to the next set of sunbathers. A group of fishermen watched her progress with open scorn and called derisive remarks.

The Dutch took a late-afternoon dhow back to town, leaving Paul with the evening to himself. He had an early supper at a local tavern on the waterfront beside Kijani. From his table on the promenade, he could watch the antics of Shela's cats scavenging along the beach. The scrawny creatures — lean, feral and Egyptian-looking — patrolled the shoreline with an arrogant gait, acting for all the world like lions of the Masai Mara. Fishermen were scaling their catch and a feline scrum developed, circled by timid kittens and even an inquisitive donkey. A marabou stork, professor of birds, came flapping in with loud wing beats and strode over in his scruffy overcoat to see what could be plundered. He sized up the kittens, but changed his mind at the last moment: not enough meat and too much fuss.

The next night, Paul felt like treating himself to a better meal. He chose Peponi, the grandest establishment on the island. It was reached along a coastal path with water lapping a metre below. In the evenings, with the horizon lightly gilded, Peponi's terrace was a bewitching spot. Before dinner, Paul sat with his notebook and a glass of wine, Shela's dhows bobbing a stone's throw from his wicker chair.

Beside him was a coral seawall topped with rusty cannons guarding the channel; behind lay the hotel's manicured lawns and tropical gardens. A white sloop with raking lines, dated 1929, was anchored alongside a Mozambican double ended dhow, rare in these waters. Both craft belonged to the hotel.

There was an air of decadence about the place and Paul could overhear conversations about yachts moored in the Cote d'Azur and polo games 'back home'. The appearance of the odd lord or duchess, wrapped in a kikoi and going native for the summer, only added to the white-mischief atmosphere. Barefoot waiters discreetly monitored the progress of Paul's drink, while Peponi's two Staffordshire bull terriers went from table to table, greeting guests in a most affable manner.

'Bru, thank God there's some oke here I can actually talk to.'

Doug, at Peponi! He swaggered over and plonked himself beside Paul, ignoring the poised pen and feigned faraway look. 'Lamu is so effing boring, 'scuse my French. No babes, no nightlife, expensive dope. Anything doing here in Shela?'

Doug's usual scruffy garb would've had him thrown out, but he'd put on trousers and a clean shirt. The backpacker was running low on dosh, so a free drink, courtesy of Paul, wouldn't go amiss. 'Dude!' he exclaimed to the waiter, 'you're charging a fortune for this wine and you're pouring less than half a glass. Ask your barman to fill it to the top.' He winked at Paul.

The glass reappeared, fuller this time, but still not to Doug's satisfaction, so he sent it back again. If Paul could have made himself any smaller, he'd have slipped through the gaps in the wicker. Their waiter remained polite and unruffled. Paul tried to read the man's eyes. The staff had been well disposed towards him, but would they reappraise him? Returning with a brimming glass of Chardonnay, the waiter's eyes met his with what could have been anything from sympathy to disapproval.

'Good to see we're about to nail the fuckers, hey,' said Doug.

Paul thought he might be referring to the cricket. 'What's the score?' he asked.

'Nah man, the bombing. We're going to plaster the Taliban. Soon, man, soon. Bin Ladin will be a rabbit trapped in his own stinking hole. Nowhere to run.'

There was the 'we' again. Technically, South Africa — being kind of capitalist, democratic, sympathetic to the West and mostly Christian — was pro-America. But to be placed squarely in their camp was disconcerting. George Bush had said, 'You're either with us or against us.' Paul had taken this to be war-mongering humbug, but maybe Doug was right and some sort of collective 'we' was about to bomb Afghanistan.

'We've been patient,' said Doug, 'asking nicely for Bin Ladin to be handed over. Now they're gonna get what's coming to 'em. Revenge is our right, don't you think? After what they did to the Big Apple, it's a no-brainer.'

To change the topic, Paul told Doug about his wish to sail to Somalia.

'Pirates, dude!'

'Yeah, so everyone tells me,' said Paul. 'But I hear they only really hassle the fishermen. It's very low-key piracy.'

'Maybe. Maybe not. Could get yourself into lotsa trouble. Why'd you want to go up there? You looking for buried treasure or something?'

'I suppose so, in a funny sort of way.'

'You ever read *Treasure Island*?'

'Yes, as a kid, it was one of my favourites. Long John Silver, Billy Bones —'

'The Black Dog, Captain Flint, Blackbeard —'

'X marks the spot, shiver me timbers, fifteen men on a dead man's chest —'

'Yo, ho, ho, your money or your wife, ha-ha-ha. Jolly fucking rogering.'

CHAPTER 17

USA is big terrorism! The graffito, painted in red on the wall behind Kijani, greeted Paul the next morning.

In the breakfast room, guests learnt that America had launched first strikes on Afghanistan during the night. A table of American tourists was overly polite and a little embarrassed, as though one of them had peed in their bed and everyone knew. Almost everyone. One tourist — big as a house and dripping with gold jewellery — loudly and lengthily berated the waiter for not bringing the coffee at the same time as her toast. *On today of all days, you should hold your fat tongue,* thought Paul.

'I've just phoned the police in Lamu,' Pierre said, coming over to pour his tea. 'Just to check that the mullahs aren't getting restless or anything. All seems quiet, so there's nothing to worry about.'

Paul didn't think there would be. The world's political waves were much dissipated by the time they reached these shores. After all, this was Lamu.

But now, further down the lane, here was another: *Fuck USA + Israel + Britain world terrorism.*

A shadowy figure watching him from the end of the street ducked into a side alley. Paul kept seeing him: a man in a brown shirt and black kikoi, who appeared to be following him. At first he found it mildly amusing, intriguing even, but now he felt a little worried. If things turned ugly in the Gulf, Westerners could become targets, even in a peaceful place like Lamu.

At Ali's hole-in-the-wall kiosk, the proprietor had placed a television on a crate in the alley and brought from home a sofa and some chairs, which he lined up along the opposite wall. There was just enough space between television and audience for a fully laden garbage truck — in the shape of a donkey with rubbish baskets on each flank — to squeeze past. Paul stopped to watch a live CNN broadcast from Islamabad. Ali, round, gregarious and bespectacled, immediately cleared a place for him. Paul declined.

'No, no, no, you are my guest,' said Ali, ushering him to the sofa. 'Big troubles, eh?'

'*Asante*,' said Paul. 'Yes, big troubles.'

'It has begun,' said Ali, crossing his arms and frowning.

The proprietor offered Paul a cold drink, as a guest, not from the shop.

The television beamed images from another world. Black specks drew vapour trails across a porcelain sky. The camera zoomed in to show waves of aircraft sowing their seeds from high in the stratosphere. Barren mountainsides exploded into dust. There were images of C-17 cargo planes dropping thousands of 'culturally neutral' food pouches. Vitamin-fortified rice cakes from heaven. A talking head from the Pentagon held up a dollar bill and pointed to the image on the back. 'Our eagle clutches an olive branch in its right claw and arrows in its left,' he said. 'Food aid and firepower in tandem, that's our mission. The United States wants to send two messages to the world simultaneously. We want to show that we are on the side of good.'

A report crossed live to the bridge of the USS *Kitty Hawk*, where troops were being airlifted into battle. An embedded journalist on the flight deck was saying something about a marine amphibious task force being prepared. Meanwhile, a thousand light-infantry troops of the 10th Mountain Division were shown winging their way to Uzbekistan. To Paul, much of this had all the reality of a computer game. He spent the morning glued to the television, then took a breather for lunch and to digest the images of destruction he'd been witnessing.

Over the ensuing days, the alley kiosk would be a regular port of call. Sometimes it was just him, Ali and the CNN or Al Jazeera presenter. At other times, there'd be a throng of viewers, often just out of mosque and hungry for news. The opinions expressed around the television were close to his own.

In the days to come, the ideological positions became blurred as bombs failed to be as surgical as promised. Anti-American heckling grew louder round the fringes of the group. Ali, however, tried to maintain a tight and moderate ship. When one teenager rode past on his donkey, fist in the air, chanting: 'Bin-la-din! Bin-la-din!', he was shouted down and told to piss off.

Paul felt strangely at ease: here he was, on a tropical island, ensconced in front of an outdoor television set with a group of Muslim men watching high drama unfold across the ocean. He saw night skies streaked with green tracer fire, Muslim shells groping for Christian B-2s. Advancing Northern Alliance tanks lumbered creakily into frame, bound for Mazar-i-Sharif. Smart bombs and propaganda leaflets rained down on Kabul and their smooth-talking host, Mike Chinoy, tried to make sense of it all from far Peshawar. That little screen, in that particular context, felt surreal. There was, too, the vertigo of peering over the edge into a dark chasm.

He watched students in Lahore burning the stars and stripes. There were demonstrations against Westerners in Indonesia, Palestine and Pakistan ... and also in Mombasa. An effigy of

Bush stuck on a pole was set on fire, to the delight of a chanting crowd. All the while, Ali kept serving cardamom-flavoured coffee for the viewers and chatting about Lamu things.

CNN had the biggest news story of the young century and was milking it to the full. Each credit sequence showed slo-mo images of the two aeroplane impacts and the towers toppling. What had driven those Arab men to such lengths? What, exactly, were the messages they sought to convey? The virtue of martyrdom for a cause, certainly. But what else? How powerful was their faith, thought Paul, compared to his own wishy-washy Christianity and that of most of the West.

However George Bush wasn't being wishy-washy at all. His marionette-like head on the TV vowed that America would be 'ending countries' and 'smoking the enemy out of their holes'. Had George been smoking out of his own hole? His 'crusade against the evildoers' sounded like just as much gobbledegook as Bin Ladin's rants.

Ali fingered the remote, flicking between Al Jazeera and CNN. A bombing raid on some remote village had resulted in the deaths of Afghan women and children. There was anger in the group gathered around the television. Paul stayed at the back. Ali came and stood beside him.

'We do not hate the Americans,' he said. 'They are doing what they have to do. It is just some of their policies, especially the Middle East. The Palestinian question goes on and on and America always sides with Israel. For us Muslims, this is important. It is a symbol. What do Bush or Rumsfeld know about the pain their policies cause?'

Just then, Paul noticed a figure on the screen, sitting at a computer behind the newsreader — one of those shadowy presences who conjure the news from the wings. He went cold.

'Hannah.' Paul said her name aloud, feeling as though he'd been kicked in the stomach. He made his excuses and hurriedly left.

Paul walked back to Kijani in a daze, not paying much attention to his route. As he turned a corner into a narrow lane, an arm grabbed him from behind and dragged him into a doorway. Rough fingers pulled at his hair, yanking his head back. A knife blade touched his neck. He went stiff with terror.

'Fuck you, American, you die!' hissed a voice in his ear.

'Please, I … I … I'm not American,' he rasped.

The man's hand was rifling his pockets. Paul could feel coarse breathing on his neck.

'Wallet, American pig!'

His passport and wallet were locked in the safe at Kijani House.

'I have no wallet.' The knife pressed against his Adam's apple.

'I cut you.'

'Please, please, no, I have dollars!' Paul reached into his back pocket and pulled out a handful of notes. The man grabbed the money with his free hand.

'Not enough. You must pay for —'

'*Mwizi!* Hey, thief, stop! STOP!' The shouting came from the top of the alley.

Paul's face was thrust against the coral wall and the man made a dash for it. The corpulent Ali was running towards him, out of breath and wheezing. A figure in brown shirt and black kikoi disappeared round the corner.

'Are you all right?' said a panting Ali, one hand on his knee, the other on Paul's shoulder.

'Yes, thank you, Ali, you arrived just in time. Thank you.' His body was trembling and he found he could hardly stand.

'Come back to the shop. I'll make you something sweet.'

Ali put his arm around Paul and they walked slowly back.

'I haven't seen that guy before,' said Ali. 'He's not from Shela. I will report it to police. Do you want to make a statement?'

Paul thought for a moment. 'No Ali, I don't think so. I don't want to get involved with the police.'

'Okay, but still, I am going to talk to them and we will keep a lookout for that guy.'

At the shop, Ali led Paul through to the back and made him a cup of very sweet, strong tea.

'If you hadn't come along, I really think he was going to knife me. There was real hatred.'

'It's what he sees on TV.'

'That's what I thought.'

Back in his room that night, Paul found that Pierre had left a few books on his bed that might be useful for the movie. He was too wound up from the mugging to sleep, so he opened one on Vasco da Gama and began reading.

He was struck by the brutality of the early explorers. Set against Swahili Islam, the Christianity introduced by Da Gama and his men seemed to Paul a violent imposition. Their obsessive hatred of Muslims had its roots in centuries of religious conflict on the Iberian Peninsula: Portugal had been in a state of holy war with the Moors for generations.

The Muslims of the Indian Ocean were shown no mercy and the massacres began as soon as the caravels and carracks entered the Indian Ocean. On one occasion, Da Gama stopped a large trading dhow, the *Merim*, laden with riches and crammed with passengers. On board were noblemen and a large number of women and children returning from Mecca to Calicut. Da Gama had the cargo transferred to his ships, then ordered his men to massacre all seven hundred passengers. The women pleaded, offering their gold jewellery and holding up their babies, begging for mercy. To no avail. The dhow was set on fire and soldiers were lowered in rowing boats to finish off the survivors in the water with their lances. The ocean turned scarlet with their blood.

CHAPTER 18

At Ali's the next day, Bin Ladin droned on, blaming America for the killing of Muslims in Bosnia and Somalia and, through the Israelis, in Lebanon and Palestine. 'Infidels walk everywhere on the land where Mohammed was born and where the Koran was revealed to him,' said the bearded figure. The messianic face stared from the screen and called down damnation on the West: 'Merciful Allah, shatter their gathering, divide them among themselves, shake the earth under their feet and give us control over them.'

Ali and the television had begun to depress Paul. He needed downtime, so when the Dutch suggested a trip across the channel to visit the Takwa ruins on Manda Island, he was happy for the diversion. His friends were coming to the end of their stay in Kenya and he wanted to be close to Lorike, even if he couldn't exactly be with her.

When he emerged from Kijani the next morning, the mashua *Pernille*, bearing the Dutch, was luffing in the shallows. He waded out to the dhow. Lorike sat on the gunnel looking beautiful in a grey T-shirt and yellow kikoi, her hair scraped into a ponytail.

'One love, bruddahs and sistahs!' shouted *Pernille*'s skipper as the South African pulled himself over the rail.

Oh dear, thought Paul, *we're back in Kingston Town with our Rasta brothers.* Although the reggae fad was infectious, Paul couldn't help feeling the locals were short-changing themselves. Kenyan and Swahili music and style had so much to offer. As for fashion, a faded Burning Spear T-shirt could hardly compare with local fabrics.

The crew cut into his thoughts with an off-key rendition of Bob Marley's 'Redemption Song', which Paul found, despite himself, strangely poignant:

Emancipate yourselves from mental slavery;
None but ourselves can free our minds.
Have no fear for atomic energy,
'Cause none of them can stop the time.

A northerly breeze had picked up and they sailed *joshi*, beating into the wind across the channel. The crew slid an outrigger plank into position, allowing a couple of lads to clamber outboard, like a Hobie Cat's trapeze, but without the safety of a harness. The plank was loosely jammed between rib and thwart and wobbled precariously. The person at the end of the contraption had a rope to hold on to, but this would be of little use if he lost his footing. The Rastas were eager to please the Dutch, who'd become their regular taxi clients and seemed to have the lads wrapped around their fingers. Katja and Lorike asked to have a go on the trapeze and shimmied out. It required considerable agility, particularly in the fluky conditions: scrambling up the plank as the vessel heeled over in the gusts, sliding quickly inboard as it levelled in the lulls. If the gust died abruptly and they weren't smart about it, they'd be dunked in the water or lost overboard.

Pernille slipped into the calm of a creek lined with mangroves whose leaves glittered in the sunlight. The dhow sailed up an ever-narrowing inlet and soon ran out of wind. Fortunately, it was shallow enough to use the *pondo* — the pole. '*Jah* man, we go poly-poly, ha, *pole-pole!*' called one of the crew.

When the dhow touched bottom, they disembarked and waded up the creek to a walkway on stilts which led to the site entrance. Takwa had been a stone-town, abandoned three hundred years ago, possibly because the fresh water had become too saline. It was a typical Swahili settlement of tightly packed dwellings surrounded by mangrove swamps and encircled by a wall for protection. On its seaward side, tall sand dunes kept it safe from the prying eyes of passing ships.

Paul didn't have much interest in Takwa. The town wasn't important enough to feature in the movie and the ruins weren't particularly impressive. He was there for Lorike. They wandered among the remains of houses until they came to the sultan's palace. This was in better repair and still had a tower fashioned from coral blocks. He took a picture of Lorike with a provocative expression as she leant against a wall. In the cistern of the mosque, Paul spotted a blue-and-white Portuguese majolica plate bearing the cross of the Order of Christ. Ironic in this place of Muslim pilgrimage, he thought. Elephantine baobabs and acacia trees had sprung up among the ruins and goats clambered over the walls, hastening their destruction.

A pillar tomb stood all by itself at one end of the site. 'Let's go have a look,' said Lorike.

The others had drifted off in another direction. It was a chance to be alone for a few minutes.

Lorike gave him a meaningful glance and disappeared behind a wall. They were in an isolated part of the ruin complex and there was no one about. She leant against the grey coral wall of the tomb, eyes smouldering. He took both her hands in his, she lifted her chin and they kissed.

Paul sat on Ali's couch. Herat was in the process of being bombed. Cut to images of food packages being dropped from C-17s; cut to warships in the Gulf. There were whistles of awe from the crowd in front of the television as F16s swept off a carrier deck and Apache helicopters attacked in formation. Cut to Muslim bodies at a bomb site, which brought silence and a few mutters of anger.

Footage of the military's 'shock and awe' tactics was interspersed with advertisements for dotcom companies and Sheraton hotels. Then the viewer was whisked back to American talking heads giving their version of events to the world, to Lamu, to Ali's crew. The format was similar to a post-football-match assessment by a team of studio experts, but how to reconcile AT&T access with Kabul ack-ack fire?

Mary, a forty-something guest at Kijani, joined them for the twelve o'clock news. She was a vacationing music teacher from San Francisco who worked at an international school in Nairobi. Like Paul, she was happy to be in Lamu at this time and experienced no animosity from locals. She, too, was embarrassed by the tenor of the CNN reporting.

'On the morning of the first bombing, an angry man stopped me in the street,' she said. 'He blocked my path with arms folded and legs apart, shouting, "You, lady, are American!"'

'Must have been scary.'

'Sure was. So I replied: "Yes, and I didn't drop any bombs last night."'

'What did he say?'

'Nothing. He just put his arms around me, gave me a hug and walked on.' She tossed a mop of red hair over her shoulder. 'On that same morning of the bombing, there was a woman from LA staying at Kijani who paid a local guy to clean the anti-American graffiti off the wall. Can you believe it? She's paying in dollars for a Muslim African ... I mean, you just can't do that.'

The Dutch came to say goodbye. Paul felt he'd had far too little time alone with Lorike, and now it was over. They stood in Kijani's garden exchanging small talk and email addresses. Paul shook hands with Pieter and gave Katja a hug. He kissed Lorike on the cheek. They kept their voices neutral as Lorike's fingernails bit into his hand.

The Dutch scrambled on to *Pernille* and poled away from the shore. Paul stood waving for a long time.

CHAPTER 19

Walking back to Kijani, Paul wondered whether it wasn't time that he, too, thought about booking a flight home. Before returning to South Africa, he wanted to make one last attempt at finding a passage to Somalia. Pierre knew of a dhow owned by a friend who was sometimes game for unconventional charters. Apparently, *Jamal* was a jahazi that could accommodate the entire documentary crew for overnight shoots and sounded just right. Pierre had been making enquiries, but the vessel was currently at Pate.

'I have some good news for you,' said the Swiss as Paul walked into reception. 'My friend has just returned from the north and says he might be able to help you. This guy has been sailing the waters of the archipelago since he was a kid. I've told him to come for tea this afternoon. Make sure you're here at four.'

Paul sat waiting in Kijani's garden. When the skipper of *Fayswal* stepped through the gate, he did a double take. Husni had swapped his shorts and T-shirt for a white kanzu and looked every bit the ancient nakhoda.

'What on earth are you doing here?'

'Hello, Paul. Pierre sent for me. I told you I was going to see my family in Pate and the crew would sail *Fayswal* home.'

'So *you're* the skipper of *Jamal*?'

'Sort of. It is our family dhow. When I heard you were still in Lamu and still trying to sail north, I talked to my father and uncles. So here I am.'

They sat in the dappled shade of a frangipani tree, sipping tea and discussing the possibilities.

'I'm trying to get to a town called Galoh,' said Paul. 'I read an article that said there might still be a mtepe there, you know, one of those old sewn dhows?'

'Yes, I know mtepes.'

'If there is one there, it would be fantastic for my documentary.'

'Well, you are in luck. If we do go to Somalia, I would stop at Galoh anyway. My brother lives there and I have not seen him in two years.'

'So you think there's a chance we could go?'

'There is a chance, if the price is right. My family needs the money.' Husni ran a finger along his thin moustache.

'How long would it take?' asked Paul.

'About a week, depending on the wind. My crew will do some fishing. I will visit with my brother —'

'And I will try to find my mtepe.'

'Yes, this is not impossible.'

They discussed the details of a hypothetical trip that might just, against the odds, come off. Paul could barely contain his excitement. The price of $350 was reasonable, given the distance. It would consume the rest of his budget with not a cent to spare, but he reckoned it was worth it. Paul named all the places he wanted to stop along the way for his research. Husni was amenable to his requests. They looked at a map, traced a route, listed provisions and settled for a proposed departure two days hence, assuming Husni could muster a crew and organise everything in time.

'Are you sure it'll be okay sailing into Somali waters?' asked Paul.

'Yes, sure. I know that coast. Don't worry, you're not the first foreigner I've taken up there.'

'Really?'

'Sure. Actually, you might be interested in this for your movie. The man was an archaeologist, a Hungarian. It was many years ago, before things turned bad in Somalia. He was looking for Rhapta. You've heard of it?'

'Yes, the mythical African port.'

'That's the one. This Hungarian guy, Halász, had a theory. He said archaeologists had all been looking too far south. I thought he was a bit crazy. He was old, sick — cancer, I think. But we did find some ruins south of Galoh.'

'Did he dig?'

'A little. We all helped. Halász found a couple of Roman coins. He was very excited, jumped around like he had a snake in his pants. The man wanted to return with a team and excavate properly, but he died soon after he got back to Hungary — and then Somalia went bad.'

Of course, Rhapta. Paul had forgotten about it in his excitement about mtepes. Come to think of it, reading about Rhapta in the *Periplus* was how he got on to mtepes in the first place. In fact, he remembered from his reading that the name Rhapta actually referred to sewn boats.

Back in his room, Paul dug up his old notes on Rhapta: *Men of the greatest stature, who are pirates, inhabit the whole coast and at each place have set up chiefs...* Rhapta's wealth had been built on ivory. As the opulence of Rome grew during the first century AD, so did the town's fortunes: the Romans began to use the tusks not only for statues and combs, but also for chairs, bird cages and carriages. The emperor even had a stable built out of ivory for his favourite horse. Rhapta's other exports, such as rhino horn and turtle-shell, also grew and were exchanged for iron goods, weapons and glassware. Arab agents set up shop as the town's middlemen and the wealth poured in. Rhapta became so important that Ptolemy referred to it as a metropolis, the capital of an African state independent of Arab suzerainty. With the fall of Rome, Rhapta withered and disappeared from memory. No trace of the city has ever been found.

Until now. Just think, both the mythical mtepe and the proto-Swahili metropolis of Rhapta, found and presented to the world by intrepid South African adventurer, Paul Waterson! The great archaeologists and historians of the colonial world had conjectured about and even searched for Rhapta. To no avail. Along comes an amateur and trumps them all!

There were risks, of course, but the payoff would certainly be worth it. Somalia was lawless and many parts had spiralled into anarchy, but they were going to one small fishing village in the deep south, far from the troubles. He was on to an idea that would transform the documentary, even change it completely.

His heart was pounding. Could Rhapta be his big break? Johan would be thrilled. National Geographic, CNN, BBC — they'd all want a bite of this. Then again, perhaps he should keep the idea under his hat. Maybe this was a chance to go solo, to launch his own career as a director?

A man in a blue kikoi summoned him to reception. There was a phone call from Joburg.

'Howzit going, Paulie boy?' It was Johan.

'Good, good. All good, thanks.'

'The research?'

'*Ja*, no, we're getting there.'

'Details Paul, I can't read your bloody mind.'

'It's going well. Lots of solid material. Great locations. Amazing architecture, boats. I'm busy organising a dhow for shooting around the archipelago.'

'When you coming home?'

'Not immediately. I'm on a bit of a roll at the mo. Probably a couple more weeks.'

'You're not getting up to mischief, going off on one of your tangents?'

'No, Johan, honestly, I'm sticking like glue to the brief.'

That night, Paul went to sleep feeling both calm and excited.

He is under water, kicking desperately towards the light, his lungs screaming. He breaks the surface, gasping for air. A dozen men are floating around him. Allah has preserved them, but his dhow has disappeared. There are planks and some debris and the sailors rope together a makeshift raft. They begin to paddle using scraps of wood. To the west. That is where Azania lies. They paddle and paddle.

Eventually, land wobbles into view and the men stagger ashore. They are quickly surrounded by savages who bind their hands and deliver them to the king. He stands before them on a scaffold, a powerful brute with enormous arms.

Bowls of food arrive and the sailors gorge themselves, but his stomach revolts at the fare and he only pretends to eat. The green herbs his men consume soon turn their heads to madness and reason departs them. They laugh uncontrollably and grow increasingly ravenous the more weed they devour. Meat and coconut oil is laid before them. The sailors become immobile, fattened for the cannibal feast to come.

During siesta, he manages to steal away and makes for the east. He runs as fast as he can, but his step begins to weaken. They are surely after him. He trudges up a dune, feeling hope drain with each footstep. At the crest he looks down. His vision is blurred from sweat and the shimmering heat. There are men down there. A beach, a moon-shaped bay. Beyond them lies an anchored dhow. Merciful Allah! He runs down the dune into the arms of a surprised sailor.

'You must return with us to our island,' says the nakhoda when he is taken on board. 'Our sultan will find a ship to bear you back to Arabia.'

'Thank you, kind sir. But tell me, what is the name of your home?' he asks.

'It is Lamu, the blessed isle.'

'Laa-moo, what a lovely name.'

He lays his head on a cushion, utterly drained, but safe. Lamu, amu. La-La land. He drifts into heavier, dreamless sleep.

CHAPTER 20

Paul took a dhow taxi from Shela to the north end of Lamu's waterfront, where he found the forty-eight-foot *Jamal* tied up stern to. She was a handsome jahazi and sat in the mirror water like a seabird, elegant lines embodying the spirit of nautical adventure. Her sides gleamed with reddish-brown fish oil and her blue-and-white detailing had recently been touched up. Coconut matting was attached to the railings to increase the freeboard and act as protection against the weather: they might be sailing in rough seas. A makeshift toilet — an open cubicle — hung over the stern. The Kenyan flag fluttered from a shroud. *Jamal* was everything Paul had hoped she would be.

Husni stood on the quarterdeck, overseeing the loading of provisions. The cook was busy stowing crates of food below the foredeck apron, where his tiny galley and firebox were housed.

'Permission to come aboard, Captain!' Paul called out.

'Hello, my friend, you are most welcome!' cried Husni. Paul climbed the gangplank. 'This is my crew: Rafiki, Latif, Taki and that's Nuru, my serang. And of course the doc down in the galley — he's our cook.'

Paul called a greeting and the men replied with their *salaam*s. None of them looked much older than thirty, except the doc. Paul shoved his bags under a bench and helped with the last of the loading. Soon *Jamal* was ready and Nuru started the engine before taking his place at the tiller. The boatswain was a dignified-looking man with a chinstrap beard and bright black eyes. The crew let go the mooring lines and the dhow chugged slowly away from the wharf. Paul looked astern as the buildings of Lamu began to recede. It felt like an auspicious moment and he wished he had a woman on the shore to wave to. In the absence of an admirer, he conjured up a harem comprising Hannah, Dalila, Maryam and Lorike, all standing in a line, waving white handkerchiefs.

There was hardly a breath of wind, so they forewent the sail and motored north for half an hour before turning into Mkanda Channel, which separates Manda Island from the mainland. It was just a few dozen metres wide in places and they negotiated it slowly, passing smaller vessels being poled along. Husni told Paul the channel was used by nakhodas trying to avoid the open-ocean route around Manda. 'It's very shallow here. At low tide elephants, even antelope and leopards, cross over to the island from the mainland.'

As *Jamal* emerged from the channel, they passed a yellow beach beside the upmarket Manda Bay Lodge. This was the site of the famous Manda ruins, reputedly the birthplace of the Swahili. In a wealthier country, they would be fenced off and there'd be entrance fees, manicured pathways, dioramas and tour guides. But all Paul could see were a few overgrown mounds in the bush. His imagination would have to do all the work.

The ruins stretched across a small peninsula — an easily defensible position with a mangrove creek on either side and a good anchorage in front. Paul had read about Manda. Settled in the ninth century by Shirazis from Iran, it had been a wealthy city for centuries, its inhabitants known as the 'wearers of gold'. Manda's merchants prospered from the export of ivory, mangrove poles, rhino horn, leopard skins, slaves. Archaeologists had uncovered quantities of Islamic pottery from the Persian Gulf, even objects from China.

But other than a few piles of rubble, very little remained of the town's patrician homes and towering baobabs hid most of the ruins. Paul spotted one fairly intact mosque and, as they passed a small beach, a line of coral blocks half buried in the sand.

'What's that?' asked Paul.

'It was a wall. Those blocks weigh more than a ton each,' said Husni. 'Some people think they were used to reclaim bits of the shore when sea levels rose.'

'How did they move such huge stones?'

'I do not know, but it's just like the pharaohs, don't you think?'

The story of Manda was the story of the coast. A merchant from Arabia starts a trading station, raises a multicoloured family with a local woman, begins to thrive. Friends and family from his homeland join him. A makeshift mosque is erected. More countrymen arrive on the dhows: perhaps young imams seeking converts or acolytes, maybe men who'd fallen on hard times or who needed to run from something.

Settlements grew or decayed and were refounded elsewhere, up a more promising mangrove creek or on some secure atoll. Wattle and daub were replaced by coral rag. A sultan rose to power; patrician families grew into a ruling elite. Manda is where it all began, on this very beach, with that first Shirazi footprint in the sand.

The Swahilis of old were tantalisingly close. Manda's past seemed palpable, shimmering behind a veil so thin Paul could make out the crowded streets, fishermen unloading nets, children splashing each other in the shallows, their happy cries echoing down the centuries. He could almost smell the kingfish, grilling on charcoal fires, just a wafted breath away.

A gentle breeze had begun to blow, so Husni switched off the engine. Tall Latif and short Taki raised the yardarm, pulling hand over hand on the thick halyard, helped by Paul. Taki kept up a string of jokes that all but derailed a giggling Latif from the job at hand. The sail was released and filled magnificently as *Jamal* set off on a long reach towards Pate. The three kikoi-clad deckhands then took to snoozing on the foredeck while the doc peeled potatoes down in the galley and Nuru and Husni had turns at the helm.

A moustache of white water frothing at the bows, the creaking of ropes and a giant lateen angled like a wing overhead — for Paul these elements had become a kind of mantra. He asked Nuru if he could steer for a while and *Jamal*'s helmsman was happy to oblige. The worn mangrove tiller fitted Paul's hand perfectly. He bore off in the gusts, letting the dhow surge on the short swells of a choppy sea.

'We're sailing against the tide,' said Husni, 'so stick close to the Pate shore when you get nearer to avoid the worst of it. But watch for sandbanks.'

Paul scanned the ocean ahead for the pale blues of the shallows. As the wind increased, squalls began racing across the scalloped water towards them. Paul bore off just before they hit. Nuru, the most experienced crewman, was on the main sheet, ready to pay off if the gust was too strong. Some of the heavier squalls enveloped *Jamal* in warm rain, the sea hissing around them and whiting out the land. Moments later, they'd emerge into blazing sunshine and the decks would steam with the evaporation.

Nuru took the helm again and Paul sat on the foredeck with Husni. 'How fast do you think we're going?' he asked.

'I suppose about eight knots,' said the skipper. 'This is still a small Kusi sail we're using. It's only twelve cotton panels. In summer, we bend a much bigger one — fifteen panels — for the Kaskazi.'

Although most dhows are essentially open boats, *Jamal* had an inboard engine under the afterdeck and a roofed galley before the mast. It was there that the doc — Omar Yusuf — prepared his dishes, usually fresh fish, prawns or goat, flavoured from jars of cardamom, cumin and cinnamon. The doc was sage-like with greying hair in a horseshoe around his bulbous skull. The aromas of his cooking wafted over them as they sailed, accompanied by the doc's gruff voice singing in Arabic as he balanced the pots on a heaving deck. Lunch that afternoon, eaten between squalls, comprised a vegetable curry with chapattis. Once Husni and Paul had dished for themselves on to paper plates, the crew polished off the rest, eating straight from the pot with their right hands.

Jamal cruised up the western flank of Pate, the largest island in the archipelago. Flat, encircled by mangroves, marshes and shifting intertidal zones, its perimeter punctured by long, circuitous creeks, Pate is half inundated at high tide. Sailors need to know their business here.

Less accessible and far less popular with tourists than Lamu, Pate is nonetheless thick with Swahili history. Over the course of a millennium, numerous city-states have risen and fallen along its shores; palaces and great mosques have been built, forts erected, Byzantine political games of war and trade played out. Today's peaceful, shrunken settlements belie its stormy past.

Paul asked Husni whether they could go ashore and visit one such 'city'. The two men bent over a chart. The skipper suggested that, given the high tide, *Jamal* might just be able to get close enough to Siyu and Nuru duly altered course, aiming for a gap in the mangroves.

Soon they were sailing up a long inlet towards Siyu, once a famed centre of Islamic scholarship, now a forgotten village with some very impressive ruins. *Jamal* tied up to a jetty deep inside the creek. Husni and Paul went ashore and strode through coconut plantations towards the town while the dhow headed back out to sea, lest it be grounded by the ebbing tide. Reaching the outskirts of Siyu, they came to an Omani-style fort dominating the anchorage. Paul thought the tiny bay, with its Camelot-like castle, must be one of the most picturesque spots in the archipelago.

A man named Isaam — pale skin, receding hairline, goatee — offered to be their guide. 'Here is the city wall, but as you can see, there is very little left,' he said. 'Inside the walls were thirty thousand inhabitants; now we are less than five thousand. We were once a big, famous city; now we are a poor fishing village.'

They wandered among the overgrown vestiges of houses, mosques and the sultan's palace. 'The ruling family, the Famaus, produced many famous poets,' said Isaam. 'The "Utendi wa Mwana Kupona", written by the wife of Sheikh Bwana Mataka, is the most beautiful of all Swahili poems.' He recited:

Wanangu Waislamu
Ninenayo uhikimu
Mutimizapo yatimu
Na peponi mutangiya.

O my children of Islam
Attend to the words I speak
If you fulfil them completely
Then paradise you shall enter.

There were a few pillar tombs and the odd domed vault still standing. African vernacular architecture, adapted by the Arabs; once, they would have been inlaid with hundreds of Chinese porcelain plates. Only smashed ones remained. Children played among the ruins, ignoring the illustrious ghosts who watched them.

At the town jetty, Husni and Paul found a fisherman who agreed to ferry them back to *Jamal* for a small fee. His vessel was a long, narrow, double-ended dau. She was fast and the ebb hastened their progress. With two passengers on board, her crew was showing off, constantly adjusting the yard and main sheet, tweaking the preventers, making sure the sail caught every ounce of a fluky breeze that whispered through the tops of the mangrove trees.

Back on board *Jamal*, they upped anchor and headed north.

CHAPTER 21

'Kizingitini is a very devout place,' said Husni as they rounded the top of Pate, on course for Husni's hometown. 'You can't even bring alcohol ashore.'

'And it's okay to bring a Christian?' asked Paul.

'Oh sure,' chuckled Husni. 'No problem. You know, I was making a voyage here on a friend's dhow last year with some Catholic missionaries. It was a funny thing. The crew prayed to Allah on the aft deck, the missionaries prayed to God on the foredeck and the atheist passengers sat drinking beer amidships. It was a little bit strange.'

As they approached the town, loudspeakers broadcast a melodic incantation from the Koran, followed by a sermon that echoed across the water. 'We lost time going ashore at Siyu, so we should not land here,' said Husni. 'We must push on to get to our anchorage before dark.'

They sailed through Kizingitini's roadstead, passing close to the pier. Fishermen and childhood friends waved to the crew and called greetings. Once clear of the anchored dhows, Nuru was instructed to set course for Kiwayu Island. *Jamal* bore off on to a beam reach and picked up speed. Half a dozen dhows were approaching them, racing back to Kizingitini, laden with their lobster catch. Sailors sat out on trapeze boards, calling challenges to each other and coaxing every last knot out of their mashuas. It seemed that even bringing in the day's catch was a chance to score points against a competing boat.

One dhow caught a heavy gust and heeled too far, water pouring over the leeward rail. A hand quickly freed off the main sheet, the skipper tried to bear up into the wind and the crew leant out madly, but it was too late. Within moments the dhow was swamped, the sail flogging loudly. There was pandemonium on board.

By the time *Jamal* drew alongside, only the tops of the gunnels were visible and eight men were in the water. A small fleet of dhows gathered around the stricken vessel. Only *Jamal* had an engine, so she would have to do the towing. The mast and yard of the swamped vessel were unshipped and secured to the bowsprit and thwarts by her swimming crew. Husni tossed a line to the skipper and soon the semi-submerged craft was bobbing along behind them like a weird, Da Vinci-designed submarine. At times the dhow disappeared completely, with only eight torsos wearing masks and snorkels protruding above the surface. Paul pulled out his camera and took a photo of the bizarre scene. It was a slow, tedious chug back to Kizingitini. When her keel eventually touched bottom, the shivering men shouted profuse '*Asante sanas*' and *Jamal* turned north once more.

It was getting late as they crossed the open water between Pate and Kiwayu. The dhow no longer had the protection of a windward island and the sea grew rougher. Waves broke against the palm-frond splashboards, sending torrents of water into the bilges. Rafiki, with his lithe body and youthful eagerness to please, was set to bailing, his dreadlocks bouncing as he tossed bucket-loads of water overboard.

The rescue had put them behind schedule and the sun sank into a mess of western clouds, releasing the occasional beam of honeyed light. It was cold on deck. Even for an old girl, *Jamal* was coursing along at a tidy lick, cleaving into the dusk. The rigging strained, the ropes were taught as iron, humming like a finely tuned instrument. The short, cross sea created a confusion of soapy crests. A flash of lightning turned the water an eerie green, then a clap of thunder detonated against the dhow. *Jamal* appeared to shudder from the impact.

Squalls came racing out of the gloom from the southeast. Black clouds, often bearing torrential rain, enveloped them. The vessel leaned over, taking the weight of the wind. Paul grew anxious. Just as he was beginning to think the skipper should drop the sail and continue under motor, they were struck by a squall that tore spray off the crests around them.

The first gust sent a groan through the rigging; the sail quivered as it took the strain. The second hit *Jamal* with a hammer blow. The mast creaked and canvas thundered. The dhow heeled steeply, water pouring over the leeward rail and through the coconut matting. Pots and pans came adrift in the galley with a crash. Men lost their footing and untethered items bounced across the deck into the scuppers. The air turned to water as rain came at them horizontally.

Husni shouted something, but his words were torn away by the squall. Nuru swung the tiller hard over, trying to point her into the wind, and two figures struggled to release the mainsheet, which had jammed on the quarter post. 'Allaaah!' yelled Latif in frustration. Paul stared up at the yard, which was bending like a bow, and reckoned it was about to snap or come adrift. The bulging sail looked as though it might explode into a thousand fragments at any moment.

Jamal continued to lie on her side, water pouring in.

Finally, the mainsheet yanked free, to the thunder of flogging canvas. The gust released its grip and the dhow sat bolt upright, slewing into the wind. As quickly as it had come, the squall scudded off downwind and the crew set to bailing with any container they could lay their hands on. Even the doc pitched in, using his biggest cooking pot.

They lowered the yard, furled the sail and continued under motor. After a while the wind steadied. Enough water had been bailed and *Jamal* was chugging comfortably towards the sinuous shape of Kiwayu, the white stream of their wake shot through with dancing phosphorescence. Latif began tapping a drum, his long fingers a blur on the goatskin. Husni sang a sea shanty from his home town, and the sailors joined in:

Illa yeo bandari
enda joshi,
dama kuvuta
mikondo ya mayi hupita
nenda nyuma
huya mbele.

To be in port today
we'll have to steer to windward,
draw in the sheet!
We'll leave a tremendous wake!
I'll go aft
to make good speed.

A black mangrove smudge loomed out of the darkness. Nuru was trying to find the right channel, but the keel kept touching bottom as he passed over sandbanks. Each time, with a string of curses and high-rev reversing, *Jamal* would be worked free and they'd begin probing for another gap in the tree line.

Finally they found the right channel and anchored off a beach near the southwestern tip of long, thin Kiwayu Island. The engine was silenced and night sounds pressed in. *Jamal* lay in the lee of tall dunes and there was hardly a breath of wind, just a whispering of palm fronds and the slurp of water on sand.

'What a spot,' Paul said softly.

'The island is a sanctuary,' said Husni. 'Turtles come and lay their eggs here every year. Until recently, locals hunted them for their meat and dug up the eggs. Then the WWF got involved. Now the whole community is protecting them.'

Somehow, the doc had managed to salvage supper, despite the bumpy run. They gathered around a pot of biryani prawns in the pool of light cast by a paraffin lamp strung from the yard. Paul dispensed with a plate and, copying the crew, used the fingertips of his right hand to make a ball of rice and prawn, propelling the food into his mouth with a flick of the thumb.

'Today you saw us make one or two mistakes, Paul, but Swahili sailors are usually very good,' said Husni, taking another handful of biryani. The crew murmured agreement. 'We can take dhows into places they shouldn't go and in conditions that even modern yachts struggle with.'

'Yes, like entering Lamu Channel on *Fayswal* at night on spring low.'

'Yes, that was ... interesting. In the Kusi, such a place eats boats. Shifting sandbanks, currents. The tidal range can be four metres at springs, which creates bad rips. A wrecked dhow on the beach can be completely covered with sand in a few days. It just disappears! That is why we prefer the channels behind the islands.'

After a cup of tea and evening prayers, the crew went ashore to sleep in a deserted tree house while Paul and Husni laid out mattresses on the deck. Paul found a comfortable spot between the benches amidships, Husni took the quarterdeck. The air was sticky and heavy with the vegetable scent of mangroves. Sleep didn't come easily and he lay looking at the stars.

Just as he was about to doze off, a squall passed over the dhow. Although he lay beneath a tarpaulin, raindrops drilled the deck around him and rivulets seeped under his mattress. He got up and pulled his bedding nearer the mast and further under the awning. A while later he was woken by the lid of a pot tapping to the rock of the boat and he got up to silence it. Husni was snoring at the stern. A gust of wind shifted *Jamal* closer to the shore and she kissed the sand briefly, then drifted free. Somehow, he found sleep again.

Paul woke to the sound of Husni loudly blowing a conch. The crew emerged from the tree line and waded out to the dhow. It was a grey, windless day. *Jamal* motor-sailed up the western flank of Kiwayu, gliding through a viscous sea and sending an arrow wake into the web of mangrove roots on either side the channel. A bigger awning was strung across the deck to protect them from regular showers.

Mid-morning, the doc dished up a breakfast of toast and bananas, fried on a jiko charcoal cooker, washed down with mugs of strong Kenyan coffee. All was soporifically peaceful on board.

'Fire one!' came a bellowed command from the Kiwayu shore.

'Merciful Allah, we're under attack!' shouted Husni. 'Hard a port, full throttle!'

Nuru swung the tiller over and the dhow slewed round. A black projectile hurtled through the air towards *Jamal*. The dhow responded sluggishly. It was too late. The ball struck the sail and exploded. Water rained down on them.

Paul stared at the crest of the dune in disbelief. A grey-haired man dressed in a white admiral's uniform stood with a sword raised above his head. Beside him was an enormous catapult. Three men were pulling on a long, thick elastic. A fourth was loading another plastic water bomb into a pouch. 'Look lively,' cried the admiral, 'they're getting away!'

'Ready, Sah!' called the loader.

'Fire two!' His sword came down with a flash of silver and the projectile arced skyward.

'Hard a starboard!' yelled Husni. Nuru responded instantly, allowing the sail to flog as the dhow jagged through ninety degrees.

The bomb hit the water a few metres behind them with a splash. *Jamal*'s crew let out a cheer.

'Load, load, load, you lily-livered landlubbers! Where the hell did you learn artillery? The scum are getting away!'

By now, they were out of range and the third projectile landed in their wake. Everyone on board was laughing. Taki pulled off his red kikoi and waved it at the enemy, chanting something derisive.

'Old Jim,' said Husni. 'At least he only got one on target. He's an eccentric English lord, or something like a lord. He's got a lodge up there on the dune and shoots at all the dhows using the channel. Everyone gets into the spirit.'

Later that morning, *Jamal* anchored off Mkokoni, a mainland village opposite the northern end of Kiwayu. The clouds remained low and gentle rain continued to fall. A few dhows were fishing in the channel, but nobody was venturing into open sea due to the lack of wind and a big swell. There was little to do but laze about the boat. Paul wrote in his notebook, scripting a Pate scene for the movie. A rotund and ever-smiling Taki listened to tinny Arab music on a windup radio, the doc fried white snapper for lunch and Rafiki grated more coconuts.

When the weather cleared in the late afternoon, Paul and Husni went ashore to have a look around Mkokoni. They landed in the middle of a game of beach soccer: Manchester United versus Arsenal. Most Kenyan boys supported an English football club and took premiership games seriously, explained Husni. There was a communal television set, run off solar panels, that screened important games in a village clearing. 'In this country, soccer is politics,' said Husni. 'You never see any of our coastal players in the national side. It boils down to tribal prejudice and corruption. The Swahili don't count in modern Kenya.'

Mkokoni was a typical rural settlement of coral-rag and makuti-roofed buildings set back from the beach among cultivated shambas and coconut-palm groves. The villagers were welcoming, calling out '*Karibu*' as the two men strolled by. Passing the school, Paul noticed there were far more boys than girls. Husni said this was because, from a young age, girls had to start tilling the fields and tending to the house.

'Some of my family live here,' said Husni. 'You'll find that most island people have relatives spread throughout the archipelago. Come and meet my granny.'

They ducked through an open doorway into a dark interior partitioned by walls of cloth. Husni was warmly greeted by family members within, a young relative jumping up to give him a hug. He introduced Paul to his blind grandmother and a handful of female cousins in long kangas. One of them was weaving a grass mat, the other crafted jewellery from discarded slip-slops made in China. Paul was offered a bowl of bhajees the girls had just cooked. They tasted like smoky doughnuts.

The two men continued their stroll through Mkokoni. 'Seeing as you're so interested in dhows, do you want to meet a mtepe fundi?' asked Husni.

'Gosh, is there still one alive? I'd love to meet him.'

They walked to the far end of town and knocked on the door of a stone building. The housekeeper opened and a short conversation in Swahili ensued. They were ushered into an anteroom and the woman motioned Paul to sit in a straight-backed wooden chair. There was a rug with a geometric design on the floor, a chest in the corner, a second high-backed chair and not much else by way of furnishings. Husni excused himself and the woman reappeared with a tray of tea, which she placed on a low stool beside Paul without saying a word. After a few minutes a stooped man entered the room at a shuffle. He wore a blue kanzu, skullcap and slippers. Paul stood up.

'Sit down, sit down, Mr Paul, pour us some tea,' he said in a creaky voice. 'I am Fundi Daud Bwana. Lots of sugar. Pleased to meet you. They say you are interested in mtepes.'

'Yes, very much. Husni told me you were a mtepe fundi.'

The man laughed, his face crumpling into a topographic map. 'Husni exaggerates. When I was young, I was an apprentice to a great fundi from Lamu. He taught me everything I know. It was before the European war. The second one.'

Bwana's mind was still sharp and he'd forgotten nothing. He explained in detail how the mtepe was constructed. 'You see, Mr Paul, in European shipbuilding, the ribs are the first to be put in place, then the hull is attached to them. But with a mtepe, the shell of the hull is made first, then the ribs put in. The reason is simple: you cannot stitch the planks together if the ribs are in the way.'

Initially, Bwana explained, mangrove timbers had to be bent into shape over open fires, then laid edge to edge and fastened together with wooden pegs. Next came the sewing. Holes were drilled with a hand auger and the rope was passed back and forth by two men, like the lacing of a shoe. The rope was stretched, and each stitch secured by a peg knocked in to wedge it. Then the hole was plugged with tree gum.

Lastly, a paste of pounded mangrove bark and vegetable oil was smeared on everything as a preservative. This had to be done every few months for the rest of the mtepe's life to stop the hull from rotting. It was a painfully laborious process.

'No nails, Mr Paul. That is the beauty! In the old days they believed that when a ship built with nails sailed over a magnetic mountain on the ocean floor, its nails would be drawn out like teeth and she would sink. Not with a mtepe! But one bad stitch can sink a ship, Mr Paul, and the hull has more than four thousand of them. Every plank has to fit together perfectly,' said the fundi, laying his calloused hands together. 'Exactly. Over a length of sixty feet. Not even a gap the size of paper, understand? In a nailed boat, if there's a gap in a seam you just hammer in some caulking. If you do that in a sewn boat, you open the gap wider. Then you sink.'

'Do you think there are any fundis who could still build a mtepe?' asked Paul.

Bwana took a slurp of his tea. 'Perhaps one or two old fools. But they would need my help,' he said with a wink.

'Did you ever sail one?' asked Paul.

'I made a few voyages as crew when I was young,' said Bwana. 'We mostly worked the inshore channels, carrying cattle, boriti, salt, pottery … in my grandfather's time, they carried slaves. But never coconuts.'

'Why not coconuts?'

'Bad luck — they loosen the stitches!' said the old man. 'We mostly travelled using poles and oars. We had a sail, of course, square and made from palm fibre. Unfortunately, mtepes are not very good sailors. They are leaky boats too. We had to bail water out every hour. It was hard work. But mtepes were good for beach landings. The hull is more, how can I say, forgiving than one built with nails. And they were graceful, Mr Paul, the most graceful of all dhows.'

Returning to the beach, Paul and Husni saw a motorboat waiting in the shallows, a WWF logo on its side. A teenager hopped out and sprinted up to them. 'Come quickly, they are hatching!' he cried.

The motorboat sped them the short distance across the bay to Kiwayu. A game guard met them on the beach and led the group hastily up a sandy path, over a hill to the island's wild eastern shore and north along a line of low cliffs. By now, the sun had set and waves pounded the rocks below in loud detonations. When they came to the crest of a dune, the guard stopped and crouched down. A stick marked an indentation in the sand. 'It's here,' he said to the teenager.

The lad began gently scraping away the soil. Just then a miniscule turtle popped to the surface like a cork. Soon, there were a dozen of them hurtling down the dune, using their flippers to paddle across the sand, the roar of the waves acting like a magnet. Paul walked beside them, brimming with emotion. He would be their escort, making sure they reached the water safely. The baby turtles came to a wave-cut ledge and, without hesitating, tumbled over the precipice, their white bellies flashing in the dusk as they cartwheeled to the beach below. For a human baby, this would be the equivalent of a five-metre fall within a minute of being born, Paul reckoned.

He glanced across the beach and noticed that each man was herding his own flock of hatchlings and shooing away the ghost crabs. The cove had become one big maternity ward. The teenager came over and told him to resist the temptation to pick up the turtles and carry them to the water, as all their geomagnetic imprinting took place during the mad dash for the surf: this was what allowed them to return to that very beach, years hence, when they were adults.

Paul's batch of reptiles neared the water, leaving caterpillar trails in the hard sand. A wave broke on the shore and he jumped back so as not to wet his shoes. When he looked again, the backwash had swept the beach clean. Somewhere in the surf, infant turtles were swimming for their lives into a darkening deep, thick with predators.

CHAPTER 22

After a quiet night in the Mkokoni channel, *Jamal* motored to the north end of the bay and anchored off Kiwayu Safari Lodge. Paul had asked to be put ashore for twenty-four hours to reconnoitre the resort where the film crew would be staying. While he was on land, *Jamal* would do a short fishing trip.

Paul stepped ashore and Trisha, the manager, walked down the beach to meet him. 'Welcome to paradise!' she said, handing him a cocktail adorned with a paper umbrella and fruit kebab. Trisha was an attractive, resourceful, thirtysomething Kenyan; barefoot, blonde and blue-eyed, wearing a red bikini top with a green kikoi. *Paradise indeed,* thought Paul, trying not to let his gaze drift to her curves.

The lodge was Robinson Crusoe chic and comprised a line of reed-and-thatch bandas overlooking the beach. Even better than the brochure, he reckoned. Conches, calabashes and cowries adorned pathways that led to the main building, reached along an avenue of immaculate palm trees that leant inwards, as though bowing to the guests. He knocked the trunk of one to make sure they weren't fibreglass. The lodge was an open-plan, makuti-roofed enclosure. Mahogany logs had been fashioned into chunky tables and a bar counter. Skulls, horns and turtle shells formed a motif intended to evoke conservation.

'Much poaching around here?' asked Paul.

'Sure,' said Trisha. 'This place actually started out as a hunting camp back in the seventies. In those days, elephants still walked the beach and foraged on the islands, but by the mid-eighties they'd all been slaughtered. Fish stocks got hammered too.'

'Really? I thought the fishing was good,' he said, thinking of all the dhows he'd seen.

'Much of it got wiped out a few years ago by a Japanese fleet with thirty-kilometre lines,' said Trisha. 'They bought the fishing rights from the Kenyan government — the right to rape and pillage, more like. They took out everything. We used to be able to catch three marlins in a morning; now you can't get one. But the fishing in Somali waters is still great.'

Trisha showed him to his room. The grass-walled banda had an enormous bed set beneath a mosquito net, a two-person hammock and colourful throw cushions scattered everywhere. The shell of a giant clam stood in the doorway to wash beach sand from one's feet. This was a dream Africa, a fantasy Swahili-land which Paul found both seductive and unreal.

After unpacking, he joined Trisha for a beer in the lounge. She was witty and charming, interspersing her enquiries about food preferences and entertainment needs with titbits about the WWF turtle project and etiquette when visiting the local village. She dropped in all the prerequisite eco and conservation soundbites: the lodge cleaned the beaches, employed local people, protected the wildlife and fought the charcoal burners destroying the forest. Paul pretended to take notes.

Being so near the border, he asked about the situation in Somalia.

'It's a bit wild and woolly up there right now,' she said, scrunching up her petite nose. 'I wouldn't advise going.'

'We're not sailing very far north, and for the most part we'll be staying a long way offshore.'

Paul discovered that Trisha was also mad about dhows and was considering organising charters along the coast for the lodge's guests. He filled her in on the details of his documentary project and his own dream of one day sailing down as far as Mozambique, maybe even South Africa, on a dhow. Trisha said she'd be game to join such a venture and hauled out a 1966 Admiralty Chart of the coast.

They traced a possible route and anchorages, discussing where to sail far offshore and where to slip inside the reefs. Their animated talk and mutual encouragement made it seem almost possible. If they found a sponsor and made a movie about it, maybe they could even pick up a dhow in Oman — in Sur or Muscat — and sail to Africa on the Kaskazi. They'd need a rubber duck to scoot across shallow coral and land on desert islands. They'd dress in turbans and galabias. Their very own *Arabian Nights*.

Paul liked Trisha a lot. She was down-to-earth and no nonsense. There was none of the unpredictability and drama of Hannah. In place of his initial sexual attraction, he now thought she might become a friend, a lasting friend, maybe even a future shipmate.

Returning to the business at hand, Paul made arrangements for the film crew and did a walkabout with Trisha. The lodge had everything they would need. She offered to show him their exclusive, $1000-a-day honeymoon suite, called The Baobabs of Kitangani, situated across the bay on the northernmost tip of Kiwayu.

The motorboat sank its bows into the sand and they stepped ashore beside a gazebo with hammocks, grass mats and throw cushions. On a hill above the deserted beach stood a couple of bandas reached by a sandy path through the trees. The lower one was nestled among baobabs and housed the largest bed

Paul had ever seen. It would have been just the place to bring Hannah. They could have emailed each other from opposite sides of the bed.

'The staff are a few hundred metres away,' said Trisha. 'You can call them on a walkie-talkie for meals, a water taxi or whatever you need. Otherwise, you're completely private. Some guests go naked from the moment they set foot here. This is really the place to come with a lover or a sugar daddy. Honeymoons usually mark the end of high passion, don't they?' She winked. Paul just smiled.

Mkokoni lay around the corner, so prying eyes couldn't see the naked lovers as they frolicked about in paradise. But what did the conservative Swahili villagers make of all this? Back at the lodge, Paul spent the rest of the afternoon sailing a Laser around the bay. The dinghy was a fun craft for the light airs, and he tacked out through crumbling surf to the reef where a bigger swell broke and reformed. It took him back to his teens, racing on the brown waters of the Vaal. A hollow wave broke just ahead of him so he gybed and ran from it, letting the white water spend itself. The wave was catching him, so he tried to harden up quickly and take it head on. The Laser didn't come around fast enough and the wave enveloped the dinghy, knocking it over like a toy.

Splash! He went under.

Paul broke the surface to find the boat turned turtle beside him. Fortunately the wave was a rogue and he had enough time to heave on the dagger board, right the dinghy, sort out the lines and get going again before another one threatened.

Over a supper of charcoal-grilled lobster that evening, Trisha teased him about his undignified flip. She told him of a much more tragic capsize that happened recently in almost the same spot. 'It was a dhow filled with refugees from Somalia,' she said, the candlelight flickering in her eyes. 'They were trying to enter the bay at night and the boat hit a reef. Twenty of them drowned and the hull washed up next to the lodge.'

Paul glanced at the calm waters of the bay, the feathery lines of surf at the headland, and tried to picture the horror of a boat grounding on the reef, the sound of wood splintering, waves broaching the vessel, the terrifying tilt of the deck, women and children spilling into the water, the cries for help.

After supper, Paul considered asking Trisha to join him on a walk to the headland, but thought better of it and turned in. His banda lay far down the beach and he followed the beam of his torch as ghost crabs in their thousands were parted like the Red Sea by his footsteps.

He climbed into bed and began reading one of the history books Pierre had lent him. In the early seventeenth century, the Portuguese captain of Fort Jesus had organised the murder of Mombasa's sultan. The sultan's heir, a lad of seven named Yusuf, was dispatched to Goa for a Christian education, and later sent to sea to learn the arts of war. When the authorities deemed the boy, now named Dom Jerónimo, ready to fulfil his role as vassal, they prepared him for a triumphal return to Mombasa.

The strange chameleon who stepped ashore in Mombasa wearing doublet and hose was not exactly welcomed. He was trusted by neither Portuguese nor Swahili. When he was spotted praying 'in the Moorish manner' beside his father's grave, it was decided he should be arrested as a traitor and shipped back to Goa for trial. However, the young man got wind of the plot and visited the captain of Fort Jesus in his bedroom. After a heated exchange, the captain was stabbed to death. Next thing, a force of Arab soldiers and African archers rushed the gates, killing every Portuguese in their way. Fort

Jesus fell in minutes, and more than 150 Christians sought refuge in the Augustinian convent. Dom Jerónimo took his old name and returned to Islam with a vengeance. Mombasa was his.

The Portuguese men were ordered to leave the convent so that they could be 'sent to Christian countries'. No sooner had they emerged than they were massacred in the street, their limbs severed and their bodies roped together and thrown into the sea. Yusuf extended an olive branch to the women and children: those who converted to Islam could return home, those who did not would be banished to Pate. The women all chose banishment. An Augustinian friar later recounted how, as the ship pulled away, the sailors sliced the throats of 'those innocent sheep', tearing children from their mothers' arms and cutting them to pieces.

Yusuf then loaded up two captured vessels and set off into the blue. With the monsoon filling the sails of his hijacked ships, the King of Mombasa set a course into the uncharted waters of his new career: piracy. For seven years he plied the Indian Ocean, wreaking havoc. The Portuguese couldn't catch him: they'd taught him far too well. Yusuf became a legend of the coast, slipping into Swahili ports where he was feted as a hero, then disappearing over the horizon again. He was eventually killed in a battle with Arabs in the Red Sea, still defiant, still on the run.

When Paul glanced at his watch, he saw that it was past midnight. There was a big day ahead. He switched off the light and lay listening to the sea, but sleep would not come. The bed was too big for one person and the sting of longing — for Hannah, for Dalila, for Lorike — was sharp. In fact, the bed could have accommodated all three. Paul stared up at the mosquito net. He was a fish swimming into its great web, trapped in a net of regret, lost infatuation, stupid lust, impossible love. Thrashing about, suffocating.

He got up to take a leak and found a frog in the toilet. Peeing against the porcelain to spare it the indignity, Paul wondered whether he should flush or leave the creature bobbing in urine all night. A little worse for wear, the amphibian was fished out with Paul's sandal. It flip-flopped into the night to find its mate, relate its near-death experience and then copulate furiously. *Lucky bastard,* thought Paul, slipping back under his net and finally to sleep.

CHAPTER 23

Paul woke to the sound of an anchor splash and peered through the mosquito net. *Jamal* lay fifty metres away in a bed of glittering diamonds. He walked to the lodge where he drank a quick coffee. Trisha gave him a brochure and her card. They would see each other early in the new year when he returned with the crew for the shoot. He gave her a hug, then boarded the dhow.

No sooner had his feet touched the deck, than the sail was unfurled and *Jamal* put way on. Paul felt elated: Somalia beckoned, adventure beckoned. The baggage of the previous weeks could be left behind. This was his voyage now; the movie was only incidental. It was as though he'd crossed a boundary in himself. He stood on the quarterdeck beside Husni and waved at the blonde figure on the beach. Perhaps one day he could make a life with someone like her.

Jamal cleaved away from the shore, bending to a light breeze from the east-northeast. They cleared the headland and prepared to harden up into the wind. First the weatherside *sharutis* were tightened to give the mast better support, then Husni gave the command: '*Kaza demani!* Sheet in!' Latif and Taki hauled on the mainsheet and the dhow heeled further over. Husni was at the tiller, pointing *Jamal* as high as she would go.

They sailed straight out to sea for an hour, the land diminishing to a smudge, until Husni decided to head back inshore and called for a gybe. Paul had been on board mashuas for wearing ship; now he could take careful note of how it was done on a jahazi. His Nikon was at the ready. The crew took up their positions as Husni bore away from the wind and *Jamal* wallowed exaggeratedly into a run. The sail flogged in thunderclaps as the foredeck team manhandled the yard into a vertical position, then twisted it around the front of the mast. At this precarious point in the manoeuvre, there were few ropes to control the sail. It was like trying to turn a circus tent inside out, without dismantling it, in a stiff breeze.

There was an awkward moment when the yard, standing vertical, bounced up and down like a battering ram, threatening to impale the deck or the men grappling with it. The crew tried desperately to keep the butt under control as clouds of sail ballooned around them. Agile Rafiki quickly carried the mainsheet around the front of the rig and trailed it aft. The yard was allowed to slide forward, back to its diagonal position, Husni gradually hardened up on the other tack and the flogging sail was brought under control. *Jamal*'s mainsheet was secured on the port side and water began to boil along the flanks again. The manoeuvre had been deftly handled and Paul had got some decent photographs.

Having left the archipelago's 'interior sea' at Kiwayu, they remained outside the protecting *kizingiti*, the barrier reef that created a line of safe anchorages in its lee. The wind was warm and steady. *Jamal* drew a white chalk line through an azure sea. There was not another vessel in sight. Paul lay on the deck gazing up at the triangle of cotton and listening to the sound of creaking rope, the chafe of yard against mast, the happy splash of the bow wave and the murmur of the timbers. It sounded like a prayer, his own oceanic adhan.

A chain of calcareous islets stretched away to the north. Flocks of gulls and terns rained down on them like confetti. Many of the atolls were really just pieces of permanently dry reef. Local fishermen often mended their nets on these kiwas, or took overnight shelter there in makeshift bandas. Behind lay a low, uninhabited shore of mangrove swamps.

After lunch, they passed Kiungamini, the northernmost island in Kenya. 'People call it Tanga la Mnara, place of the tower,' said Husni, coming to sit beside Paul. 'It's got a tall pillar tomb. Look there! You can just make it out. Locals think it is the grave of an *ifriti*.'

'What's an *ifriti*?'

Husni explained that it was a dangerous jinni. The tomb was actually that of a British lieutenant murdered in the 1800s. In revenge, the Royal Navy attacked Kiungamini and destroyed everything. The locals abandoned the island for the mainland and built the tomb to appease the foreign ghost.

They sailed on in light airs, keeping well clear of a cluster of mushroom-shaped coral outcrops. Paul perched on the windward rail, shirt off, gazing over the bows and thinking about pirates and the anarchy of Somalia. Even the Chinese, sailing here many centuries ago, were terrified of this coast where humans could change themselves into birds, beasts or fish and strike the fear of death into travellers. If your commercial dealings with the Somalis went awry, sorcerers would cast a spell on your ship so it couldn't be budged until the dispute, or rather the price, was settled.

Could the ruins found by the Hungarian archaeologist really be the famous port where Arab sailors came to barter metal tools for ivory and turtle shell? And who were its ancient inhabitants? Could they have been Bantu-speaking people from West Africa, as some historians suggested? For Paul, these questions were tantalising and the prospect of finding pre-Islamic ruins thrilling.

Ahead of them lay the promontory of Ras Kaambooni: Somalia. The wind had freshened and *Jamal* was creaming along handsomely. Flying fish broke the surface and glided through the air beside them like escorts. They were sailing closer to a shore that looked completely deserted. The green coastal fringe of Kenya had disappeared and the coast was barren, dominated in places by tall sand dunes. Inshore islets were covered with smaller dunes and bushy scrub. None bore any sign of humans.

Paul needed the toilet. There was no prospect of touching land for some time, so he was forced to use the open-top box that hung over the stern. He grabbed a roll of toilet paper and climbed inside. *Jamal* was sailing with an awkward, corkscrew motion and Paul found it hard to keep balance as he squatted over the hole. Aiming his buttocks at a gap that offered a window on to sluicing water was most unnerving. One moment he was centimetres from a dunking, the next he was soaring high above the waves. Eventually, his business done, he emerged from the box feeling queasy.

'Next time you can drop me on a beach,' he muttered to Husni, who wore a wide grin but passed no comment.

Young Rafiki shouted something from the bows and pointed to a grey shape on the eastern horizon.

'American destroyer,' said Husni. 'Hunting Osama. They are probably looking at us right now; maybe took pictures of you on the toilet.'

'More gunboat diplomacy,' said Paul. 'Do you think Al-Qaeda is here?'

'Yes, probably. We have heard there are training bases. The refugee camps in Kenya are terrible places that breed trouble. There are thousands of Somalis in them. These things make me worry. It touches all of us.'

The afternoon wore on. Husni was steering; Paul sat next to him. The crew lay sprawled on the deck amidships, whipping and splicing rope or simply dozing. Husni told Paul how he went about selecting his men. He chose those whom he'd sailed with before, men from his own village or whose families he knew. Foredeck hands like Rafiki and Latif were usually happy-go-lucky youngsters, while those on the quarterdeck, like Nuru, took the sailing more seriously. Perhaps one day he too might skipper a big, coasting dhow. He, too, might acquire the skills of *usukuni*. More than mere helmsmanship, this was an art that involved reading wind and tide, steering with the least amount of helm, trimming the sails perfectly and having an understanding of coastal navigation that was elevated to a form of instinct. Few dhows carried charts, compasses or even binoculars. Bringing a vessel safely home was a matter of knowing the currents, the weather, every feature of the shoreline and which stars to steer by.

'My younger brother was the best skipper in Kizingitini,' said Husni. 'He's a natural. You'll meet him in Galoh.'

'You said you hadn't seen him in years?'

'Mohamed is a wanderer. He was always the bright one. Good at school. He was going to do great things, but he never kept his focus. After high school he went to university in Nairobi, but only lasted a year. He became very religious for a while, ended up at an Islamic college in Sudan. We did not have news from him for a long time. When he moved to Galoh, we heard he'd found a woman, settled down. He is the skipper of a fishing dhow. My mother wants to know everything. She says I must instruct him to come home for Eid. It is her wish. If he has a wife, she must come too.'

'Are you looking forward to seeing him?'

He shrugged. 'You never know what you will find.'

Towards sunset, *Jamal* edged closer to the coast. Husni frequently called for a change of course, seeing sandbanks where Paul saw only monochromatic blue. They found a gap in the barrier reef and turned inshore. Nuru steered them into a cove in the lee of a big atoll covered in scrubby foliage with palms and baobab trees on its eastern shore. Long-limbed Latif climbed on to the foredeck and tipped the anchor over the side. There was a splash and Paul watched the hook sink to the bottom through water mottled with coral outcrops. *Jamal* came to a gentle stop and turned to face her anchor rope. Paul scanned the shore: there was no sign of life. The mainland lay a few hundred metres to the west, equally wild and deserted. The island's small, moon-shaped bay almost completely encircled the dhow, creating an ideal anchorage.

Donning a mask and snorkel, Paul jumped into the warm water and swam towards the shore. He spotted a few Moorish idols, a shoal of chocolate dips and one busy parrotfish. Reaching the atoll, he climbed out on to a powdery white beach. His were the only footprints. He scrambled up a coral outcrop on the northern headland to watch a scarlet sun dip behind the mainland dunes. Paul could see the bowed figures of the crew at evening prayers on *Jamal*. They'd rolled out their mats on the quarterdeck and were all facing north, to Mecca, kneeling and prostrating themselves. The sound of their voices reached him faintly across the water.

Walking back along the beach, he came upon a bone washed up on the high-tide line. It was bleached and brittle, the femur of some animal. Could it be human? He kicked it with his foot. Probably baboon.

Back on board, Paul helped Taki and Latif drag the yellow tarpaulin over the lowered yard as rain clouds were threatening again. With its ends tethered to the gunnel, the tarpaulin created a makeshift tent amidships. Nuru's radio played Somali pop music, Rafiki set to grating more coconuts and the doc busied himself cooking a shark they'd caught off Kiwayu while Paul had been ashore. Taki was telling another string of unfunny jokes and Latif's deep laugh burbled across the deck. Husni and Paul sat in the bows watching the first stars dance in the water.

'There aren't any more dhows from Arabia, are there?' asked Paul.

'Just a few from Yemen to fish or sell dried shark. They arrive with the Kaskazi. It takes them about a week to sail down to Mombasa and they normally motor back up.'

'It's progress, I suppose. Container ships, tankers, airliners.'

Paul thought how the Swahili were, once again in their turbulent history, being subjected to dramatic change. They'd been on the back foot for centuries, it seemed. And yet the culture still thrived in pockets, even on the Somali coast. It was evident in the makuti-and-coral architecture, in the language and poetry, cuisine and dress. And of course there were still the dhows, the most beautiful of all African boats. Paul pictured *Jamal* surfing down a long ocean swell, her white lateen etched against the sky. Yes, a civilisation born on the monsoon, and one that learnt to prosper from it.

Spicy aromas from the galley drifted across the deck, making everyone's mouth water, even Paul's, who wasn't keen on shark. The flesh had been deboned and boiled in sea water. Now the doc was crumbling it into small pieces and adding onions over a charcoal fire. He tipped in chillies and tinned tomatoes, along with tamarind and crushed cardamom. When it was finally served on the windless, moonlit deck, Paul had to admit it tasted heavenly.

Supper done, he left the crew to make their beds in the waist and lowered himself over the side. The dhow had drifted close in and he could wade ashore with his borrowed sleeping bag held aloft. He found a comfortable spot on the beach, dried himself off with a T-shirt and crawled into the bag. There could hardly be a better place to spend the night, with a bed of soft coral sand and the ocean chafing the shore just metres from his feet. The cove was an enchanted disc of silver and black. *Jamal* lay in a patch of mercury moonlight. It was like the painting of a dream. *Somalia,* he thought, *I'm sleeping on a beach in Somalia.*

CHAPTER 24

'Good morning, did you rest well?' called Husni, striding up the beach towards him.

'Better than ever,' said Paul, sitting up on one elbow and rubbing the sleep from his eyes.

'Breakfast?' Husni handed him a Tupperware with papaya slices.

'Thank you, delicious.'

'Seeing as we are here, why don't we go and find Rhapta?'

'It's here, on this island?' said Paul, amazed. 'Why didn't you tell me?'

'I thought it could be a little surprise.' Husni had a wicked grin.

'You bastard, let's go find it!' Paul said, getting out of his sleeping bag and pulling on a T-shirt and shorts.

Husni led him over a dune and through a coconut grove on the seaward side of the atoll. After twenty minutes they came to a promontory overlooking a cove. The area was dotted with baobabs, a few scattered doum palms and a stand of mango trees. They looked down on a picturesque beach with lime-green shallows, neatly contained by a line of coral. Beyond was the dark blue of the deep. On their right, the mainland stretched away to the southwest in one unending stripe of sand.

'I think this is the spot,' said Husni. 'It was more than a decade ago ... all these thorn bushes have grown up in the meantime ... but look, can you see those low mounds? They're actually the remains of buildings. Here —' Husni pointed to a collapsed trench. 'We dug these for Halász, the archaeologist. He hired a bunch of men from Kiwayu to come and help. We worked all the daylight hours.'

'Why the rush?'

'Halász was old, very sick. He knew he was dying and there was very little money. It was a hunch, a gamble. Sort of a dream for him. Like buried treasure.'

As they explored the site, Husni explained how the biggest job had been clearing the bushes — days of back-breaking labour. Then digging the trenches, three metres deep. At the deepest level, they found wonderful things. Glazed pottery, glass beads, an amphora: trade goods from both the Mediterranean and the Persian Gulf. 'He was very happy about the money we found: three Roman coins.'

Paul understood why Halász was excited: imperial coins might suggest this was Rhapta. But if Paul was completely honest with himself, the site was too small to be a 'metropolis'; the ruins weren't grand enough. Most experts believed the city to be way further south, anyway. That big National Geographic Rhapta special might not be on the cards after all.

But it was certainly a very old settlement. Definitely pre-Swahili. The Romans and Greeks traded with a number of African ports, and this was probably one of them. After the fall of Rome and the collapse of that market, many towns along the coast would have died off, along with Rhapta.

'There was broken pottery spread over the whole area,' said Husni. 'There would have been stone buildings in the centre, huts surrounding it — just like Lamu, or any Swahili town. And here, look at this.' Husni pointed at a toppled pillar made of coral. 'It's part of a tomb. Halász was very interested in it.'

Paul and Husni sat on a fallen palm-trunk and shared a bottle of water. The pillar reminded him of the one he'd seen with

Lorike at the Takwa ruins. Beside the column was a low mausoleum of sorts, adorned with panels of asymmetric, geometrical patterns. Pre-Islamic, but what were its origins? They had similar obelisk-like stelae in Axum in Ethiopia at that time — he'd seen photographs. Perhaps the Arabs had taken over this African tradition and turned it into an Islamic one.

Birds chirruped in the trees. The light reflecting off the sand was blinding. A stone-town surrounded by wattle-and-daub structures set on an island for security: the classic Swahili pattern. The sheltered anchorage would have been packed with the small sewn boats, forerunners of the mtepe, mentioned in the *Periplus*. Some would have been for fishing, others for coastal trading. He imagined larger, square-rigged vessels in the roadstead, a wondrous array of Roman, Greek, Egyptian, Arab and Persian craft.

There would have been a marketplace somewhere close to the beach. He saw tables, awnings, a pile of elephant tusks. In a cordoned-off section stood a group of near-naked slaves, tethered to one another, bound for Iraq to work on the reclamation of the southern marshlands. A trader had laid out two pale leopard skins and a handful of turtle shells in the shade of a baobab. On his lap he held a rhino horn, wrapped in blue cloth. It was sure to fetch a good price.

An Arab dhow had been warped into the shallows and its cargo of glass jars and bolts of cotton cloth was being unloaded. Goods from a Roman vessel that was moving back into deeper water were being sorted on the beach. Paul could see a pile of boxes filled with metal objects — iron tools, swords, spearheads — and a few amphorae of wine. A merchant in a colourful caftan was shouting something about the price.

'But is it really Rhapta?' muttered Paul, mostly to himself.

'Who knows?' Husni shrugged. 'I think we must get back to *Jamal.*'

The sun was high. They'd spent most of the morning standing over their own reflection in breathless conditions. Now *Jamal* was beating slowly northward in fluky airs. The crew lay about the deck; Husni was perched at the tiller. Paul sat cross-legged on the quarterdeck and wrote in his notebook:

VISUAL: *Bustling harbour scene. Water-line images of dhows cleaving through the roadstead, men leaning out, graceful lateens filling, quivering, alive. Slo-mo helicopter shot from directly above: a jahazi coursing through limpid green water, leaving a wide wake.*
A gust strikes the vessel. It heels, accelerates. Cut to a camera in the bows looking ahead, under-cranked so we appear to be flying across the water...

A popping sound interrupted his writing. He looked up. The sail above his head was riddled with holes. The punctures began to tear grotesquely.

'*Maharamia!*' screamed Rafiki from the foredeck.

Paul dropped the notebook and scrambled to his feet.

There was utter confusion on deck. The skipper yelled incoherently. Taki ran to start the engine. Paul looked astern. The boat was a hundred metres off their port quarter, approaching at high speed. There was no way they could outrun it.

The vessel was a white fibreglass skiff, about eight metres long. Paul counted five men. One was driving, another stood in the bows with a red keffiyeh wrapped around his head, its end trailing in the wind. Two men amidships carried AK-47s, a third pointed a rocket-propelled grenade-launcher at *Jamal*.

The skiff came tearing up to them, the outboard engine deep and throaty. Moments later they were alongside. Their driver decelerated and the skiff settled back into the water like a pelican landing. The man in the bows shouted something in Swahili.

'What's he saying?' asked Paul. His hands were shaking, his voice high and unsteady.

'We must let them come aboard or they'll shoot,' said Husni in a dead tone.

Paul stared at the attackers in disbelief. This couldn't be happening. The skiff bumped against *Jamal* and four figures climbed over the rail. Teenagers charged with adrenalin; their eyes wild. It wouldn't take much for one of them to pull a trigger. He desperately hoped none of the crew did anything foolish.

'Nobody move! Shut up!' screamed the pirate with the red keffiyeh.

The rest of the crew held their hands aloft, except Husni, who continued to steer. Paul copied the others, putting his arms high in the air. It was only then that he noticed Latif lying on the foredeck, a stream of blood pouring from his arm.

The red pirate was obviously the leader. He mounted the quarterdeck and struck Husni in the face with his pistol. The skipper fell to the deck and Paul leapt to grab the tiller to stop *Jamal* veering off course. The pirate smiled, pressed the pistol against Paul's temple and shouted something in Swahili. The ugly, pockmarked face was close to his. Black, bloodshot eyes. A sprig of khat protruded from the side of the man's mouth and his teeth were stained green. Paul smelt foul breath, the stale sweat of his body. The pirate was excited, enjoying himself. *'Mmarekani?'* — American. Paul went cold with terror, his body stiffened, expecting at any moment the shot he would never hear. His mind raced, but could find no purchase.

Husni was pleading, repeating something over and over. His voice came from the bottom of a deep well. '*Mmarekani*' again. The gunman laughed, patted Paul on the cheek with a rough, fisherman's hand and turned to the crew, shouting orders. Nuru took the helm and the rest of the sailors were herded into the waist, where two men guarded the group. The third took up a position on the foredeck aiming his rifle at them. The red pirate stood on the quarterdeck beside Nuru. 'You are now prisoners!' he shouted in English. 'If you do anything wrong, we kill you. Keep heads down. Do not look at us. No talk!'

The pirate ordered Nuru to follow the skiff, which had drawn ahead of *Jamal*. 'Do not fall behind,' said the pirate. 'Do not change course. I shoot you.'

The crew sat with hands on their heads. Two pirates moved among them, checking their pockets and patting them down for money or weapons. After the search, they were allowed to tend to Latif, who lay on the deck behind them. The young sailor's upper arm had been torn open and the wound was a mess of ugly flesh. Taki tried to staunch the bleeding with a kikoi. Husni found some painkillers, disinfectant cream and bandages in *Jamal*'s rudimentary first-aid tin. They propped Latif against the mast. His eyes were closed and he moaned through dry lips.

Nuru remained at the helm, trailing the skiff. The sail was riddled with holes, but with the engine's help they were still making good speed. Paul was forced to sit at the stern, away from the rest. The adrenalin had left him and he felt drained, exhausted. His body still shook.

Once Latif was made comfortable on a pile of mattresses and his arm bandaged, Husni took the helm.

'How's he doing?' asked Paul under his breath.

'I don't know,' whispered Husni. 'The bullet went right through his arm.'

'Silence!' shouted the leader, vaulting the steps to the quarterdeck and grabbing Paul by his hair. The pirate punched him in the face with his pistol, opening a cut across his cheek. 'American pig!' he screamed. 'I tell you, quiet!'

He dragged Paul by his hair the length of the dhow and on to the foredeck, forcing him to kneel. 'Hands on head, face front!'

Paul closed his eyes, expecting another blow. Blood ran down his cheek, but there was no pain. The pirate turned to the sailors and began shouting in Swahili. He heard another blow and the thud of a body hitting the deck.

Then there was silence for a long while and the drone of the engine took over. Paul's knees began to burn, his arms ached. The pain of keeping his hands on his head hurt more than his cheek. He needed water. After an hour or two — Paul had lost track of time — he was allowed to go and sit with the others on the main deck. A bottle of water was passed around and he drank sparingly, aware that it was meant for all of them. Rafiki sat with Latif and was given an extra bottle of water. The wounded sailor appeared to be drifting in and out of consciousness.

The pirates piled all the crew's luggage in the middle of the waist and began opening bags, flinging possessions everywhere. Soon there was a small heap of booty in the shape of wallets, knives and sunglasses. Two of the pirates were now wearing Paul's T-shirts. One of them unzipped his toiletry bag and pulled out a pack of condoms. He tore open a sachet and blew a condom balloon which he released into the air. All the pirates laughed. Paul felt the humiliation flushing his face.

The red pirate found his Nikon and watch, as well as the dollars hidden in a sock at the bottom of his backpack. He came over and slapped Paul across the wound on his cheek.

'Please, I'm not American —'

'No, you liar. Shut up!'

The pirate gathered up the booty and shared it among his cohorts, careful to divide the spoils equally. *Jamal*'s crew was ordered to repack their bags and stow them.

The sun dipped towards the cursive horizon of a dune-lined shore. The skiff drew alongside and a bag of ingredients was handed aboard. One of the pirates descended to the galley and prepared the evening meal which was served at dusk. The pirates squatted around a pot on the foredeck and told the crew to turn their backs while they ate. When they were done, the pot with the remains of the food was returned to the galley.

The wind remained light and most of their propulsion was derived from the engine. The moon threw a silver path across the water as the dark shadow of the skiff led *Jamal* ever northward. Their stomachs grumbled and the water bottle was long empty. They tried to sleep but without mattresses the deck was hard.

Paul woke from semi-slumber to hear a pirate hoiking up a gob of phlegm and spitting into the pot with a ghastly rasping sound. Then another followed. Paul pictured the green teeth of his captor. There was much giggling, then the food was served cold. None of the hostages was able to eat and the pot was returned to the galley.

'You not hungry!' shouted the leader. 'You no like our food. We will see.'

The pirates retired to the foredeck and Taki was sent to the tiller to steer for the rest of the night.

'It's a new group,' whispered Husni, lying on the deck beside Paul. 'They're operating much further south than I was told. Because we have nothing of value, I thought no one would bother us. I'm so sorry, Paul.'

'It's not your fault. What can we do?'

'Nothing. We must do as they say. They normally steal the cargo of Kenyan dhows, then let them go. Unfortunately, they probably think you might bring a ransom.'

'Me? But I'm an African, just like them. I'm not a Westerner. I'm worth nothing. Shit, do you know how much a freelance scriptwriter earns in South Africa?'

'You are white, you look European. It is enough for them. They won't treat us too badly.'

'They shot Latif.'

'That was a mistake.'

'They might make another mistake.'

'We must hope they do not. They only want money. We will negotiate. Others will negotiate. Perhaps your government will pay.'

'For me? Not likely.'

'Maybe your family can pay.'

'My parents live in a small house in a lousy Joburg suburb. Jesus Christ. We have no access to any kind of real money.'

'Try to get some sleep. Tomorrow will be a long day.'

'Today was long, Husni.'

They fell silent, the pulse of the deck passing through their bodies, willing them into a reluctant sleep.

CHAPTER 25

Paul opened his eyes to the sound of a pirate banging about in the galley. The morning was bright and he sat up, shielding his eyes from the sun. The crew were stirring around him. Husni rolled over and groaned, taking in their circumstances with a disbelieving look. The youngest pirate, a small lad with light-brown skin and a pinched face, swaggered over with the pot from the previous night. 'Breakfast,' he said, tossing it to the deck.

It was a mess of congealed rice and brown beans cooked in milk. There was whitish scum on top. Each took a small handful from the edge, where the muck looked slightly less revolting. Paul watched his shipmates pulling faces as they swallowed. This might be the only meal they'd get that day. He ran a finger along the rim of the pot, put it to his lips and found that the cold goo didn't taste as bad as he'd feared. They all forced down a few mouthfuls before handing the pot back.

The morning grew hot. Paul's cap was in his bag and there was no way he could get at it. His face was already bright red from the previous day's exposure and he moved surreptitiously to follow the shifting shade of the sail. Husni was permitted to clean and dress Latif's wound and give him more painkillers. The first-aid tin was now almost empty.

'Want money, you hide money!' screamed the youngest pirate, coming down the ladder to where they were sitting bunched together on the main deck. Despite his youth and diminutive size, he had the swagger of power. Striding between them, he yelled: 'Give more money!'

'You took all our money yesterday,' said Husni. 'We are fishermen.'

'You lie, I know you! Don't look me, look down!'

'We are just Lamu fishermen.'

'And him?' The pirate pointed his rifle at Paul.

'He is my friend, from South Africa,' said Husni.

'You lie, he American!' The pirate jabbed the barrel into Paul's chest.

'Please, leave him, he is my friend.'

The young captor swung the rifle butt and Husni ducked as it struck him a glancing blow. Then the pirate walked to Latif and prodded his arm with the rifle. The man screamed.

'No, no!' the crew shouted in unison. 'No money! We have no more money!'

When the pirate saw the reaction from all the captives, he wavered and, swearing at them in Somali, retired to the foredeck to sit with his mates. Paul looked at the two groups, five Somalis on the foredeck and five Swahili in the waist. He wanted to believe the pirates were simple sailors just like his shipmates. If he could understand them better, he'd be able to handle the situation better.

Both Husni and Paul needed to go to the toilet. Husni called to the red pirate. They were given permission but were not allowed to use the latrine box. They had to do it together over the port rail and were not given toilet paper. Both men pulled down their trousers and sat with their bottoms over the gunnel. As the boat rolled, the water came high enough for Paul to scoop handfuls and clean himself, the red pirate looking on with a bemused expression.

As Paul was finishing, the man came over and held his jaw in a firm grip. His eyes were glazed and bloodshot. Rough fingers scraped Paul's cheeks as he tried to drag on his shorts. The man's other hand reached between his legs and started to squeeze his testicles. He gasped as the pain shot through his body. The pirate laughed. His hand was like a vice. Paul felt his legs begin to give way. 'South African American,' he whispered. The pirate let go and Paul dropped to the deck. He half-walked, half-crawled back to the others, tears smarting from his eyes.

The day wore on. Paul sat in the midst of the sailors and kept his head down, trying to look unobtrusive. Nuru was at the helm, still following in the wake of the skiff. In the late afternoon, they turned towards the shore. By sunset it became obvious they were indeed making for Galoh.

Paul noticed Husni's growing apprehension as they neared the village. Had Galoh been taken over by pirates? Was Husni's brother a prisoner too?

The skiff circled back and drew alongside. The red pirate ordered them to anchor in a channel about a hundred metres wide between a small island and the mainland. There was a scruffy village on the shore, a line of palm trees and a few fishing skiffs pulled up on the sand, and a handful of mashuas anchored just off the beach in translucent water.

Husni called for the yardarm to be lowered, the sail furled and secured. The pirates took up positions around the deck, their rifles pointing at the crew, and grew more agitated as the dhow neared the shore. *Jamal* proceeded slowly under motor until they were told to drop anchor. Nuru switched off the engine and a deathly silence eddied around them. The crew were instructed to gather their bags. Heads bowed, they looked like zombies as they climbed into the skiff, rifle muzzles tracking them as they gathered in a group at the stern.

Paul was surprised by the sudden rush of speed as the boat accelerated towards the shore. The driver didn't slow down as they closed with the land and the crew had to hold on tight as the pirate ramped the skiff up the beach. There was much heckling and shouting as the prisoners bailed over the rail with their bags and were led across the sand towards the palm trees, watched by a group of chattering children and a crowd of adults standing on a low dune. Behind the rise, they came to the village: a few dozen whitewashed houses surrounded by makuti-roofed, wattle-and-daub huts, many of them patched with pieces of corrugated iron, cardboard and plastic sheeting.

One of their new guards prodded a rifle into Paul's back and peeled him away from the group. He tried to resist, not wanting to be separated. The guard hit him between the shoulder blades with the butt and Paul sprawled on the sand. Looking back, he caught Husni's eyes. They told him to go quietly.

Paul was directed down a sandy path. His escort wore camouflage fatigue trousers, a black shirt and a black-and-white keffiyeh around his head, showing only the eyes. A bandolier was draped over his shoulder, the rounds glinting like chunky jewellery across his chest. Paul thought it excessive — one bullet would be enough. Perhaps it was a modern version of the traditional eye patch and peg leg.

They came to a hut and the guard shoved him inside, pointing to a wooden bedframe strung with rope and covered with a grass mat. There was a tin bucket and a small, barred window set high in the wall. No chance of escape there. The guard sat on a stool in the doorway, watching him for a while. Paul's stomach was grumbling. When he asked about food, the guard pretended not to understand English, but pointed to his wrist, which Paul took to mean 'later'. Then the guard banged the door shut and secured it with a chain and padlock.

Paul made a pillow out his jacket and a few T-shirts, then lay on the bed staring up at the palm-frond roof. His mind was blank: being a prisoner, there was no need to think.

Sometime later, a woman in a kanga arrived with a plate of chicken and left it in the doorway without saying a word. Paul scoffed it down with his hands. It was delicious.

Once he'd eaten, the guard took away the plate. Paul lay back on the rudimentary bed, deciding that he needed to try to get some rest. Halfway through making the decision, he was fast asleep.

Paul woke with hands locked around his throat and was dragged from the bed by his neck, the back of his head smashed against the wall. Two thumbs squeezed his windpipe. It was the red pirate.

'Fuck you, *Mmarekani*!' he screamed.

'Please, I told you, I'm not American, please, I'm *Muafrika*!' he gasped. 'Nelson Mandela, Bafana Bafana!' Paul couldn't breathe and was unable to prise the hands from his throat.

The red pirate released his grip slightly. Paul sucked in air, his throat burning, breath rasping. He could smell alcohol. The only light came from a paraffin lantern in the doorway. He could just make out his assailant's venomous eyes.

'Why the fuck you in my country, *Mmarekani*?' spat the pirate. He released his hold so the prisoner could answer. Paul slid down the wall and slumped at the man's feet, tears pouring down his cheeks.

'Please, I ... I'm an African like you —'

A swinging rifle butt connected Paul's temple with a terrific blow. Everything went black.

CHAPTER 26

Paul came to with a throbbing ache behind his eyes. He winced as he ran a hand over his temple and felt a crust of dried blood. How long had he been out? It was dark in the room and he crawled across the floor, feeling for the bed. Every movement sent a painful pulse to his head. When his hand found a bed-leg, he levered himself on to the grass mattress and lay drifting in and out of consciousness, his mind returning to the ugly face of his assailant, the stink of his breath.

A cock began to crow, followed by another. Then came the adhan from a nearby mosque. No Tannoy, simply an unamplified voice in the still morning air. The muezzin must have been close, just a few houses away, perhaps standing on a roof, for Paul had seen no minaret.

A bowl of breakfast fruit and sweet tea was placed on the floor through a half-open door. Paul ate mechanically, hoping it would help his headache. Then he stood staring out of the tiny window. All he could see was the back of another house and a window into a bedroom. There was no one inside.

For the rest of the day, he sat on his bed. Termites were building a nest using red soil and fashioning long tunnels across the wall. Paul watched their industry for hours. As his watch had been stolen by the pirates, he tracked the passing of time by the progress of a patch of sunlight across the floor. Darkness came swiftly at the end of the day and he had no light or candle. Supper comprised spaghetti with a few vegetables and hard, sweet biscuits. The pirates had not taken away his notebook, but it was too dark to write. Besides, he found he had nothing to say.

Early the following morning, Paul's guard with the bandolier kicked open the door.

'You, come.' So the man did have some English after all. The guard's keffiyeh was partly unwrapped, revealing the handsome, craggy face of a man in his fifties. He led Paul a few paces down the street to a stone house that stood beside his hut. The guard knocked and a muffled voice called from within. Paul was guided into a darkened room by the muzzle of a rifle.

'Please, a seat,' said a voice.

It took a moment for Paul's eyes to adjust to the gloomy interior. The room was bare, save for a large television set balancing atop an Arab chest in the corner. A man sat cross-legged on cushions, propped against the wall. Beside him was a tray with a samovar of sweet shah and a bowl of khat. There was a cushion in the middle of the room and Paul assumed this was where he should sit.

'You are Paul.' It sounded like a command. 'I know everything about you.'

Paul was scared and disconcerted. There was something uncomfortably familiar about this imposing figure, something about the eyes and the strong jaw. Paul studied him carefully: a tall man, probably in his early forties, with a gaunt face and a beard dyed with orange henna. There was a scar across his forehead, almost like a deeply etched worry line. He offered a smile that revealed a set of large, white teeth.

'Are you —'

'Yes, yes, I am leader of this group. My name is Mohamed.' The man took a bushel of khat, selected a few of the softer shoots, placed them ostentatiously on his tongue and began to chew. 'We are the *badaadinta dabah*, saviours of the sea. We are Somalia's volunteer coastguard.' He stroked his beard.

Paul felt anything but saved.

'Your crew tell me we will get no ransom for you, that you are worthless. Worthless. We must simply let you go. What a crazy idea!' His voice was amiable, but his eyes were cold.

'Please, Mr Mohamed, I'm from Joburg. I write scripts for documentary films. My parents are not wealthy. They are old, retired. There's no money anywhere in my family, I promise you.'

'Silence! Do not promise me anything!' he shouted and got up to stand over Paul. He grabbed him by the hair.

'What's this?' He stuck his thumb roughly into the wound on Paul's temple. The pain lanced through his head. 'Ah, yes, my skipper visited you. He has moods. He will not hurt you.'

'He did —'

'He and his boys are new. They are still learning. We must make allowances. So, to return to our topic, perhaps a couple of hundred thousand dollars? Just to cover our, ah, running costs?' He chuckled, turning the pulpy green ball around on his tongue.

'I beg you, we don't have that kind of money. I live in a two-room flat, smaller than this house. I get paid in South African rands, a worthless currency.'

'There is always your government.'

'They don't care about a stupid white boy messing about in Somali waters.'

'So you just want me to let you go!' Mohamed bent forward, giggling loudly and almost spilling tea on his ma'awis. His expression grew suddenly angry: 'Set you free? No, Paul, that is not what I have in mind at all. Farid! We will talk again. Go now.'

Paul was led back to his hut. The lock and chain clanked loudly and he heard Farid taking a seat outside.

Another day passed with no news. Paul's only contact with the outside was Farid, who brought food and walked him to the long-drop toilet. Their conversation, however, was largely non-existent. In the evening, Farid gave him a plate of sticky rice and grey stew. Paul picked at the meat, but after trying it found the taste not too bad, somewhere between fish and goat. When Farid came to take the plate away, he asked what kind of meat it was. The man put one hand on top of the other and wiggled his thumbs. It was unmistakeably turtle.

Paul paced the room, wondering when Johan would begin to get suspicious about the long silence and make some calls. By phoning Kijani House or Kiwayu Lodge, he would learn about the Somali voyage and soon diplomatic and military processes would begin, both in South Africa and Kenya. But Paul also knew there was little that could be done to rescue hostages in remote lairs on the Somali coast.

After three days, Paul received a handwritten note from Mohamed: *You are permitted to walk in the town as long as Farid is with you.*

A chance to be outside: his spirits immediately lifted. Perhaps even a chance to make an escape. The door had been left slightly ajar. Paul joined his guard outside and they stood staring at each other for a moment, unsure what to do. Farid pointed his rifle up the street and Paul began walking, his minder following a few paces behind.

Sandy footpaths led from house to house beneath coconut palms. They passed a group of men playing bao on a porch and women sitting in doorways chopping cassava and tossing it into pans of sizzling oil. A game of street soccer took up a whole block in the village centre: dirty, smiling kids and a ball made of plastic packets bound together with string. He'd seen the same, happy scene on all his African travels. At the end of the road stood a small school with bullet-holed walls. Paul could hear children behind a fence chanting verses from the Koran in singsong voices. Despite the marks of conflict, Galoh was a picture of village harmony.

A tin-roofed house, only slightly larger than the rest, caught his attention. Two rows of shoes lay at the door and Paul glimpsed worshippers on their knees within. The house served as a mosque. It was the absence of trappings, the simplicity of the act of communing with Allah, that struck him. The faces of the men were soft; they had discarded worldly thoughts. This prayer was not a mere formula, but a heartfelt communion with God.

He saw a shop exterior covered with murals advertising the produce within, the images depicting essentials such as cans of oil and bags of flour. It was doing brisk trade. Poking his head through the doorway, he was surprised to see expensive items on the shelves. There was good whisky, imported tinned food, sunglasses and even a couple of iPods on a shelf. The Somali equivalent of Woolworths.

At the end of town, they came to a cluster of more affluent houses. These were made of cement blocks and had pitched roofs and steel windows. Some had satellite dishes. A handful of brand-new, black Toyota Hilux Surfs with tinted windows were parked outside. With one dusty main road and a couple of sandy side streets, Galoh didn't seem prosperous enough for cars like these. Pirate economy, he reckoned.

Just then, a truck bounced into town, the driver sounding his trumpet-like horn. Two guards rode shotgun on top of the load. A crowd quickly filled the street and a scrum of buyers crowded round the tailgate as leafy bundles were unloaded. It was the daily khat delivery. There was shouting and shoving. The merchants, mostly tall women with colourful headdresses, had first pick, wrapping the rectangular bushels in canvas and setting off to sell to their clients.

Farid pointed at the beach and said, 'You, come.'

Did the man have only two English words? Maybe the guard didn't want him to witness the khat frenzy. In a strange way, Paul was beginning to warm to his keeper. The man's silences were almost comforting. At least there was a kind of constancy there, a dependability even.

The sand was sparkling white and the shallows aquamarine. They walked along the water's edge, the wavelets making a crisp slapping sound on the sand. Hoping to have a dip, Paul pointed at the sea and made a swimming motion with his arms. Farid shook his head, frowned, and pointed down the beach. Walking was clearly the designated activity and they were not to be deflected.

They passed piles of reeking nets and a flotilla of white skiffs drawn up on the sand with powerful Yamaha engines attached to their transoms. Despite himself, Paul was impressed at how the pirates were able to navigate vast distances in these small, open boats. Again, he thought of the benign monsoons and the predictable weather of the north-western Indian Ocean. Trying the same thing in a wilder corner of the Indian Ocean, such as off South Africa, would be too dangerous, even in the relatively calm summer months.

A rusty Kenyan fishing trawler lay at anchor beside the island. Waiting for a ransom payment? A dozen mashuas bobbed just off the beach. They looked no different to the Lamu dhows he was by now so familiar with. In their midst was *Jamal*, her yardarm lowered and the yellow tarpaulin rigged to protect her deck and fittings from the sun's rays. She looked forlorn and abandoned. Paul felt a pang to be at sea again, far from the mess of Galoh, sailing south to Kenya and freedom.

After a few hundred metres, they came to a large grey container that had washed ashore. The side was split open and it was empty. Farid pointed at the lettering with his Kalashnikov: *Rifiuto Pericoloso*. Even if you didn't understand Italian, the skull and crossbones made it clear the contents were hazardous. Why Italian?

Farid stopped beside a square, coral-block structure in the tree line and chatted to a teenager sitting on a plastic chair at the door. The youth wore dark sunglasses, chewed a sprig of khat and a pistol lay in his lap. His teeth were green with slime and he was obviously high. The two talked for a while in Somali, then the guard stood up and motioned Paul towards the hut. The seat of his pants had the words 'play boy' stitched across it. 'Come, Mister, I show you my tings,' he said in a drawl.

The teenager ushered Paul into the building. A makuti roof let through thin shafts of dusty light. It took Paul a moment to register what he was looking at. The walls were lined with shelves full of weapons: AK-47s and AKMs with their banana-shaped magazines, a dozen TT-30 semiautomatic pistols and a row of RPG launchers, good enough to stop a tank. The entire mud-earth floor was crammed with boxes of ammunition and grenades. A shoebox contained a satellite phone and a couple of GPSes.

'You like?' said the teenager with a big, mossy grin. He picked up an AKM and took aim at the prisoner's head.

'Yes, very nice,' Paul said quickly and took a step back.

'We make any ship go boom. Nobody fuck wid us.'

CHAPTER 27

Paul's guard opened the door and said: 'You, come.'

He got up groggily and stepped into the sunshine. Farid led him north along the beach. Where was he being taken? If his guard could be distracted for a few seconds, Paul might be able duck over the dune and outrun the older man. Find the right moment, make for the trees, but where could he go? The pirates would easily track him down and there'd surely be retribution.

The pair swung left over a dune and back among the palm trees. They emerged at the far end of town and came to a derelict stone house with a rusted tin roof. A guard at the front door opened and Farid indicated with his rifle that Paul should enter. He hesitated, suddenly afraid. The muzzle gave the base of his spine a jab and he was propelled into the cavernous space.

There, resting on mats around the edge of the room, was the crew of *Jamal*.

Husni leapt to his feet and gave Paul an awkward hug. There was joy on the skipper's face.

'*Nzuri mbingu*, what have they done to you!' he cried, looking at the black bruise on Paul's temple.

'I had a visit from the red pirate.'

'I am so sorry.' Husni held Paul by the shoulders. 'We will do everything we can. I will ask for medical supplies for you.'

'No, don't worry, it's just a bump. It looks worse than it is. Where's Latif? How's he doing?'

'He is all right. They put him with a family. The woman of the house has medicines. She was a nurse before. Latif will be okay.'

The rest of the crew crowded round, chattering and shaking Paul's hand. 'Thank goodness you are safe,' said Omar Yusuf, slipping him a handful of nuts.

'Thank you, Doc.' The old man smiled. There was strong emotion in his eyes.

'What are we going to do?' asked Paul.

'This is such a mess,' said Husni. 'I never dreamt my brother would turn to this.'

It struck Paul like a physical blow and for a few moments he was unable to speak. How had he not seen it immediately?

'Mohamed is your *brother*?'

'Yes, did he not tell you?'

'No.' Paul's cheeks flushed, stung by betrayal. 'No, he didn't.'

'Mohamed has brought shame on our family,' Husni blurted out, not looking at Paul. 'He has gone mad. He is not one of us.'

The room was silent. He stared at Husni, aghast, weighing up this man he'd put his faith in.

'Paul? Please, my friend —'

Paul turned away, his mind playing back the voyage and capture. What had he missed? 'This is not your fault, I guess,' he said at length, anger still in his voice. 'At least it's your brother, I suppose, not some unknown pirate.'

'Mohamed is very unpredictable.'

'I told him they won't get much ransom for me.'

'I said the same. He is thinking about it.' Husni grasped his hand. 'Listen, I will speak some more to him. I will talk him round, I promise.'

'But what about the other pirates?'

'It is a worry. I will do my best.'

At Paul's next meeting with Mohamed, they sat in the courtyard. An elegant young woman dressed in a long guntiino of red cotton served him a glass of warm Chardonnay. Paul glimpsed the label: Nederburg. He caught himself almost asking for ice. Mohamed drank shah from a narrow glass with a gold rim.

'Wine from your country, the Cape.'

'Thank you, Mr Mohamed, it's good of you.' The wine was badly corked. For a moment, Paul thought it might be poisoned.

The woman was tall and slim, her hair swept back from a high forehead in tight braids. He noticed a delicate floral pattern of henna on her hands.

'Come and sit with me, *thamani*,' said Mohamed. She went and sat side-legged next to him. Mohamed cradled her head in one hand and bent it into his lap. Paul couldn't decide whether it was an act of tenderness or ownership. She closed her eyes, almost dutifully, and a big hand began to stroke her braids.

'Seeing that you are worthless — which I do not believe for a minute — I am thinking about doing something different with you.'

Paul looked apprehensively at his captor. The gentle voice was pure menace.

'I am going to educate you.'

Paul ran through a likely list: cat o' nine tails, keelhauling, hanged from the yardarm. No other form of pirate education sprang immediately to mind.

'First, I will teach you why we are guarding our coast. We want the world to know our story and you will be the one to tell it. You will be our, what do you call it, PR man? Our agent in Johannesburg.

'I want to tell you about pirates,' said Mohamed, his voice deep and sonorous. 'Not us; the real pirates. For five hundred years, foreigners have come here to steal. First the Portuguese, then the Dutch, the English, the Italians. All pirates.'

'But that was so long ago. You can't still —'

'After colonialism, we thought we were free,' Mohamed interrupted. 'But no. When Somalia fell apart in 1991, the international community washed its hands of us. But it wasn't exactly hands off, you see.' He grew agitated, running a deliberate finger across the scar on his forehead. 'We have the best fishing grounds in the world. It is our national treasure. Like thieves in the night — I like this expression — the foreigners crept back into Somali waters. Trawlers from everywhere. They chased us out of the sea, poured boiling water on our fishermen in their canoes, cut our nets, rammed our boats.

'I am a man of principle, a man of God, Merciful Allah be my witness. When I came here two years ago, I saw what the foreigners were doing. It would have been wrong of me not to act. Now, when a ship's ransom is paid, the whole town celebrates. Food and khat for everyone. We slaughter goats. We pay good money for everything, double the going rate. A year ago the people were starving; now there are generators supplying electricity, our shops are properly stocked, builders have work. We have television. Soon we will sponsor a clinic.'

'But what about the violence?' said Paul softly.

'Don't you talk to me about violence, *mzungu*!' Mohamed leapt to his feet and stood over him. Paul cowered, expecting a blow. 'How dare you speak to me about violence, you white pig!'

'I'm sorry.'

Mohamed stepped back, still looking down at Paul with contempt, then returned to his cushion. 'Do not misunderstand us.' Mohamed's voice was matter of fact again. 'We are religious, but this is not jihad. They are calling us terrorists. It is an old story. Our grievances are about life and death. *Our* lives, *our* deaths!'

Paul's throat felt constricted, as though hands were wrapped around it again.

Mohamed stared at him for a long time. 'Our people were starving. So we intercept the foreigners and levy a tax, you understand.'

'Modern-day privateers,' said Paul.

'What is that?'

'It's an old word. A privateer is a boat — or its commander — authorised to attack shipping. Sort of like piracy with the blessing of your own government. Sir Francis Drake was a famous English privateer.'

'I like the word. I will use it.' Mohamed took a sip of tea and continued, telling Paul how Italian fishing boats brought barrels of toxic material, threw them overboard, then filled their nets with illegal fish: two crimes for the price of one voyage. When there was a storm, drums came ashore all along the coast and broke open on the reefs. Whatever was inside killed everything in the water. Dead fish by the thousand washed up along the coast. They even dumped rubbish from European hospitals. Mohamed had seen syringes on the beach. Children had developed breathing problems, bleeding mouths, hair loss and skin diseases.

'We have even seen malformed babies.' Mohamed shook his head. 'The ransom money we get is nothing compared to the damage they have caused. Do you know the saying "He that sows the wind, shall reap the whirlwind"?'

'It's from the Bible,' said Paul, thinking how much his interrogator reminded him of Dom Jerónimo.

'Yes, it is Christian. It was taught to me when I was young. I am a man of the sea. I like this saying very much. *He that sows the monsoon, shall reap the cyclone.* It has already begun. The last few years are nothing compared to what we have planned. I have met with my brother leaders from Hobyo, from Eyl. Chief Afweyne, my friend in Harardheere, has this idea to form the Somali marines. He is raising funds and training men. My friend Garaad, in Kismaayo, is doing the same. We are of one mind: the foreigners must go or else the cyclone will blow them out of the water.

'Up till now, we've concentrated on the trawlers, but they are heavily armed these days. Since we took a Korean cargo ship a few months ago, the game has changed. We will now go for more commercial vessels. For the bigger ships, we'll get millions of dollars. Not bad money for poor fishermen. Cargo ships, oil tankers, cruise liners, luxury yachts: they are all there for us. What do you think we could get for a tanker carrying half a million tons of oil?'

'But those ships are enormous,' said Paul. 'How will you get aboard?'

'Simple. Like we did with you, only on a bigger scale, maybe with two or three skiffs. We point an RPG at the bridge and order the captain to stop. The boarding skiff carries a long ladder or grappling hooks. We take the bridge and it's all over in a few minutes. We bring the ship back here and wait for the ransom. The hostages are treated well. It is all very easy.

'We are ready to take the fight further, into the Gulf of Aden. We will hijack dhows and turn them into mother ships.

Then our marines won't be stuck on the beach during the worst of the monsoons. We'll operate throughout the year; our men will be able to spend months at sea. If we keep the crew hostage on board, we have a human shield. We'll hit shipping as far as India and Mozambique, yachts and cruise liners in Mauritius, the Maldives. The potential is very great.' Paul thought of his trip to the Seychelles and imagined modern-day pirates swarming aboard the *Hispaniola*, striking the Jolly Roger and running up the Somali flag. Just one such act could cripple the yacht-charter industry of the entire Indian Ocean.

'Mr Mohamed, this is madness. Surely this will bring down the world's vengeance?'

'Listen to me, Paul, I do not like this picture of the future.' His eyes were cold. 'I do not want it, but the foreigners will not hear us. We will grow stronger. More and more young men are joining us. The volunteers get lots of money, they have power, they get the most beautiful girls, they build big houses, they drive new 4x4s. And so it grows.'

His hand lay on the woman's throat as she rested her head in his lap. Her eyes were open. Paul couldn't read the expression. 'There are threats,' said Mohamed. 'Al-Qaeda is taking a cut of the ransom in the north. There are warlords from upcountry who want to be part of us. It is no longer just fishermen. Ransoms will not be met. Warships will come. People will die. Billions of dollars are already being wasted. Each step in the process gives the foreigners more reason to destroy us. They will say we are Muslim fundamentalists. They will come with their lies and their bombs, just like in Afghanistan.'

'Your actions make it very difficult to see things differently.'

Mohamed brusquely lifted the woman's head and stood up to pace the courtyard, circling Paul. 'That is why we need people to publicise our situation, our legitimacy,' said

Mohamed. 'We need the world media to know who we really are and what we are fighting for. We need international navies patrolling the Horn of Africa, but not to fight Somalis … to fight the real pirates.'

A man entered the courtyard and said something to Mohamed.

'Enough,' he said to Paul. 'You do not understand yet. I have a meeting with my marines. Go!'

CHAPTER 28

Later that evening, Paul and Farid strolled down the road towards a building that issued the pulse of music. Drawing closer, he saw that it was a makeshift restaurant with a counter and a few tables. The interior was dark save for one bare light and a glass-fronted fridge emitting a blue glow. There were a few pirates slouched in plastic chairs and a handful of scantily clad women.

A man called him over from the corner table. Paul recognised him as one of the pirates who'd attacked *Jamal*. The teenager waved a beer bottle at him, pulled a garden chair closer and motioned him to sit. Old friends, it seemed. Farid stood at the door with a disapproving look on his face.

'Sit. You want beer, my friend? I am Dalmar.'

'I'm Paul.'

'I know.'

'I don't have any money,' said Paul.

'I know.' The teenager laughed. 'No worry, I pay. Budweiser?'

'Sure.'

Dalmar was dressed in camouflage cargo pants and a collared, pin-stripe shirt. The heavy chain around his neck looked like real gold. They sat sipping their bottles for a while in silence, regarding the room and its occupants, the girls mostly. Dalmar offered him khat.

'You try miraa.' He pushed the bushel across the table. 'Make you happy.'

Paul took a couple of leaves, rolled them into a ball and began chewing. The leaves were bitter and after a while he spat them into his hand and on to the floor when his newfound friend wasn't looking.

'You like Ethiopian girls?' asked Dalmar, sweeping the room with an unsteady arm.

'Very pretty.'

Paul's eyes fell on a young woman in skin-tight jeans — tall, slim, high cheekbones. Naomi Campbell's sister.

Dalmar tracked his gaze. 'That one I take tonight. Expensive, but she fuck like animal. Christian girl very good. They all want to ride pirates. We the cargo ships; them the skiffs.' He guffawed. 'Christian girl the best. With Muslim girl, we have to marry. *Nikah misyar* — a traveller's marriage. Really, it's a fuck marriage, no complication. Us pirates, we travelling men, just like you.' He gave Paul a nudge.

The music had changed. George Michael's 'Careless Whisper' wafted into the Somali night. A woman stood up and teetered over to sit on a pirate's lap. The man was drunk and draped an arm over her shoulder, cupping a breast roughly with one hand. She looked uneasy, but didn't remove it.

'You want one?' asked Dalmar.

'One what?'

'One pussy. I organise. Nice clean one. Mountain girl, fresh import from Harar.'

'No, thanks.'

'Come on, when last you fuck? You on that old jahazi with smelly fishermen for how long?'

'I've got a girlfriend in Holland,' he lied.

'*Bal, bal.* But you miss out, man.'

Paul downed the beer, thanked Dalmar and joined his guard outside. Farid had kept aloof. Maybe he was one of the old school — a purer, more principled pirate.

Paul lay on his bed mulling over Mohamed's version of Somalia's history. What exactly did he think of it? How much of it was true?

And what of these twenty-first-century pirates, these latter-day buccaneers in their open boats? Where did they fit into the picture? Young men getting rich, getting drunk, getting high. Fancy cars and all the girls they could sleep with. Danger, adventure, life on the ocean wave and seemingly not a care in the world. What would he choose if he were a young Somali?

Paul rolled over and blew out the candle, but he was still awake. He began thinking about a treatment for *People of the Monsoon II*. The movie would focus on a band of defiant figures prepared to take on the might of the world's navies in jumped-up jolly boats. Like African wild dogs, they hunted down their prey, nipping at the flanks and stern until the great beasts were brought to a halt. It was an African solution to an African problem. Outboard engines and Kalashnikovs were technical innovations that had slightly shifted the goalposts, but the principles of good seamanship and resourcefulness on the open ocean had remained the same. It was a fascinating evolution, enforced by circumstance. Now *that* would make an interesting documentary.

His thoughts were interrupted by the sound of a woman laughing outside his window. He got up to look, standing on tiptoes to peer through the bars. The voice came from the bedroom across the lane. There was a lantern flickering within. A tall woman stood talking to a man, who was out of frame on the bed below her. Paul knew that heart-shaped face. The prone figure must be Mohamed. She was speaking softly. The man made a comment and she smiled, then began to disrobe. She was in no hurry. Paul thought it looked like a feline act as the flowing guntiino dropped to the floor. Her body was lean yet curvaceous. A silver bellybutton ring glinted in the lamplight. Her bra was lacy and red. She reached a hand behind her back to undo the clip, hunched her shoulders and let it fall. Paul instinctively took a step back to make sure no reflected light gave away his presence. Even his breathing was too loud. She was, after all, only metres away.

Mohamed said something and the woman laughed again. She hooked her thumbs under the waistband of her panties, slipping them off in one motion. She stood looking down at her lover with hands on hips. Her nails were long and manicured; the henna tattoos went all the way up to her elbows making her forearms look like weapons. Paul was rooted to the spot, mesmerised.

She stepped on to the bed and stood over Mohamed, staring down at him as though he were prey. Paul could just make out the head of a penis above the windowsill, like a mole peeping from its hole. He stifled a giggle. Paul was sure no sound had left his mouth, but the woman suddenly looked up. Could she sense his presence? Her eyes bored straight into him. He was in pitch darkness and there was surely no way she could see him. His body stiffened. He held his breath and narrowed his eyes, lest their whites betray him.

She turned back to Mohamed and slowly began to squat. Mohamed gave the moan of a wounded animal. There were feral sounds and the scrape of a bed against linoleum. It was going to be a long night.

Paul woke in mid-air. The red pirate had entered silently, grabbed him by the shirt and hurled him across the room in one movement. All was darkness, flailing limbs and terror.

'Fuck *Muafrika*, you die!' shouted the pirate, dragging him to his knees. 'Hands on head! Open mouth for gun.' His voice was high-pitched and excited.

Before Paul could react, the pistol struck the side of his head, almost knocking him unconscious.

'Which gun you want?' The man undid the front of his trousers.

'Not like?' said the man. 'Maybe time to die?'

'Please! Mohamed said —'

'Fuck Mohamed! Sometimes it simple.'

The pirate forced Paul's lips open with his thumb and jammed the pistol against his teeth. He resisted. The pirate drove the muzzle hard until his teeth parted and the barrel dug into his mouth. He felt icy steel against the back of his throat and started to gag.

'Warships, helicopters, dollars,' hissed the pirate, his breath reeking of alcohol. He was stroking himself with his free hand. 'You think you so powerful. Enough of games: now you die.'

He pushed down on Paul's jaw and rammed the muzzle and trigger guard as deep as they would go.

'Say prayers, *kafiri*. Ten ... nine ... eight ...'

Paul's mind raced from his mother to Hannah and back to his mother. *Oh, God, there's no time.* He closed his eyes. If only he could —

'Three ... two ... one!' The pirate pulled the trigger. Paul heard the deafening click inside his mouth.

He opened his eyes. There were tears streaming down the man's cheeks. He was laughing delightedly. 'Oh, *Mmarekani*, that was good joke! You play really nice. Thank you. Just like the movies. We must do it again. Thank you, thank you.'

He tucked away his cock and buttoned up his trousers. Giving Paul a kiss on the cheek, he patted his head and staggered out of the door, still giggling.

Paul crumpled to the floor in a foetal ball.

CHAPTER 29

Paul woke before dawn with a start, terrified. He lay with his arms wrapped around his knees. He had to be strong; he could not let this derail him. It had not been a nightmare, but he was going to treat it as one and banish it from his mind. In a situation like this, there was no place for dreams or colourful imaginings, no place for heartache or grieving.

He lay on his bed, listening to the cocks crowing and goats scuffling outside the hut. Soothing, domestic sounds. Eventually he got up. Two oil cans, fashioned into wash buckets, had been placed inside the doorway during the night. Where had Farid been during the attack? Silently listening outside the door, or had he been told to make himself scarce? Paul took off his clothes and emptied one bucket over his head, ignoring the pool of water left on the earthen floor. It was his first proper wash since capture and layers of encrusted salt, dust and grime melted off his skin. He carefully washed his hands and feet, as though a ritual ablution. Then he put on a clean pair of khaki shorts, a white T-shirt and sandals.

He would stay on the surface, not letting his mind sink into that which threatened to engulf him.

All day he waited for something to happen. He was prepared; he could take whatever came. Nothing happened. The waiting ate at him. He mustn't think. His armour was on; his defences were up. But please let it come, whatever it is. Darkness fell. Farid avoided his gaze and said nothing as he delivered a plate of rice topped with tinned tuna and a bowl of camel milk. Paul took a few mouthfuls.

He found it impossible to sleep, fearing that if he closed his eyes, he might wake to the red pirate again. His mind paralysed, he sat watching the door, feeling the painstaking drift of the night. At first light, he slipped into a sleep plagued by nightmares.

Late morning, Farid opened the door: 'You, come.'

'Ah, Paul, good of you to come. Please, sit here.' A disconcertingly affable Mohamed patted a cushion on the ground beside him in a corner of the yard. Paul sat down feeling decidedly wary. The man handed him a sheaf of paper. 'These notes list our grievances.'

It was Mohamed's manifesto: *The Real Pirates of the Horn of Africa* by Mohamed Issa, Captain of the Galoh Coastguard. Some of it was merely in note or bullet-point form. The handwriting started neatly and became untidier as it progressed. The first heading was 'Fishing Piracy'.

'I have tried to summarise the crimes and give solid proof. Facts, facts, facts. As you know, the West wants facts.' Mohamed took a pair of wire-framed spectacles from a red case and placed them carefully on the end of his nose. He half read, half summarised: 'Every year, foreign fishing companies steal 300 million dollars' worth of tuna, shrimp and lobster from Somalia, ignoring seasons and quotas. The mother ships never enter local ports, never get searched and remain in our waters for months. The illegal catch is laundered through places like the Seychelles and Mauritius. These criminal governments do nothing about it. And so on and so on. All these things I cover in the first section of my document.'

Paul turned a few pages and came to the next heading, *Toxic-Waste Piracy*.

Mohamed tapped the document in an agitated manner. 'Okay, this is very important. It's about the dumping. Our fishermen have recorded the names of ships, the places and dates of their crimes. We have evidence. Look here, on page nine.'

Paul saw a list of ships with their call signs, type and nationality. There were GPS coordinates next to many of the entries and a brief description of each illegal activity that had been spotted. Mohamed looked over Paul's shoulder and read aloud, squeezing his elbow for emphasis. Paul didn't like the sudden intimacy. 'Mr Mohamed, you are being —'

'As you well know, my South African friend, there are consequences. Do they really expect us to stand around in puddles of nuclear waste and watch them steal our fish for the restaurants of Paris and London?' Mohamed stood up and paced the courtyard, punching the air with his finger and appearing to address a far bigger audience than Paul. 'Why does the UN do nothing? Because its members want to protect their illegal fleets. They are making a fortune in Somalia! Britain, Spain, Italy, Russia, Japan, Egypt, all the other villains — they are the enemies of the Somali people. We will take the fight to them!'

'But Mr Mohamed, the consequences for your own people will be terrible,' said Paul. 'You can never fight the West in open boats. It's madness.'

'They have forgotten Somalia!' Mohamed was shouting now. 'If we capture a hundred ships, they might begin to remember us. If we capture a thousand ships, maybe they will sit up and listen!'

Mohamed stopped pacing and looked at Paul with a dazed expression. For a moment, it was as though he didn't know where he was. He came to sit next to Paul again. 'If you page a bit further on ... here ... these are our demands.' His tone was gentle, almost pleading.

Paul read the demands: *The rich nations must immediately stop their piracy, must help negotiate a political solution, must send aid to alleviate poverty, must help set up a government.*

'If there was a stable government and proper employment in Somalia, there would be no need for piracy,' said Mohamed.

Paul shook his head sadly. 'The rich nations aren't interested, Mr Mohamed. This is a forgotten corner of Africa.'

Mohamed ignored him and read aloud from the document: 'The EU has the authority to stop the fishing fleets. The owners of big companies must be arrested and tried in the international court. The UN must send experts to clear the toxic and nuclear waste —'

'Mr Mohamed, you have no chance. Stop now, before they come after you. Return with your brother to Kenya. Husni will be able to organise things. Husni says —'

'I don't give a damn what my brother says!' hissed Mohamed. 'You and he are *such good friends*.' His eyes were wide, his voice mocking. 'Are you completely blind? Bad pirate Mohamed, good nakhoda Husni! Please, Paul, please, tell me you are not so naïve. You disappoint me.'

'What do you mean?' Paul's voice faltered.

'Where do you think Husni got the money to buy *Fayswal*? How do you think a poor family like ours can afford a big jahazi like *Jamal*? Now he plays innocent: the defender of Mr Paul!' He burst into his high-pitched laugh.

Paul sat in silence. Farid entered the room and nodded to Mohamed.

'Ah, thank you,' said Mohamed. 'I have a meeting with Husni. Go to your room, read my document and think about what is written. Think about what you can do for us.'

Paul sat on his bed, heavy with doubt and a sense of betrayal. Mohamed's manuscript lay crumpled on the floor. It was useless. Husni had probably been a pirate — probably *was* a pirate. Husni had brought him to Galoh. Husni knew. The afternoon drained into dusk and with darkness came the fear again. The red pirate would return. It was only a matter of time. If Husni was one of them, Paul had to find a way to escape on his own.

He paced the room, unable to sleep. The direction of his escape would be simple: follow the beach south. How many days would it take to get to the Kenyan border? What would they do if they caught him? He could not afford to think about that.

Paul waited until the early hours of the morning before he tried the door. As he suspected, Farid hadn't used the padlock. Very gently, Paul pushed it open, making sure the hinges didn't creak. He stepped over the legs of a sleeping Farid, his AK-47 propped against the wall beside him. Paul made himself walk painfully slowly down the path to the beach, ears and eyes alert to any movement. He carried only a bottle of water and some stale injera bread in his pocket.

The night was tomblike. Palm trees stood like shaggy ghosts against the stars. Although the air was warm, Paul shivered. Over the rise, making sure his feet avoided the dried leaves. Now he was on to the beach, a wide runway of white leading to the southern horizon. He began to run, down to the water's edge, where the incoming tide would hide his footprints, and south. Sprinting, trying to put as much distance between himself and Galoh as possible. Soon he was out of breath and forced himself to slow to a trot. There was a lot of running to come and he was unfit. The eastern sky began to purple. Before it got too light, he'd need to find a hiding place. But the beach was featureless. Inland was no better: a flat wasteland of low scrub.

On he ran, scattering the ghost crabs. He passed a dead creature, perhaps a dolphin or a seal, and a couple of abandoned dhows rotting where they stood above the high-tide line. He ran past grey containers, broken open and spilling their toxic contents on to the beach. Paul's world narrowed to the rasp of his breathing and the crunch of his sandals on the wet sand. *One foot in front of the other. Keep going.*

After half an hour he stopped at the water's edge, hands on his knees, trying to catch his breath. The crunch of waves on the beach produced explosions of phosphorescence. The horizon had turned salmon. *How lovely,* he thought.

Just then, he heard a crackling noise, the hollow puncturing of air. He looked back. Galoh was lit up with flashes. It was rifle fire. The alarm had been sounded. He set off at a sprint, whimpering as he ran. The red pirate would lead the chase. Paul was just prey to them now. After a few minutes, there was the sound of vehicles racing inland. Out to sea, he saw a white dot and heard the whine of an outboard engine.

Up ahead a dark object lay stranded at the top of the beach; he made straight for it. The jagged lump turned out to be a large, wrecked dhow. He placed his hands on the rail and pulled himself up. The white dot had resolved itself into a skiff and he could make out a tall figure in the bows. Paul dropped into the hull and hunkered down between the ribs. If the men came ashore, it would be over in moments.

The noise of the engine grew until it filled his hiding place like an angry wasp. Suddenly it stopped and the motor puttered undecidedly. There was an agitated conversation, shouting, a voice he thought he recognised. The engine flared and the skiff continued south at high speed.

He was trapped. It would soon be sunrise and there was no way he could show his face in daylight hours. He would have to sit it out until nightfall and then push on. Hopefully they wouldn't return and search the wreck. He drank some water, took a few bites of injera and tried to make himself comfortable. Just before the sun lifted above the horizon, he drifted into a fitful sleep filled with flight: running and running, but never outstripping his dark pursuer.

CHAPTER 30

Paul opened his eyes to find the hull bathed in clear orange light. He lay motionless, listening. The sun peeped over the gunnel and the air was alive with the twitter of birds. He could not have slept for long, but he felt refreshed.

Trying to find a less angular place to lie, Paul became aware of something strange about the hull. He looked more closely at the planking. Surely not…

He could hardly believe his eyes: the timbers were stitched together. It was the mtepe.

Paul was overcome by a giddy wave of emotion and felt tears brimming. Here, now, of all times. He crawled along the inside of the hull like a worshipper, running his hands over the worn stitches of coir rope. Each plank and rib was tightly bound together as though the boat were one enormous Zulu basket.

He guessed the vessel to be nearly twenty metres long. It had rotted badly and the wood was bleached grey. Some of the seams gaped open and many stitches were split. The wreck had obviously been plundered for wood and spare parts, but the shape was unmistakeable. Both bow and stern were raked at steep angles, the long prow carved in the shape of some sort of bird. He could still make out flecks of red, black and white paint.

The deck housing and rigging had been removed, leaving the ribs exposed. It was like being inside the carcass of a whale. He perched on one of the large ribs amidships, sensing that he was inside a maritime fossil. An intact mtepe, resting on her old bones, still dignified in death. He tried to picture her construction, many decades earlier, perhaps on this very beach. This vessel was in all likelihood the last mtepe ever built.

Paul imagined the elaborate ceremonies during the laying of her keel; the sacrifice of a black goat to the mizimu spirits; the haunting recitations of the maulidi by village children. He pictured the stately craft moving down the beach on mangrove rollers, hungry for its first taste of ocean. The whole community is gathered, turned out in their finery; there dancing and beating of drums, the noise growing to a crescendo. The hull kisses the water and floats free to raucous shouts of '*Harambee!*' The last mtepe has been launched.

He found a comfortable spot in the shade between two ribs and allowed himself to nod off again.

'Paul?'

His eyes snapped open. Panicked, he scuttled forward into the cleft of the bows and tucked himself into a ball, covering his head with his fists.

'Paul, it's okay! It's me.'

He tentatively lowered his arms. Husni was peering through a hole in the side of the hull, his face framed by splintered wood.

'You!' said Paul.

'My friend, you have misunderstood. I am not with them.'

'What are you doing here, then?'

'Mohamed let me help with the search —'

'The hunt.'

'He knows I will not flee. He has my crew and my boat.'

'And the red pirate?'

'No, no, Mohamed has dealt with him. He will not harm you again, trust me.'

'Trust you? You knew what your brother was doing here! You were in Galoh with him before!'

'Yes, I was here two years ago, but I left. I am a sailor, not a pirate.'

'You kept the truth from me.'

'Paul, we sailed into Lamu Channel on a spring tide together. We are brothers.'

Paul stared at the mtepe's pale, sun-bleached ribs, remembering *Fayswal* surfing the night wave. Where, exactly, had betrayal occurred?

'I don't know, Husni.'

'I am telling you the truth. Come back to Galoh. We can talk there. My brother thinks you can help him. Everything will be all right.' Husni reached through the hole and put a hand on his shoulder. Paul's body shook. He could not speak.

'So you found your mtepe,' said Husni eventually.

'Yes, I found it.'

'Is it what you hoped for?'

'Yes, exactly.'

The door to Paul's room burst opened. 'You come, now!' said his guard.

'Jesus, Farid!' cried Paul, sitting suddenly upright.

'You come,' the man said more gently.

Paul dressed quickly. He'd stayed up late, reading through his notes and writing about the old mtepe, although the documentary seemed a distant prospect now. Outside, the morning was cool and a rind of golden light adorned the horizon. A few stars still glittered above a blue-black sea.

Mohamed paced the courtyard, waiting for Paul. 'The crew are on the beach, getting ready to leave. Our fishermen have repaired your sail, so there is nothing to keep you. Today you sail back to Kenya.'

'Mr Mohamed, thank you! You are —'

The man held up a hand to silence Paul. 'Tell them what you have learnt here. Tell them who we are. Tell them. Now you must go. *Safari salama*, safe journey.'

'*Asante sana*, Mr Mohamed.'

It took Paul only a minute to stuff his belongings into the backpack. A black-and-white ma'awis, a gift from Mohamed, had been left on his bed. He pulled off his shorts and wrapped the ma'awis around his hips. Farid carried his backpack as they walked down the sandy street. Husni and the crew were already on board *Jamal*, bending the repaired sail to the yard. They looked like ants silhouetted against the rising sun.

'Goodbye, Farid,' said Paul, reaching out a hand.

The man stepped forward very formally and gave him a hug. Paul felt the cold metal of the rifle against his arm.

'*Safari njema*,' said Farid. 'May Allah preserve you, my friend.'

Paul smiled and looked into the older man's eyes, then turned and walked down the beach towards the waiting skiff. There were so many things he could have said to Farid in their time together. Perhaps it had not been necessary.

The skiff bumped against *Jamal*'s side and the South African scrambled aboard.

'Morning, Paul!' shouted the crew.

'*Salaam,* everyone! Latif, how are you?' he asked. The young man's arm was in a sling cut from a kikoi and he wore a big smile.

'The wound is getting better,' said Latif.

'No deck work for you, you lazy bastard,' said Paul.

'No, *mzungu*, you can do all my work on the way home.'

'I'd be happy to.'

'Okay, Paul, stop slacking!' called Husni from the quarterdeck. 'Get on that halyard or I'll have you flogged.' Clearly, the skipper couldn't wait to put sea room between himself and the Somali coast.

'Aye, captain,' said Paul, joining the rest of the crew at the mast. They leant their backs into the hauling as *Jamal*'s yard squeaked skywards. Short strips of coconut rope had been tied to the repaired sail to keep it tightly furled. The doc led the singing of a Swahili shanty as the men heaved.

Oh Allah, fill our great sail with wind.
Allah helper! Allah helper!
Rise up, great yard,
Give strength to our arms,
Swell out, great sail!

The singing was powerful and masculine, even Rafiki's young voice had found a deep resonance. Paul joined in where he recognised the words. Sweat dripped off the haulers as blocks and halyard creaked and protested. Once the yard was in position, the engine coughed into life. Paul and Taki heaved on the anchor rope, the wet line coiling around their feet as *Jamal* slid slowly forward. Up came the chain, coated in transparent green weed and then the anchor with its muddy flukes, which they yanked over the bows and on to the foredeck.

Husni prodded the engine into gear and swung the vessel in a wide arc to starboard, close by the island. Paul looked back at Galoh. Farid and Mohamed were standing on the beach, both wearing white kanzus. Paul remembered it was Friday, mosque day for the people of the coast. He made a grand wave, swaying his whole arm back and forth in an arc. The two figures returned the greeting — a slow, almost ceremonial sweeping of their arms through the air. Behind them, the little village seemed a place of timeless peace. Paul felt a pang, an undirected yearning for something he couldn't properly define. Everyone else was silent, looking back at the shore. Only Husni looked east, seeking the best course through a gap in the barrier reef.

Just then, Farid raised his rifle to the sky and fired three shots. *Crack, crack, crack!* The hollow sound echoed off the island, rending the morning air. The sailors on *Jamal* responded, shouting '*Allahu Akbar!*' The hair stood up on the back of Paul's neck. '*Allahu Akbar!*' he shouted at the top of his lungs. The sailors continued calling until the two men on the beach were reduced to tiny white specks.

'Okay *vijana*, enough jihad,' said Husni. 'That goes for you, too, Paul. Get ready to unfurl the sail.'

The men prepared the lines and mainsheet, and loosened the shrouds on the starboard side. As *Jamal* chugged through a gap in the reef, the water changed colour from jade to dark blue. Waves crumbled on either side of them. Black serrations showed above the surface and Husni chose his course carefully. Once they were clear, the captain shouted: '*Chia damani!* Sheet in!'

Paul and Taki yanked on the mainsheet and one by one the palm strops parted with a pleasing snap as wind filled the canvas; the sail looked like a shirt whose buttons were being ripped by an overzealous lover. There was a bang of impatient cotton as the lateen ballooned. The two men brought the sail under control, hauling in the mainsheet and taking a turn on a bollard for purchase.

'Not too much, we'll be sailing *tingi*,' said Husni. He bore off, allowing the breeze to fill the cloud of canvas above their heads. The doc let out an ancient cry:

*Let us go, oh Allah,
let our good ship go,
for we are bound for home!*

Paul looked to the northeast, his mind filling the sea with a fleet of every kind of dhow that had ever existed. Beautiful ghost ships decked with bunting and silken flags, the horizon studded with a thousand triangular sails. The great armada sailed down the sunlit sea towards them. Mighty baghlas with horned figureheads and tall spreads of canvas, Indian kotias flying extra jibs and kites, date-laden booms from Kuwait and sambuks with proud scimitar bows from Oman and the Red Sea. And in the centre of the fleet, a mtepe, leaning gracefully to the breeze.

Jamal picked up speed and, for a moment, rode a swell. White water boiled around the prow and gurgled down her flanks. The men were looking around, smiling at each other. This band of blue-water brothers was back where they belonged, thought Paul, returning home to lives that followed the rhythms of Islam, the rhythms of wind and ocean.

Husni was looking south, a firm set to his jaw. A man of the sea, not of the land and its complications. An older brother trying to undo the mess of a younger sibling. Or maybe a much, much more complicated story.

A gust caught the dhow and she heeled over, bowed for a moment by the force of the wind. Then *Jamal* responded, accelerating, her prow lifting. She rode a big, Indian Ocean roller, racing down its face. The doc and Rafiki were in the bows, crying out in delight.

'Is this the Kaskazi?' Paul asked.

'Yes,' said Husni. 'The summer monsoon is here at last.'

A NOTE TO THE READER

Dear Reader,

Thank you for taking the time to read *Whoever Fears the Sea*. I do hope you enjoyed it. The problem of piracy along the African coast is a perennial one, and the troubles in Somalia have spread to Kenya, West Africa and, more recently, northern Mozambique. The origins of these conflicts are complicated and things are seldom as they seem. I wanted to convey this complexity in my novel, but also something of the beauty of the East African coast and its rich maritime and cultural history.

Strife on the high seas, particularly of an African variety, holds an abiding fascination. Much of my writing involves such nautical themes and my latest novel, *The Cape Raider*, is the story of a minesweeping flotilla, led by Lieutenant Jack Pembroke, operating off the southern tip of the continent during World War II.

I will be tracking Jack's story through World War II and although each novel in the series may be read as a stand-alone, the next one will follow on directly in time from *The Cape Raider*. It will tell the story of U-boats off the South African coast during the winter and spring of 1941, attempting to disrupt Allied convoys bound for North Africa. Jack and his ship, the *Gannet,* will head to sea once more to try to stop this mortal threat.

In this series, I have chosen a British hero and placed him on a South African ship in a Royal Navy base at the Cape. It has provided me with the opportunity to marry parts of my own background: my time in the South African Navy as a citizen-force officer, my university education in England and my love of the Cape and its stormy ocean.

Since I was a boy, I've adored nautical yarns and grew up reading the likes of Alexander Fullerton, Nicholas Monsarrat, Patrick O'Brian and Douglas Reeman. But I always lamented the fact that none of these naval adventures were set in my home, the Cape, despite the presence of an important Royal Navy base in Simon's Town. The Jack Pembroke series is an attempt to bring the South African maritime story of World War II to life. Future books could see Jack serving in the Mediterranean at Tobruk, Malta, Sicily and Greece, and even in the oft-forgotten Madagascar campaign.

Nowadays, reviews by knowledgeable readers are essential to an author's success, so if you enjoyed *Whoever Fears the Sea* I shall be in your debt if you would spare a moment to post a short review on **Amazon** or **Goodreads**. I love hearing from readers, and you can connect with me through my **Facebook page**, **Instagram**, **Twitter** or my **website**.

I hope we'll meet again in the pages of the next Jack Pembroke adventure on the high seas.

Justin Fox

Sapere Books is an exciting new publisher of brilliant fiction and popular history.

To find out more about our latest releases and our monthly bargain books visit our website: **saperebooks.com**